snapped

snapped

pamela klaffke

MIRA®

MIRA®

Please Recycle — This Product is Recyclable

Recycling programs for this product may not exist in your area.

ISBN-13: 978-0-7783-2746-2

SNAPPED

MIRA Books acknowledges use of excerpt from the back cover copy of *The Single Girl* by Walter C. Brown (Monarch, 1961).

www.MIRABooks.com

Printed in U.S.A.

First Printing: January 2010
10 9 8 7 6 5 4 3 2 1

Parrot Girl

I hate the girl with the parrot on her shoulder. I don't want to but I do. She's nineteen, maybe twenty, smoking as she waits in line at the restaurant. There's always a line now for Sunday brunch and I know it's my fault. Sometimes I should just keep these things to myself. But the Parrot Girl. She's wearing shiny blue short-shorts with white piping, soccer socks with the stripey tops pulled up to her knees. I can tell her cowboy boots have been scuffed and distressed on purpose, the leather warped and discolored by water, they're scratched and dirty—she probably dragged them behind a car through an unpaved alleyway then invited her friends to stomp on them with their filthiest shoes. I know all the tricks. Still, the boots are too stiff. She wears a short gold satin jacket that the parrot keeps snagging with its claws every time it readjusts itself on her shoulder. From where I'm sitting I can't see what's underneath the jacket and the way the sun is reflecting off the satin, I can't get a clear view of her face. Plus, the parrot is in the way. Ted has a better view and assures me her face is good, so I polish off my third champagne cocktail and grab my camera bag from under the table.

Up close I see Parrot Girl has a tiny diamond stud in her nose. Her makeup is perfect: smudgy kohl eyes and sticky mascara, smeared lips, classic morning-after face. But her hair is too clean and smells like apples, her face freshly moisturized. I wonder how long she spent getting ready this morning, if she had a fitful sleep editing all the possible combinations of outfits in her head.

"Excuse me." I tap Parrot Girl on the shoulder. "My name is Sara B. and I was wondering if I could take your picture?"

Parrot Girl turns to look at me. Her friends titter behind her. She lights another cigarette and I notice her hands are shaking slightly. She knows who I am, I'm sure of it. She takes a deep drag and shrugs. "Yeah, okay, that's cool."

I lead her away from the line and ask her to face my camera. The satin is tricky in the sun and the parrot won't look at me. I think for a moment that the parrot is smarter than either of us—it knows how ridiculous this all is, and doesn't want any part of it. I get the shot and Parrot Girl signs the release allowing the magazine to use the photos however we see fit. She doesn't ask the obvious—it never occurs to the ones who try so hard to be a DO that they could possibly be a DON'T.

I push my way back through the line and to our table by the window, which is open onto the busy street. A couple of people call my name and wave. I have no idea who they are, but smile and wave back anyway. One of them yells, "Sara B.! Take my picture!" I smile again and sit down.

Genevieve is breast-feeding the baby in the washroom. She won't do it at the table anymore after last week when a woman in bad camouflage pockety pants that emphasized her puffy abdomen berated her for drinking one champagne cocktail, then feeding the baby an hour later. According to Genevieve, this was typical. The situation was made worse when the Bad Camo Woman broke from her rant and narrowed her eyes at Genevieve. "You!" She pointed a finger in Genevieve's face. "You! You're that singer! Gen-Gen! You had that song—what was it called? 'J'taime, J'taime something…'"

"'J'taime My Baby Tonight,'" Ted spoke up. Genevieve glared at her husband.

Bad Camo Woman snapped her fingers. "That's it! Wow! I used to listen to that song over and over when I was a teenager! You're Gen-Gen! Andrew, look, it's Gen-Gen!" Andrew, who had been hanging sheepishly in the back, nodded a quick hello. He, too, was wearing bad camouflage pockety pants. "So do you think I could get your autograph? Here." She shoved a crinkled receipt in front of Genevieve and produced a pen from her fake Louis Vuitton bag. "Sign this."

Genevieve obliged, scrawling *Best Wishes, Gen-Gen* across the crumpled paper.

"Wow, thanks. I can't wait to call my friend Angela. She was my best friend in school and she loved you, too. We're not that close now—she lives in Vancouver—but we try to keep in touch, you know. It's hard, though, with our kids and our jobs and—"

"How would you feel about me taking a picture of you two?" I interrupted. I couldn't take it anymore.

"Of us?" Bad Camo Woman brought her hand to her chest.

"Sure. But let's do it outside. There's not enough room in here," I said as I ushered the Bad Camo Couple to the door.

"Check it out." Jack nods toward the table behind ours. We're silent, we listen. They have the magazine open to the DOs and DON'Ts fashion page and I can see my shot of the

Bad Camo Couple staring out as the man holds it up to take a closer look. They are the featured DON'T, the biggest DON'T of the week, more DON'T than the unitard juggler or any of the three other DON'Ts on the page. "Could be a good look for us," the man jokes.

"Ugh. Put that thing away." The woman snatches it out of his hands. "It's so *mean.*"

Jack leans into me and whispers, "I like it when you're mean." Then he kisses me on the neck. I order another drink and he does the same. Ted asks for the check.

"What? No more champagne, Ted? Oh, yeah. I guess you've got that long drive ahead of you," I say. I'm tipsy and when I'm tipsy I can't help needling Ted about having moved to the suburbs.

"It's not that bad, Sara. You should come out sometime. You might even like it."

"We'll see about that," I say. I've refused on principle to visit Ted and Genevieve's new house. Jack says I'm being stubborn and immature but Jack's young and doesn't get it.

As soon as Genevieve and baby Olivier arrive back at the table, Ted announces it's time to go. He has to mow the lawn. Genevieve's parents are coming for a barbecue supper. She has to make potato salad. Genevieve hands Olivier to me, freeing her hands to pack the baby gear and pop open the stroller. I grip the baby firmly, but not too close. Jack tickles Olivier's nose with his finger and makes goo-goo baby-talk sounds that I hope I'll be able to block out the next time we have sex. Which won't be for three weeks, I remind myself. Jack's leaving for his home in Toronto late this afternoon.

Hugs. Kisses on both cheeks all around. Safe drive, have a great time. Give my best to your parents, Gen. Call me tomorrow. I'll see you at the office, Ted. They're gone and I slump back into my chair, knocking back the champagne cocktail that's been placed in front of me. Then Gen suddenly reappears. She's frantic. Olivier is wailing. His pacifier has disappeared. We look between plates, under napkins. Jack finds it on the floor and hands it to Gen. She gives it a quick wipe on her shirt and pushes it into Olivier's mouth before scrambling back out the door. I shudder. Doesn't it have to be sterile or something?

Jack looks at me but says nothing. His smile is crooked and his eyes are warm. "That is one cute baby," he says.

"Yup," I say, my eyes darting around, trying to find a waitress, a hostess, a bus boy, anyone who can get me a drink.

"Do you ever think about it, Sara?"

I can't look at him. I catch the eye of our waitress and point to my empty glass. She nods.

"We've never talked about this, you know." Jack is not letting up. I hate this conversation more than I hate Parrot Girl.

"That's true."

"I have to be honest with you, Sara. And you need to be honest with me. You're thirty-nine and you know I'm totally cool with that, but I also know that, well, your time is…"

"Running out?"

"I guess, yeah." Jack's voice is very quiet.

I laugh. "Jack, I don't want to have a baby, if that's what you're worried about." He looks relieved. My drink arrives and I immediately suck half of it down. "I'm not one of those women."

"I know *that*. I just thought that we've been together for almost a year so maybe we should make sure we're on the same page with this." I am certainly not on the same page with anyone who says *on the same page,* but I say nothing and smile. "I mean, I love kids, my nieces and nephews are great and Olivier is adorable, but it's not for me. I've never wanted kids of my own."

"Great. That's just great, then." I raise my near-empty glass to clink Jack's, down the last of it and instruct him to order another round as I excuse myself to use the bathroom.

I squat above the toilet to pee and wrestle my cell phone out of my purse. I dial Gen's number, but click the phone shut before it has a chance to ring. I can't call her about this, about Jack not wanting to have kids and me not wanting to have kids and how great that should be but how I feel mysteriously winded and sad and I don't know why. I can't call her and we can't spend hours dissecting my feelings and his feelings and still not really know why I feel like this by the time one of our phones starts to die. I can't call her about this because she has Olivier and her parents are coming for a barbecue supper and she has potato salad to make.

There's a girl sitting in my spot, laughing with Jack. "Hello," I say.

The girl stands. "Oh, my goodness, Sara B. I saw you over here and I didn't want to be rude or anything, I just wanted to meet you—you're, like, my idol, seriously. I want your job. What you do is amazing. I mean, you're *Sara B.*"

"You can just call me Sara." I stick my hand out to shake hers. "And you are?"

"Eva. Eva Belanger."

"That would make you Eva B., then."

"Gosh, yes. I guess it would." Eva's face is bright red. She looks away from me and to Jack.

"Go ahead," Jack says. "She won't bite. Well, not unless you want her to."

"You're funny," I say to Jack. "So what can I do for you, Eva?"

"I just, well, I was wondering if you'd ever consider letting me tag along, shadow you for a day, see how you do it."

"It's not magic. It's just a job."

"No, no, it's *important*. You know, I have almost every issue of *Snap*. I had to get the older ones off eBay, but now I'm only missing issues six and eight, when you were still only monthly."

"Nineteen ninety-three," I confirm. The first year, when it was just Ted and I and a bag of money his dad gave us. By ninety-five we were weekly and had an office. Now we have a building, six satellite offices and three retail stores. Last month, a stuffy American company paid Ted and me twenty thousand dollars to spend a day with their marketing team. Advertising agencies pay us more. We don't mention those things in the magazine. "I think I've got some of those old issues kicking around," I say to Eva. "If I can find six and eight, they're yours."

"Really? Are you serious?"

"It's not a problem," I say.

"What *is* a problem is that you're not sitting down," Jack says. "Another round?"

"Sure," I say. "Would you like to join us, Eva?"

"Oh, my! Yes, of course—if you really don't mind."

"We really don't mind," I say. I wouldn't mind anything that's a distraction from Jack and the baby talk and the talk about babies and not wanting one, and not knowing why I was spooked when he said he didn't want one when I don't want one, either. I definitely want this Eva girl to join us.

Eva tells Jack stories about me. She tells him about the time

I got into a very public squabble with a Hollywood starlet after we published a picture of her wasted and bleary-eyed, attempting to dress in what I could only guess was her misguided interpretation of Audrey Hepburn in *Funny Face*. Here to shoot a film, the starlet was on the town, trying like they all do when they come to Montreal to look French. But like they all do, she got it wrong. The striped top was not black and white like Hepburn's, but too short and striped in multicolored pastels. The black leggings were shiny and too tight and made her ass look like a big balloon. Instead of ballet flats, she wore stilettos and her trashy big blond hair was nothing like Hepburn's neat-and-sleek brunette style. To top it off, the starlet had the scarf—they always had the scarf, no matter the season—wrapped around her neck like a strangling tensor bandage. It was not French. It was sad. She was definitely a DON'T.

Eva tells Jack about how I'd started wearing shrunken kid-size T-shirts with cutesy logos and sayings when everyone else was decked out in Doc Martens and plaid. She tells Jack that when she'd read my TO DO column a couple weeks back she knew she had to meet me for real. The column was about recycling old Girl Guide and Boy Scout merit badges by sewing them onto the sleeves of the prettiest vintage beaded sweaters, and Eva said she had done the very same thing just days before the magazine came out.

I got that particular idea from Sophie, the woman who ran a thrift shop in Westmount I frequented. I didn't mention this in my column and I don't mention it now. Sophie said that the kids were coming in and rifling through a bin of old patches in search of merit badges to sew on their coats. Sewing the badges on vintage sweaters was my idea and, according to Eva, hers, too.

Indeed, she's wearing a pink vintage cardigan, buttoned up to the neck with brown triangular Brownie badges sewn in pairs down one sleeve. I recognize the one for cooking, the one for puppet-making, another for writing. They're the old-style ones, the ones from the seventies. I had all of these. Eva's wearing pearls, three strands and they're real. She wears glasses, vintage cat-eyes with custom lenses and the tiniest rhinestones clustered at the edge of the frames. She has on a brown pencil skirt that falls below her knees, panty hose and shoes that look clunky and orthopedic, something a nurse or your grandma might wear. But it's her hair—that red—that gets me. Montreal red, the color old ladies in the city dye their hair instead of trying to keep their natural color or letting it go grey. It's not red, exactly, but more burgundy, with a bit of that purple that's the color of eggplant. Aubergine—that's the word. A bit of aubergine mixed with the color of the reddest wine. It's no one's real hair color. It belongs to the old ladies and to Eva.

It's 3:00 p.m. and Jack and I are sitting at the same table we have been since eleven. I'm drunk, and so is he. Eva is still here and I'm glad. She's sober and has offered to drive Jack to the airport. If we don't go soon, Jack will miss his flight, so we stumble out into the afternoon and smoke cigarettes and wait for Eva to bring her car around to pick us up. There's still a line to get into the restaurant. We're going to have to find someplace new, and this time, I make a vow to myself, I'm not going to write about it.

"Looks like someone has a fan," Jack says as he wraps his arms around me.

"She's cute," I say.

"Not as cute as me." Jack gets cocky when he drinks. "Maybe she can keep you company while I'm in Toronto." Jack also worries about what I'm up to with whom when we're apart, even though we have an agreement about this.

I kiss him on the lips. "Nope. She's not as cute as you, baby." Jack smiles. I think I'm going to throw up. I am not a baby-sweetheart-darling-sugarpie kind of girl. Jack likes that kind of thing so sometimes I do it for him and I hate that more than I hate the baby conversation and Parrot Girl.

Eva zips up in front of the restaurant in a silver Saab convertible. Jack and I pour ourselves into the car and we head to my place in the Plateau. Jack and I race up the stairs and into my apartment. We grab his bags and we're off to the airport. "It's really nice of you to do this, Eva. We could have taken a taxi."

"No, no, don't be silly. It's no problem. I just wish we had more time to talk. There are so many things I'd love to ask you about." She bites her lower lip. "But I don't want to be a pest."

"How about you come over after we drop Jack off and we'll have some wine and talk all you want?"

"Oh, my goodness, Sara, that would be the most amazing thing."

"Then it's a plan."

I toss a packet of breath mints at Jack and straighten his shirt before he heads to the check-in counter. I feel like his mother. But he's thirty. Biologically, I couldn't actually *be* his mother.

"So how long have you two been doing the long distance thing?" Eva asks as we wait for Jack to get his boarding pass.

"Almost a year."

"Gosh, that must be hard."

"Not really," I say. It's easier than trying to explain how it isn't hard most of the time but then some of the time it is, like when I'm sick or he's sick, or at night when I think I hear something weird or I can't open an especially tight jar of kosher pickles. The worst is when I have to go to a party or dinner and it's all couples and I wish he was there so we could snicker together in the back of the room—Jack is good for that—and not feel alone and old.

"I don't think I could do it. You must really trust each other."

"We have to," I say. I don't have to tell Eva about my arrangement with Jack, that our relationship is open, that we can have sex with other people, but not date them, we can screw them, but not love them. I once told Genevieve about this and she called me crazy. I said it was practical, better than making all sorts of promises to each other only to have them broken. Gen called my attitude defeatist. I called it modern and reminded her that she told me once that she had exactly the same arrangement with the two boyfriends she had before Ted.

"Look how that worked out," Gen said.

"You were fine with it at the time."

"I could have never done that with Ted."

"I'm not saying you should have. It's different with you and Ted."

"It's never going to be serious with Jack unless you're monogamous."

"Who says I want serious? Who says monogamy is the only way?" Discussing the finer points of your open long-distance relationship with your staunchly monogamous married friend is ill-advised.

"Come on, Sara. You're almost forty."

"Yup. I'm almost forty."

I know that I'm supposed to know what this means. People say it all the time. *You're almost forty. Wow, you're turning forty. How are you with the big four-oh?* How am I with the big four-oh? The big four-oh is super, and I'm not quite there yet, but thanks for reminding me. And yes, I know I'm not married and I know I don't have a baby and I don't think I want either of those things. And yes, my boyfriend is nine years younger, so you can stop asking questions and doing speculative math in your head. I am fine with the big four-oh, but you people are freaking me out, and I already had my freak-out at thirty-five, so stop it or I will slap you.

Eva wanders over to the newsstand, leaving Jack and I a moment alone. It's always the same. I'll be ready, almost anxious for him to go, to get back to work, to sprawl in my bed and sleep alone, but then I want him to stay and I nearly cry. I kiss him goodbye at the security gate and he says he loves me and that he'll call when he gets in.

I find Eva at the newsstand thumbing through a celebrity tabloid. "That one's my favorites," I say.

"Me, too," she says. "It's so trashy."

"But not *too* trashy. There has to be a balance."

"I used to buy it at this Metro stop up in Chabanel when I'd go look at fabrics, then I'd put it inside, like, *V* or Japanese *Vogue* or something and read it on the way home. I didn't want anyone to see me with it."

We step out of the terminal and walk to Eva's car. "You can't worry about what everyone else thinks."

"Oh, I don't, not now. Especially after reading that column you wrote about embracing your guilty pleasures."

"I wrote that years ago."

Eva stops for a moment. "Two thousand and one, I think. Sometime in the spring?"

I have no idea if she's right, but I'll assume she is. "I think you know more about me than I do."

The drive to the airport and back with the top of Eva's convertible down has sobered me up and a dull headache is setting in. Eva parks and we walk to the corner and buy two bottles of cheap French wine at the *depanneur*. A couple glasses and my headache is masked by the liquor. Then there's the guilt and the phantom pain of work tomorrow. It's not even eight.

Eva walks around my apartment as if it were a museum. She looks closely at everything, every picture, every knick-knack, the title on every spine of every book on my shelves. She doesn't touch a thing. I take my camera out and upload the weekend's photos onto my computer. Of the twelve DOs for the fashion page, seven are strong enough to use. I only need five. I have fifteen DON'Ts, of which ten are hysterical, but I only need five of those, as well. And then there's Parrot Girl.

I hate Parrot Girl because I don't know what to do with her. It used to be easier when people just dressed how they dressed and it was about style, not irony and preciousness or getting their picture taken. I'm tired of Parrot Girl and all the other girls who may not have parrots but they're the same because they try so hard not to be. I hate Parrot Girl and her soccer socks and her cowboy boots and her satin jacket. But I hate her most because I know she looks ridiculous and that she is a DON'T. But it's not about me and my personal DON'Ts, not really, not anymore, it's about the perception of DON'Ts and knowing whether twenty-year-olds will think Parrot Girl is a DON'T. Stuffy American companies don't pay people twenty thousand dollars to talk to their marketing department for a day unless they can tell them definitively what a DON'T is to a twenty-year-old. *I'm almost forty.* I want to slap myself, but instead I take another swig of wine, and then I want to slap Parrot Girl, but she's not here. Eva is. I don't want to slap her. She's twenty-four. I could ask her what she thinks about Parrot Girl. She'd be thrilled, I'm sure. But I don't because I can't, because I can't fucking tell *what* Parrot Girl is. Is she a poseur or some newfangled post-post-ironic poster child for some save-the-birds society? Is she wrong or all right? Is she a test, a comeuppance for something I did last week or last year? *Fuck me.* Is she a DO or a DON'T?

My brain flips over and hurts. Get me a cold compress and a very soft pillow. Let me not care and play dead or pretend I'm a teacher, a strict schoolmarm. It's a pop quiz for Eva: who's a DO, who's a DON'T? Pencils down in three minutes! I'll check her work right away, taking my time—making her wait, making her nervous and possibly sweaty, though Eva seems likely to be one of those girls whose sweat smells like rosewater and never stains. Yes, a pop quiz could be fun, with Parrot Girl first up. No, second—I don't need Eva to sense that I need her, and that I want her to spill every secret she knows.

I'm quite sure that Eva would tell me everything—anything—I wanted. She'd be happy, I'd be happy, we could do a dance around the living room because we'd know, we'd know, we'd *know* just what Parrot Girl is. We could revel and open more wine, make a toast to the most fabulous DO or DON'T of the week. I stare at the photo of Parrot Girl and her stupid fucking parrot and my mouth seals shut. I say nothing and there will be no pop quiz. I don't need Eva, she holds no secrets I haven't heard or told before. Parrot Girl is my problem, she's a riddle, not a test, maybe even a joke.

I click through the photos and print them out. I spread them on the floor and Eva stands beside me as I decide which photos will make the column. Skinny Denim Shorts Man with the skeevy mustache is a DON'T. Skinny Pink Polo Shirt Man with the mutton chops and a kilt is a DO. Headband Girl is a DON'T. Babushka Girl is a DO. And so it goes until there is one more DON'T slot and one more DO. Parrot Girl is still on the floor. My confidence is sunk; it's not too late for the pop quiz and this is no joke. I've made a Skinny Pink Polo Shirt Man with mutton chops and a kilt a DO. He looks absurd and he's trying too hard but I know he's a DO because the boys at *Snap* keep trying to grow mutton chops and half of them are in kilts—but never sarongs—and they really like pink and girls like Eva like *them*. And there are no fucking pets at all so it's really not so complicated.

I look closer at the photo: it's technically good. I have to use it. Eva shuffles her feet. She's bored, she's waiting, one second longer and she'll know I'm a fraud. I pick up the photo and put it on the DON'T pile. I feel a rush of bravado and decide she'll be the feature DON'T. Eva's shuffling stops. Fuck Parrot Girl.

Jack calls. He's home and safe. The flight was good. No snacks or bar service, but it was only an hour and he tells me he found a half-eaten protein bar in his jacket pocket. I'm drunk and I can't believe I'm dating someone who eats protein bars. Eva's sitting on the sofa wearing gloves and examining issues six and eight of *Snap*. She told me that she carries the

gloves in her handbag at all times. She won't read an important book or periodical without them, she said. Eva is odd. I
slip into my bedroom and say this to Jack and he says, "*You're*
odd." And he's right, of course. I like her—Eva—and her
oddness. I like that she carries gloves in her bag and wears
panty hose and orthopedic shoes and has hair the color of a
Francophone grandma. Jack tells me he loves me and that he
misses me already. "I know you do, baby," I say and as soon as
that *baby* is out of my mouth I feel again like I want to vomit.

Eva is too drunk to drive so I tell her she can stay here. I
make up the spare room that's so rarely used. I lend her a black
cotton camisole and a pair of boxer shorts printed with
grinning flowers. They're Japanese and they were free. They
look cute on Eva. I rifle through my sleepwear options and
decide on a long black silk chemise with lace trim and a
matching robe. I keep my bra on so my breasts won't flop
around. I catch myself in the mirror. I look like a madam, but
the silk feels cool and soft against my skin. At home, I'm
usually in long johns and T-shirts, my hair tied back in a
ponytail and my glasses on. I swipe a neutral gloss across my
lips before heading back to the living room.

As we finish the wine, Eva tells me all about how great and
important and influential I am. Sometimes I ask her about
herself. She grew up in Pointe-Claire with an Anglo mother
and a French father, not far it turns out from Ted and
Genevieve's new house. I look up their address in my book
and Eva knows the street, it's about six blocks from her parents'
place. She's living there now, just temporarily she says. She
has a job, an office PA for a French film company, but the
pay is shit. She hates it, says the producer is a prick who wears
a fedora and a trench coat every day and does nothing except

play video games and look at porn on his cell phone. I tell her I'll take his picture and make him the featured DON'T one week. She laughs until her eyes tear and I do, too. Eva tells me she went to private school, with uniforms that she started altering at thirteen. She says she makes clothes she sometimes sells to friends, but mostly she's a stylist and a writer—like me. Except when I was twenty-four no one knew what a stylist did and no one knew our names. I tell her this and she goes on about how it's about time people— but mostly me—were recognized for our talent. We're the ones who spot and set the trends, not the movie stars, not the pop stars. Eva is very passionate about this. I'm fading and my eyes are heavy, but Eva keeps talking, telling me how remarkable and inspiring I am. "Look at all you've accomplished— look at everything you've done. And you're not even forty." Eva says this and it's better than sex, it's better than a lullaby.

Red wine is crusted around the corners of my mouth and looks nearly black. I scrape it off with my fingernail and splash water on my face before pinning my hair up and stepping into the shower. Under the water I'm dizzy and hot. I feel like I'm sweating. I step out and wrap myself in an oversize towel and sit on the edge of the bathtub for a long time, still and silent. If I move my head I fear it may explode. I reach for my body cream and rub it in all over. It has a faint vanilla scent, but I can still smell the toxic odor of yesterday afternoon's champagne and last night's wine on my skin. I spritz myself with extra perfume. I spray my hair with a citrusy refresher that absorbs the smell of smoke, then I work it into two low pigtails. Ted will know I'm hungover. I always wear my hair in pigtails when I'm hungover. It used to be, even five years ago, that I'd often be asked for ID in bars, liquor stores, buying cigarettes at chain stores with signs declaring Anyone Who Looks Under 30 Will Be Asked For Identification. I examine my face. No one will be asking me for ID today.

My face sucks up the first layer of moisturizer in seconds, so I slather on another. It's the eyes. The eyes are the biggest problem. It's not so much the wrinkles, but the skin—it's like the thinnest tissue paper, delicate and soft, never totally smooth, which makes concealer an issue. Applying it evenly on the puffy, papery skin is next to impossible and no matter how much blending and dabbing I do, it's never perfect. Still, I grout the area around my eyes with concealer, set it with a light powder, then attack with an expensive moisturizing spray gel that I nabbed from the Swag Shack at the office. I feel my skin suck it in and I wait for the promised youthful, reenergizing glow that after five minutes doesn't appear, so I give up and brush my teeth again. My tongue is still dark with wine. I brush it raw with my toothbrush, which looks too gross to ever use again, so I toss it in the trash and want to climb right in with it, but the pail is too small. I don't have a garbage pail big enough anywhere in the apartment. I could probably fold myself into one of those black plastic jumbo bags I use to dump all bottles into after a party—the ones I leave around back of the building for the bottle-picker with the beard and the giant tricycle who I always try to smile at but can never quite look in the eye or say hello to. The jumbo bag is problematic, though. I'd need someone to twist-tie the top for me and get me to the Dumpster and Ted isn't strong enough to lift me. Jack is, but he wouldn't do it. I could ask Eva if she has any big-guy friends, but that might seem weird since we just met.

Eva's not in the spare room, but I can tell she slept there because the bed is made just so, all crisp corners and symmetry. I find her in the kitchen slicing fresh bagels from the Fair-mount Bakery, which is not close by, but she says it was no big deal to nip up there and back. She's also picked up cut flowers and opened the blinds to the day.

"I have Mondays off," she says between bagel bites. "We shoot Tuesday to Saturday."

I remember now. She's a film office PA. She lives in Pointe-Claire with her parents. There's a guy with a hat and porn on his phone. "So what are your plans for today?" I ask.

"I don't know. Just hang around, I guess. But should probably go home and change. I used your shower, though. I hope that's okay."

"Use whatever you want. And if you're looking for something to wear, I'm sure you could find something at my office—we've got piles of stuff." It is true. The Swag Shack is full of free stuff companies send us in hopes that we'll write about it, put it on our IT LIST. Most of the stuff is crap that no one could possibly want, but sometimes it is such spectacular crap we put it on our ICK LIST. Then the publicists at the companies—the very people who sent us this crap stuff in the first place—call up whining and angry and we laugh at them and ask them if they've ever actually read *Snap* and they get all flustered and say yes, of course, but are suddenly nervous and polite and have a call they have to take on the other line, so goodbye.

There is good stuff, too. Cute clothes, but it's been ages since a pair of pants that fit me have come in and I could use new pants. The free-stuff publicists call up our market editors and ask about me, about Ted—favorite colors, hated colors, sizes. I haven't gotten around to telling anyone that I'm not an eight, but a ten now, so none of the pants they send over fit. If they ask, I tell our market editors I don't like the pants—any of them—even if I do. It's better than sending some internal e-mail that's sure to end up on someone's goddamn blog announcing that my ass is fatter. Like they haven't noticed. But skirts, if they're A-line or pleated, they fit. My waist is still an eight—it's my ass that's a ten. And tops are fine. Shoes and handbags are the best. I don't wear jewelry so I couldn't care whether it's free or not.

I take Eva to work with me. It's exciting for her and I'm happy that she drives and that I don't have to walk or contend with the Metro today. My legs are achy and my knee cracks as I cross it over the other in the passenger seat of Eva's Saab. She presses a button and the top comes down. I'm grateful for this because I worry that the smell of my hangover has defeated that extra spray of perfume.

The *Snap* building is squat and two storeys, a former embroidery factory in the east end. The first floor is reception and production, there's a fully equipped photo studio, and piled high to the ceiling in one corner there's a heap of old Macs that looks like it could tumble down at any moment, but really they're all superglued together and affixed to the wall. Sometimes when Ted and I are taking corporate clients though we tell them it's art.

I spin Eva around through production, the studio, mumble a few introductions. She seems impressed and keeps saying, "Oh, my gosh." Eva doesn't swear, I've noticed. She says *goodness* and *gosh,* and I'm waiting for a *golly-gee.* This could annoy me, but it's Eva so it doesn't.

We take the freight elevator to the second floor. I can't face the stairs even though I know my ass will never shrink riding an elevator. Today I'm a lazy bitch and I couldn't care. I've brought a CD with the DOs and DON'Ts fashion photos for the week. I'll give it to Layout, then show it to Ted, who will laugh and sign off and we'll get proofs of the entire issue and mark it up one more time before six when it has to go to the printer. By noon tomorrow it'll be in record stores and fashion boutiques and cafés in Montreal that we've personally approved. On Wednesday, it'll be in more record stores and fashion boutiques and cafés across the country and in the States that I suppose someone at some point has visited and approved on our behalf, but that's Ted's responsibility, not mine.

My office, like Ted's, is an actual office, with walls and windows and a door that locks. When we first moved into the building it was all open and chaos. Music blared and people smoked at their desks, although even back then it was against city bylaws. There's still music and chaos and it's fun to watch through the windows of my quiet, sound-proofed office, but I have to smoke on the roof.

Music and chaos is good for business, so we built the board-room in the middle of it all and glassed it in. Ted's in there meeting with our branding team. I wave and he nods. I lead Eva to my office and collapse immediately into the swiveling fuchsia chair I received as a gift from a boring furniture man-ufacturer that made a splash in the market by hiring a flam-boyant women's wear designer to create a line of equally flamboyant home and office furnishings that got lots of press but sold abysmally. Our research showed the price point was too high—there are only so many people who will pay eight thousand dollars for a polka-dot leather sofa and they don't shop at the boring furniture manufacturer's stores. So they can't say we didn't tell them so.

"I love your chair," Eva says.

"Here—give it a try. It's stylish *and* ergonomic." Christ. I'm an infomercial. I muster all my strength and lift myself out of it, placing both hands on my desk in front of me for balance. I hear my knees crack—both of them this time. Beside my desk there's an empty garbage pail. It's larger than your average office garbage pail, but I know I can't wedge my ass into that one, either.

Eva spins around in the fuchsia chair. "Mmm. Comfy."

"Free," I say. Like that explains anything. I think I may be retarded today, but I know enough to know I can't say that because this isn't junior high when Ted and I called everything *gay* and *retarded* and we called each other *gaylord* and *retard*. You can't say that unless you created *South Park* and you're saying it through those animated kids that are surprisingly still funny, because you never know who's gay or has a retard in their family.

Pleased with my self-censoring restraint, I walk Eva to the Swag Shack. It's the Swag Shack because that's what's burned into the plank of wood above the door. It's a room, the office Ted and I were going to give to the fancy financial executive we never got around to hiring. Instead, we beefed up our in-house accounting staff and none of them are fancy enough for an office. But we may have to rethink this because they keep complaining about the chaos and the noise and someone quits what seems like every second day, but is actually more like every five months according to Ted, and Ted would know because they report to him.

The Swag Shack is jammed with racks and shelves. There's free stuff everywhere. I let Eva loose and tell her to grab what she wants and come back to my office when she's done. I think she's going to freak—her eyes are all buggy and glazed, her mouth twisted in wonder. I've seen this look before—on girls the first time they enter the Swag Shack, on guys who are fucking me right before they come and on drummers, particularly the ones who are good.

"Sara, oh, my goodness! I don't know where to start," Eva says. She hugs me and I pat her shoulder. "Thank you!"

"Take as long as you want," I say and lope back to my office.

My eyes swim across the page. I'm in the boardroom proofing with Ted and our art director, Brian. My head is throbbing and I'm out of Advil. I'm sticky and sweaty and if there was ever any doubt earlier in the day that I was toxic and stinky, it's gone. I want to crawl under the giant kidney-shaped table, but it's glass-tinted, completely see-through—and people will notice. I force myself to read each word, take in every photo cutline, check the folio at the bottom of the pages. I find a missing word and I'm very proud.

I get to the DOs and DON'Ts page and there's Parrot Girl, looking disaffected, slouchy and numb. It's not too late to move her to a DO, but I don't because that will just make me feel more toxic and retarded. I sign off on the issue, as do Ted and Brian, who scrams at once, pressed to make the final changes before deadline. My work here is done and all I can think about is my bed.

"Who's the redhead?" Ted asks as we're clearing off the boardroom table.

"What?"

"Her." Ted points to Eva, who is sitting in my office. It's nearly four. I've forgotten all about her. I *am* retarded today and an asshole and a very poor host.

"That's Eva." Ted follows me out of the boardroom and to my office where I introduce him to her. She's changed into a pair of skinny madras plaid golf pants that I'm quite sure are men's, and a purple blouse with a fussy bow at the neck. She's pinned a gaudy rhinestone brooch in the shape of a lizard above her left breast. Scrunched up knee-highs peek out of her orthopedic shoes. She's a DO and I can tell Ted knows it, too.

"Eva, I'm so, so sorry for leaving you this long. You should have just grabbed me from the boardroom."

"Please don't worry about me, Sara. I've kept myself busy. As a matter of fact, I just finished." Eva bites her lower lip and casts her eyes down. "I hope you guys won't be mad, but I kind of did something."

Jesus. This can't be good. What'd she do? Break something? Wreck something? Spill something on my velvet chair? This must be what Genevieve means when she says she can't let baby Olivier out of her sight for a second.

"Come here," Eva says. She brushes past Ted and he smiles in that goofy way that all men do when an attractive girl touches them by accident. I notice Ted adjust his pants as he follows Eva out. It's subtle and Ted's no perv, but still. I flash on Ted with a hard-on when we were seventeen, his purple penis and its big mushroom head. I'm dizzy and nauseous. I haven't eaten since this morning and the picture of Ted's mushroom-head dick isn't helping. He was a virgin. I wasn't. We were drunk. He actually begged, so we fucked and we never talked about it again. I wonder if Genevieve knows, but I doubt it because she tells me all about sex with Ted—at least she did until the baby—and I figure if she knew she probably wouldn't tell me so much. As I walk behind Ted, who's walking behind Eva, I contemplate which is worse: hearing from Gen about how turned on she gets sucking Ted's cock when I know that it's a weird mushroom-head cock or hearing Gen describe how Olivier peed in her face when she was changing him and about how baby balls disappear up inside their little baby-boy bodies and how babies get teeny-tiny erections. I wonder if Olivier has a mini mushroom-head penis like his dad. Incarcerate me in a giant garbage pail under the boardroom table and slap me around. Put me out of my misery, I'm a fucked-up sicko.

"Surprise!" Eva swings open the door to the Swag Shack and I'm agog. It's clean, orderly. The body and beauty products are grouped together. The men's and women's wear have been separated and, from what I can tell, organized according to style and color. Gadgets and toys have assigned spaces. CDs and books are alphabetized. I am speechless.

"Who are you and what have you done with the Swag Shack?" Ted says, shaking Eva by the shoulders. He can be such a cheese sometimes.

Eva blushes. "I hope you don't mind. It just seemed like it would be so hard to find anything in here. I wanted to make it easier for you."

I love her. I think I could, as my mother used to say, *go gay*. My mother didn't believe a person could be born gay, but she didn't think anyone would choose to be gay, either. Hence, her *go gay* theory. Much like being struck by a random bolt of lightning, she believed someone could be walking down the street and—poof!—they'd just go gay and that would be that. This could be somewhat embarrassing when I'd have my gay friends over and my mother would insist on asking them about their personal going-gay experience, but it was better than her being a bigoty homophobe like Ted's nightmare all-Bible, all-the-time Catholic parents. I could totally go gay for Eva right now, but the sex would be trouble. I'd still have to have sex with men without bulbous mushroom-head penises.

So maybe gay isn't the best option for Eva and me. Maybe I'll make her my assistant.

I've never had an assistant. Watching Ted burn through new assistants like Jack goes through his revolting protein bars has made me wary of both. The point of having an assistant as far as I can tell is to help you, but assistants from what I've seen are snaky whiners who spend more time trying to write some pathetic roman à clef than actually helping the bosses whom they so obviously hate. Eva doesn't hate me. Eva loves me. And Eva's smart and cute and she cleaned the Swag Shack.

Eva is my new assistant. It's Tuesday morning and she's at her desk tap-tapping away on her computer. She brought Fairmount bagels so everyone loves her already, except for one of the IT guys who's allergic to wheat and gluten and sugar and everything else good. It's a miracle he hasn't killed himself.

I'm feeling much better, clean almost. I washed my hair this morning and my resolve to quit smoking is strong. Day one was a breeze—I couldn't face a cigarette yesterday—and when I told Jack on the phone last night that I was done, he was pleased. He says I snore when I smoke too much. He smokes. He snores. I don't make a big thing of it. Jack can really piss me off sometimes.

But Eva is perfect. We're going out tonight to celebrate her new job at a new restaurant that has cordially invited me and a guest to wine and dine on the house. Genevieve was supposed to go with me, but sent a midnight e-mail bailing. Olivier is *acting up,* which is code for *I can't leave Ted alone with the baby.* Olivier is nearly one and Gen has yet to leave him with Ted for more than five minutes. Occasionally she'll entrust Prince Olivier's care to one of her newfangled suburban mommy friends I've never met, but not Ted. I think that's fucked up, but I'm smart enough to keep my mouth shut about things like mommy-baby codependency and mini mushroom-head penises.

I will take Eva to the restaurant. She bounced up and down on her chair when I asked if she'd like to go. She clapped her hands and said, "Goody!" I suspect it won't be long before I get that *golly-gee* I've been waiting for.

Eva helps stuff the Trend Essentials swag bags we'll be giving to the six participants in our Trend Mecca Bootcamp Weekend that starts Friday. I hate Trend Mecca Bootcamp weekends, but considering that each one of the corporate fucks that signs up pays ten thousand dollars to *experience the street life and underground of trendsetting Montreal,* I can hardly complain. No one wants to hear from a high-priced whore about the sultan who paid her a million dollars to fuck her up the ass for a weekend and no one wants to hear me gripe about the Trend Mecca Bootcamp Weekend. I don't even want to know there is such a thing as a Trend Mecca Bootcamp Weekend, let alone lead it. Maybe I'll take Eva this time. Maybe I'll wear a wig. Maybe I'll bring a rag soaked in chloroform to wipe the smirk off the face of anyone who sees me out with these guys and their pleated pants and patterned sweaters. The people who sign up for the Trend Mecca Bootcamp Weekend are almost always all guys.

Eva says she thinks it sounds fun and that she wants to learn everything she can about the business. She says she'll carry my coffee or fetch drinks for the Bootcamp suits. Eva is my dream girl until about 2:00 p.m. when she knocks on my door and asks if she can come in. She looks nervous. She's biting her lower lip again.

"What's up, Eva? You're not thinking about going back to that fedora porn guy are you?"

"No, no, nothing like that. It's just that there's this Web site—it's not important, really, but you might want to see...."

I wave her over behind my desk and lean back, letting her type the URL into my computer. The Apples Are Tasty logo comes up. "Yeah, I've seen this," I say, ignoring the screen. There are no DON'Ts walking the streets if one is to buy in to the Apples Are Tasty philosophy. Everyone is a DO in their own special way. Rid the world of negativity, embrace your individuality, pay fifty bucks to attend one of the parties we're already being paid ten grand to throw, for another thousand one of the Apples Are Tasty crew will spend a day shopping with you. But getting your picture on the Apples Are Tasty Web site is the latest and greatest in hipster validation.

In two months, the site has gone from nothing to a very biggish deal. These party-planners-cum-DJing-style-setters started getting attention and our clients started asking about them. At first we dismissed them as wannabes—we've dealt with copycats before—but when we tried to arrange access to one of their parties as a stop on the upcoming Trend Mecca Bootcamp Weekend we were rebuffed. That's how Ted puts it—*rebuffed*—but what really happened was he lost it in an e-mail exchange with the Tasty ringleader when the guy refused to cough up comp party tickets for the Trend Mecca Bootcamp Weekend. Then he posted Ted's tirade online and forwarded it to all the clients he knew we had and to every media outlet on the planet. That was two weeks ago. Things have calmed down, but Ted won't talk about it. And he's more determined than ever to ferret out whoever put that apple on his desk the day after the whole thing went down and fire their ass. We have security cameras everywhere now. It won't happen again.

I tell Eva it's important to know your competition and what they're doing, but not to get too wrapped up, not to obsessively worry about where they're going and what they're doing. There's room for all of us and we should appreciate each other's differences because that's what makes us all unique and wonderful. I'm a raving hypocrite, I know, and I don't care. I've built my career taking pictures of unfortunate-looking people wearing unfortunate-looking outfits. Like Parrot Girl. Like Parrot Girl, who's staring out at me from my computer, the same Parrot Girl who is the current Apples Are Tasty Look Girl.

Fuck me and stop the presses. But it's too late—kill me now or let me fall on the sword I bought in Osaka, the one that I had to fill out reams of paperwork to get through customs. Let Parrot Girl's parrot gnaw at my corpse.

They're right, they're right, I know they're right. I hate Parrot Girl, but twenty-year-old urbanites and suburban scenesters don't. Laminate my picture, doctor my birth date and make me sixty-five. I'll eat tiny portions ordered from special menus in restaurants, shop for groceries on certain days and ride the Metro for cheap. Book me into a home where I can be with my kind: wrinkled rock stars and one-time starlets with puffy lips and faces that don't move when they talk about the good old days, which is all anybody talks about. We talk and talk so we can remember when we knew something and weren't old and disgusting and had better things to do than clip coupons and play bridge and wait to die.

I don't want to die. I want to disappear. I want to press Rewind and give Eva a pop quiz. I want to be right. I want to care. I want to leave. I need to stop and I need to rest but the constant *ping* of my e-mail makes everything impossible. I rap the side of my computer with a curled knuckle. Eva's still standing behind me, silent but for the quiet shuffle of her feet. I knock on the side of my computer again as a burst of *ping-ping-pings* signals the arrival of yet more e-mail undoubtedly demanding my resignation. But it hasn't been twenty-five years: I won't get a watch or a shitty roast beef dinner buffet at some economy motel that must have a discount rate for seniors.

I don't need to knock on the computer again. I know they're all inside. The place is packed with girls with shiny jackets and soccer socks. Their pet birds are shitting everywhere, but they don't care as long as it's not on their boots. It's filthy and the girls are smoking and think it's all so very funny. They're talking about me but I can't hear the words over the laughter. I creep on unnoticed and over the wires and microchips and bird shit until someone drops a lit cigarette on my head and I jerk up, screaming. They all stop and look, but nobody laughs. Someone helps me to the door but I can't keep a grip on her arm because the satin jacket she's wearing is so slippery. I stumble and land at the feet of the Skinny Pink Polo Shirt Boy with the mutton chops and the kilt. I get a flash up his skirt and he's not wearing any underwear. His cock is thick and long and doesn't have a mushroom head. I smile up at him, but his expression reads nothing but pity. The Slippery Girl gets me to the door and nudges me out. It's all fine. I have to go anyhow. I have to make a call or have a meeting and buy clothes for my new job. Yes, I have to go. I have to go. I have to go.

I reach into my desk and pull out a spare set of keys for

the office front door, the back door, the Swag Shack. I can't go. I don't need to go. I have nowhere to go. I still have my keys. I hold them tightly in my hand until the metal edges dig into my skin—not enough to draw blood, but enough to hurt. My e-mail *pings* and *pings* and soon it's the rhythm of an old techno song—no, early Chicago house, which I know is back and that my vinyl is worth maybe thousands to some know-it-all DJ with a cute face and a thousand girlfriends. But he loves Parrot Girl the most and is living in the suburbs with his parents to save enough money to impress her by giving her the rarest, most colorful parrot in the world—one that's fully bilingual and shits in a toilet and knows how to use a bidet.

There is nothing worse than suburban scenesters who love girls with parrots who try too hard. I force myself to look at Parrot Girl's photo on my screen. She's standing in front of the brunch spot that now I'll truly never, ever return to— and she's smiling. We have a strict no-smile policy for our DOs and DON'Ts. Perhaps it's time to revisit that. I make a note on a yellow sticky: *Smiles?* Eva says nothing, she hovers, frozen behind me.

"I guess people love birds," I say, which is maybe the dumbest thing to come out of my mouth all day. "Hey, why don't I make a couple of quick calls and we cut out early, do the streets and grab a couple of drinks before dinner?" This is maybe the smartest thing to come out of my mouth all day.

Eva heads back to her desk and I e-mail Ted that I'm heading out to do the streets, which means going trolling for unfortunate-looking people wearing unfortunate outfits, and call Jack in Toronto on his cell. He's prepping a video for a New York electro-goth band all week. When he doesn't pick up on the third ring I hang up and straighten the papers on my desk. A call comes through on my private line.

"Did you just call?" It's Jack.

"Yeah."

"Why didn't you leave a message?"

"I don't know." We've had this conversation before.

"You could at least leave a message."

"Next time I will, then."

"You sound funny."

"I am funny."

"Seriously, Sara, are you okay?"

"Why wouldn't I be?"

"I saw Parrot Girl on Apples Are Tasty."

"Then why the hell didn't you call?"

"I figured you would have seen it."

"I just saw it now—Eva showed it to me." Admitting this is torture. I'm humiliated and bruised. All the blood in my body feels like it's rushing to my head. My eyes sting. I'm going to cry. "I don't know if I can do this anymore," I whisper into the phone. The tears come.

"Oh, baby, it's gonna be okay. We all have off days."

"This isn't about an off day." My voice is choking; I'm strangled by confession.

"Are you gonna be home later, sweetheart? We could talk more about this then. Now—it's not a good time. But I really want to talk to you."

"I have a dinner," I say.

"Call me when you get in, okay, baby? It doesn't matter how late."

"Okay." My voice is tiny. I am the crying girlfriend.

I hold the phone to my ear and face the back wall of my

office long after I've said goodbye to Jack. I examine in a compact mirror the hot splotches on my face and my swollen eyes. A coat of moisturizer cools my skin and I reapply my eye makeup, all with the phone tucked between my shoulder and ear, listening again and again to the robot operator lady say, *Please hang up and try your call again,* first in French then in English. I want to call Genevieve, but every time I do she can't talk, she's too tired, or I get the feeling that what I want to talk about isn't anything she wants to hear. I want to call Ted and he's right next door, but he's so stressed and serious these days the last thing he needs is me in his office bawling about Apples Are Fucking Tasty and Parrot Girl.

"You ready to go?" I ask Eva. She's at her desk arranging the Trend Mecca Bootcamp Weekend files. She's compiling dossiers for me about each of the participants. One of the men is not terribly discreet about his interest in rubber masks, ball gags and female domination. Eva shows me the online evidence, and scrunches up her face as if she'd discovered a turd in her breakfast cereal instead of a prize. "There's always one," I say. "Put it in the file."

We park at my place and walk through the streets of the Plateau, then over to Saint-Laurent. It's June and the tourists are starting to descend, making it prime DON'T season. Within seconds I spot no less than three socks-and-sandals men, but they're boring so we move on. We walk east and along the way encounter a beefy man with a mullet. He's wearing a mesh half-shirt and drawstring bouncer pants with a Mickey Mouse print. His sneakers have neon green laces and he's got a thick gold chain around his neck. I approach him and ask to take his picture. I click away but he won't stop smiling.

I ask in my most polite voice for him to stop and he does, but the smile lingers in his eyes. His pride is like a sucker punch. Tears well up and sting. Eva has him sign the release and I quickly wipe my eyes.

"Are you all right, Sara?" Eva asks once Beefy Cartoon Pants Man has gone.

"Allergies," I say.

"Gosh, that's terrible. Is there anything I can do? There's a pharmacy around the corner—I could get you some of those pills, those antihistamines."

"That would be great, Eva. Thanks." I park myself on a bus bench and fiddle with my camera in an effort to calm down while I wait for Eva to return. I have to shake off this psycho-spaz cry-baby thing. There's a bar across the street, one of those crappy fake Irish pubs—no affected urbanites, no suburban scenesters, no Apples Are Tasty or *Snap,* no *Sara B., take my picture!* It's exactly what I need. As I dart across the road, I call Eva on her cell and tell her to meet me there. My beer arrives just as she does. I rip into the box of allergy tablets and weasel two out their childproof packaging, then down them with my beer. I assure Eva that once the pills kick in my eyes will be just fine.

Mecca

Not everything French is chic, and Montreal isn't the zenith of cool. Part of my job on this Trend Mecca Bootcamp Weekend is to ensure that none of the six participants figures this out. I've known them for half a day now and am confident this will not be a concern.

As we tour the myth of the city—the shops and cafés, the lairs of local designers—the *über*alphas emerge from the group of type-A corporate alpha dogs and as usual the advertising people rise to the top of the shit pile. They know it all. Everywhere we go, they jostle for position—who can get an *I've heard about this* out of their mouth faster? There's a creative director from Chicago determined to *harness the zeitgeist* and one from Vancouver who's all about *the next big thing.* Then there's the woman from Baltimore who won't shut up about how she has her *finger on the pulse,* though from the way she keeps ogling Zeitgeist from Chicago I think she wants her precious finger up his ass, and from the way Big Thing Vancouver keeps leering at her, it's his ass that wants Precious Finger. I want to cut my veins open and hurl myself into the

St. Lawrence River, but I can't because I don't have a knife or a razor blade and we're not going to be near the waterfront until after lunch.

I thank God that Eva is such a small-talk enthusiast. She answers silly questions about the city and *Snap* and she sounds very authoritative. We're lunching at a popular bistro on Saint-Laurent better known for its attractive staff than its food. I order a side of mayo for my fries, which is something Precious Finger cannot deal with—the fat, the calories, the cholesterol, *your heart*—so when it arrives, a goopy dollop in a small white bowl, I'm sure to pass it around for everyone at the table to try. I notice Zeitgeist watching the waitresses and Precious Finger watching him. He is momentarily distracted by my fries/mayo offering. After one bite he declares it *genius.* He's chewing as he says this and I see tiny bits of saliva mushed potato-and-mayo spray from his mouth.

It's Precious Finger's turn and I reckon she has no choice but to risk it all—her weight, her cholesterol, *her heart*—if she has any chance of impressing Zeitgeist, ardent supporter of genius fries-and-mayo and, more important, of getting a chance to shove a well-lubed finger up his ass. I am convinced that Zeitgeist is the kind of man who has a bottle of travel-size lube beside the bed in his hotel room if not in the fake army surplus bag he's had slung across his chest all morning. Just because it's green and burlap with numbers and patches on it doesn't mean it's not a purse.

Precious Finger closes her eyes and screws up her face as she brings the mayo-coated fry to her mouth. I watch Big Thing from Vancouver watch her, rapt and eyes glazed. Zeitgeist is still watching the waitresses. Precious Finger purses her lips and makes a face. She munches fast. Her mouth is tight but her cheeks move furtively. Her lipstick has been wiped clean by her lunch—mandarin-almond salad, vinaigrette on the side, one fry-and-mayo. She looks like a squinty squirrel. "Mmm, delicious! *Genius,*" she says.

Zeitgeist stops looking at the waitresses and turns his attention back to the table and briefly to Precious Finger. He points at a stray spot of mayonnaise on the side of her squirrelly mouth. She blushes and dabs it away with a napkin.

"Good, huh?" Zeitgeist says.

"Delicious. *Genius.* You were so right." Precious Finger brushes her bangs off her forehead. "Actually, I'm thinking of ordering some more—if there's time." She looks at me. We can be late for the flea market in Old Montreal. Witnessing Precious Finger force-feed herself a plate of fries and mayo is an opportunity I refuse to pass up.

The fries come and I take out my camera. Precious Finger moves in closer to Zeitgeist, her head nearly resting on his shoulder. Big Thing scoots into frame. I coax Precious Finger to eat a fry while I snap a photo, but she won't until Zeitgeist slathers one in mayo and feeds it to her. His face is smirky. Big Thing's shoulders slump in defeat. I take the picture and Precious Finger excuses herself to use the washroom. I wait two minutes and follow her in. I don't have to go, but I wash my hands. The sound of the water does nothing to drown out the sound of Precious Finger retching in a locked stall.

I'm back at the table before she is and am surprised to find Ted there, smiling and doling out handshakes all around. Ted never comes on the Trend Mecca Bootcamp Weekends.

"What's up?" I ask.

"Nothing. Just thought I'd stop by, maybe tag along."

"Sounds great."

It is great that Ted is here. Between him and Eva they answer all the inane questions. I walk behind and take pictures that I'll delete at home. No one bugs me when I have a camera in front of my face. We push through the crowded flea market, visit the studio of an artist friend, walk some more, shop a little and the three advertising alpha dogs talk and talk and talk while the three boring corporate types take notes and ask nerdy questions. We stop for drinks and dinner. Precious Finger sits beside Zeitgeist and forces another order of fries and mayo down her throat and then we're off to see a band that Big Thing is particularly excited about. "They're gonna break big this summer," he announces like he's the Casey Kasem of alterna-everything. We flag three taxis after the show and I'm stuck with him riding back to the Bootcampers' boutique hotel. He won't shut up about the *Montreal scene,* which is not what it was five years ago, let alone ten years ago, but he doesn't need to know that. I want to strike him in the head with a giant mallet, but reconsider and think I'd rather use it on myself. I remember that I have a big wooden meat tenderizer in a drawer at home that I've never used.

The three boring corporate types go straight to their rooms and to bed, blathering about time zones and saying they have to call their wives or their boyfriends or their kids or their cats. If he doesn't call his wife, one man says—the one with the shirt and tie and high-waisted no-name big-box-store blue jeans—there will be hell to pay.

Zeitgeist, it seems, has no fear of hell or paying. Each time he lifts his glass to drink, the gold of his wedding band reflects the candlelight. Precious Finger pets his leg and Big Thing abruptly excuses himself. He settles into a seat at the bar and two women I've seen here before sidle up to him. If Precious Finger doesn't want him, he can always rent a lady friend for the night.

So it's me and Eva and Ted and Zeitgeist and Precious Finger. Eva is trying to convince Ted that now is the time for *Snap* to expand its online presence. Precious Finger is pawing at Zeitgeist, who seems sufficiently drunk and has stopped looking at every other woman in the room. But this could well be because his eyes can no longer focus or because he's now thinking seriously of Precious Finger's lubed finger in his ass while her squirrely mouth is wrapped around his cock, which I'll bet is a stubby, skinny thing.

I stir my drink with a skinny straw that makes me think of Zeitgeist's dick but longer. It's unpleasant, so I take out my cell phone and check for messages I know aren't there. I told Jack I'd be busy all weekend with the Bootcamp and that I'd call him Sunday if the whole thing hadn't killed me and if not we'd talk sometime Monday. It's Friday night and I'm annoyed he hasn't called. I check my messages at home. Nothing. Well, a call from Genevieve that I can barely hear due to the noise in the bar and Olivier's piercing screams. No wonder Ted is here. I dial Jack's number but hang up before it rings or my number shows up on his call display and we have to have that stupid conversation again about me not leaving messages.

Zeitgeist and Precious Finger say their good-nights and stumble off together to the lobby. Eva and Ted are laughing. I lean forward and rest my elbow on the table and my head on my hand, like a girl playing jump rope with friends waiting for the right time to step into the game. I order another drink and scan the busy bar. I feel someone watching me but I don't turn my head to look, afraid of the hipster boy-waif or nightmare suburban suit guy that I might find standing there. He moves closer and hovers behind me and to the left. I pretend the dodgy artwork on the wall to my right is interesting.

"Hi, there. Can we help you?" Eva asks.

"Oh, yes, perhaps. We'd certainly appreciate it." It's a woman's voice.

I turn to face her, relieved. I smile and look up and then down again, stirring my drink with the Zeitgeist-skinny-dick straw. They're ladies—old ladies, old ladies with orthopedic shoes and red hair the same shade as Eva's.

"It's so crowded and we noticed you weren't using all of your seats. We don't mean to impose, but—"

"Sit, sit, by all means, sit," says Ted as he leaps from his chair to pull back two for the old ladies.

The old ladies thank us too many times and offer to buy us a round of drinks, which Ted refuses and instead says that he'd be honored to by *them* a round. Ted's using his chuffy voice, which means he's awfully proud of himself and I wonder why he's here and not home helping his wife with their screaming child.

The old ladies' names are Esther and Lila. Esther takes Ted's hand in both of hers and shakes it. She does the same with Eva. Then it's my turn. I tell them that my hands are really cold and Lila seems okay with this and backs away, but Esther grabs my hands anyway and now she knows I lied— my hands aren't cold, I'm just not an old-people person.

I learn things about Esther and Lila I don't want to know. Lila is divorced. Esther is seventy-five; she's six years older than Lila, who I guess that would make sixty-nine, not that I could tell a day's difference in their made-up wrinkly faces even if I could look at them for more than a second. Neither woman is married or has children. They do share an apartment, but Lila makes it clear that they're not *funny* by which I assume she means *lesbian*. Esther is quick to add that there's

nothing wrong with being *funny,* she's always simply preferred a man's touch. She looks right at me when she says this.
I look at my watch and grab my phone off the table. "I have
to call my boyfriend," I say. My voice is too loud but I can't
shove it back in my mouth so I clod off to the lobby to
pretend to call Jack, but change my mind and go outside to
smoke and pretend to call Jack.

I left my cigarettes in my bag at the table, so now there's
nothing to do except stand outside and play with the buttons
on my phone. There's a guy smoking a few feet away. I think
about asking him for a cigarette, but he's a hipster boy-waif,
the kind I was afraid might be hovering behind me when it
was really the old ladies. I weigh my options. I bum a smoke,
he'll want to talk—people always want to talk. He'll ask me
what I do and I'll tell him the truth because I'm too tired to
lie and I'm still smarting over being busted by old lady Esther
for saying my hands were cold. I'll tell the hipster waif-boy what
I do and he'll be impressed without saying so, like Parrot Girl
was when I took her picture. Then I'll be reminded of Parrot
Girl and the goddamn Apples Are Tasty fiasco and the night—
not that it's been stellar or anything—will be unsalvageable.

"Would you like one?" It's Esther. I didn't hear her come
up. Old people are quiet and sneaky.

She holds open a thin gold case filled with cigarettes. I take
one. I can't help myself. "Thanks."

She lights it for me with a gold lighter that matches the case
and I thank her again. "It's a lovely night," Esther says.

"Yup."

"The young girl, Eva—is she your sister?"

I laugh. "No. She's…" What is Eva? "We work together."

"You could be sisters."

I'm flattered, I suppose, that someone, Esther even, thinks Eva and I could be related. "We really don't look alike."

"It's not that. My sister and I looked nothing alike. It's more your presence, your mannerisms."

I shrug, not sure what to say, so we smoke in silence for a moment. "That Ted is such a pleasant young man. He said something about putting out that trendy magazine Lila and I pick up all the time, *Snap*?"

"We run it together."

"Oh, my. Well, congratulations. That's quite an accomplishment for two young people. Lila and I think it's a hoot, by the way. Those DOs and DON'Ts always have us in stitches."

"I do those." I take a deep drag on my cigarette. *It's a hoot, they say, the old ladies are in stitches.* A taxi peals up in front of the hotel and I consider throwing myself in front of it.

Lila breaks out into a coughing fit as Esther and I approach the table. It's loud and audible above the trancy music. People are starting to stare. She doesn't stop and I look at Ted in panic. Should we do something? Should we call an ambulance? Does anyone know CPR? Esther swats her friend playfully on the shoulder and the two women burst into giggles. "Oh, you," Esther says and turns to me. "She does this every time I nip out for a ciggie. She hates it when I smoke."

"Filthy habit!" Lila says.

"Sara here was telling me that she takes those photos that crack us up so much," Esther says, changing the subject as she lowers herself slowly into her chair.

"The ones in *Snap*? We love those!"

"That's what I told her."

"That's how we found out about this place—we read about it on that fun MUST DO list!" Lila says. She's awfully excitable and squirming in her seat. I hope she doesn't have a stroke.

"Lila's addicted to magazines and newspapers," Esther explains.

"It's better than being addicted to cigarettes!"

"And she keeps them all. You should see her library, Sara. Floor-to-ceiling magazines—fifty years' worth all stacked and in order."

"What kind of magazines?" I ask.

"Oh, everything. But mostly fashion. I was quite the clotheshorse in my day—used to pore over every issue of *Vogue* and *Harper's Bazaar* for inspiration then sew up my own dresses."

"And you have all of those? Fifty years?" I would kill—well, maybe not kill, but certainly maim or pay handsomely for fifty years of those magazines.

"When I was a teenager I would make confirmation dresses for girls in the neighborhood. I spent every penny I made on magazines and material."

Esther beams proudly at her friend. "Our Lila was quite the entrepreneur."

"Sounds like it," I say. I look at Lila. Her face is heart-shaped, her features are delicate and her cheekbones high and defined. Behind the mask of age and powder and blush she was probably quite beautiful.

"Perhaps you'd like to come for tea sometime and take a look," Lila suggests.

"That would be awesome!" If my status as a complete retard was ever in question, it is in this moment that I ir-refutably determine that I am. I scrawl my cell-phone number on the back of my card and give it to Lila, who accepts it, probably out of pity for the softheaded thirty-nine-year-old who says *awesome*.

There are two taxis idling outside the hotel, but Esther insists on driving us—even suburban Ted—in her old Mercedes sedan. She's only had one drink and though no one asks she makes a point of telling us that her eyesight is perfect.

"That's because she had the laser surgery," Lila whispers to me. "Used to be blind as a bat."

I notice a copy of *Snap* from two weeks ago folded open to the MUST DOs page on the backseat. The address of the boutique hotel is circled in black ink. I pick it up and place it carefully on my lap and Ted, Eva and I slide in.

Eva is staying at my place for the weekend. With the Bootcamp schedule it's more convenient than her driving to and from Pointe-Claire every day, and I like having her around.

It's late and we should probably sleep, but my soft retard head is dancing with visions of midcentury fashion magazines, their pages filled with photographs by Avedon, Penn and Hiro. I open a bottle of wine and relax into my favorite chair. Eva sits with her legs curled up under her granny nightgown. It's short, flannelette with long sleeves and a high lace-trimmed neck that looks itchy. I admire her unwavering commitment to personal style. I'm dressed in my black silk floor-length chemise again. I'm dying to take off my bra, but don't want to scare Eva with the reality of thirty-nine-year-old breasts. I sit up straight, suck in my stomach and arch my back a little. I am a lady in repose.

I'm only half listening to Eva. She's talking about online something and some Internet show that is either something she wants Ted to watch or wants him to produce for *Snap* and I'm not sure which because I'm talking about Lila's magazines and what I know is in them. I'm speculating about how much such a collection would be worth and I get up and log on to eBay and find that a single issue of *Vogue* from the fifties can go for more than twenty-five dollars. I try to do the math but it's too much for my soft head. I debate the merits of *Vogue* versus *Bazaar* aloud and decide that it depends on the decade and on Diana Vreeland, and which magazine she was with at the time. Eva's talking at the same time and I wish she'd shut up, but she keeps talking and so do I and we talk louder and faster and over each other until it's all white noise and I have to go to bed.

It's Eva who wakes me at eight-thirty. Bootcamp starts at nine. She tells me Ted called and that he's on his way to pick up his car, which he left at the *Snap* building overnight, and he'll meet us at the hotel at nine and we'll take the Boot-campers for a bagels-and-lox breakfast. I must have been out so hard I didn't hear the phone.

Eva's dressed in a sixties day dress with tiny pink flowers running along the hem. As usual, this is topped with a cardigan and her red hair is coiffed and sprayed. I can see a hint of blond roots as she bends down to hand me a coffee and three Advil. "Let me know if you need anything else," she says and skips out of my bedroom.

I heave myself up and wash the pills down with the coffee. My glamorous silk chemise is twisted up around my waist, exposing the ugly stretched-out panties I wear when Jack's not here. I'm still wearing my bra and the straps have left deep red grooves on my shoulders. Eva is humming in the kitchen.

I shower then call Ted and tell him I'm running late and

to entertain the Bootcampers until Eva and I arrive. I like Ted-the-helpful-tagalong much better than Ted-the-angry-Apples-Are-Tasty-e-mailing ranter.

I want to wear my glasses and my baggy vintage men's 501s that some crazy Japanese guy offered to buy off my ass on the spot at a gig last summer for four hundred American dollars, but I don't. I shimmy into a cute summer wrap dress. I seal the plunging V-neck with a piece of the stickiest double-sided tape until it's semi-respectable-looking and my tits aren't entirely popping out. I make up my face and scrunch up my hair until it looks artfully tousled, but it's lopsided. I want my ponytails. I strap on sandals with heels, but there's no way my contacts are going in. I put on my prescription Ray-Bans and vow not to take them off until after sundown.

Every time Precious Finger laughs her shrill laugh at breakfast I feel like someone is stabbing an ice pick into my ears. Who knew such a sound could come out of a tiny, squirrelly woman? I can only imagine what kinds of offensive noises she was making last night, undoubtedly naked and writhing with her undoubtedly shaved pussy impaled on Zeitgeist's skinny stub. I can imagine this but I don't want to. What I want to do is throw up or lie on the floor or call Jack and tell him to get the next flight to Montreal so he can make me tea and pet my head.

I pick at my bagel and let Eva tell the group about the day's itinerary: shopping, eating, music. "And tomorrow—" she's getting them all worked up now "—we've arranged an exclusive tour of the *Snap* offices and a roundtable discussion with some great examples of the city's most stylish DOs."

This is news. Trend Mecca Bootcamp Sunday is usually

homework day, when I spend time with the participants arranging their photographs and notes into a sort of scrapbook that they can take back to their bosses as proof that the weekend was ten grand well spent. And it's the day we hand out the goody bags, which is my favorite part because it means that shortly they'll all be getting on airplanes and going home. Trend Mecca Bootcamp Sunday is not for *Snap* tours and roundtables. I glare at Ted from behind my sunglasses but he doesn't notice so I kick him under the table. He points to Eva and gives me the thumbs-up sign. It takes all my willpower not to grab a serrated knife off the table, hold his hand down and saw off his fucking thumb.

"It was just an idea we came up with last night. I told her it was impossible, we could never assemble the right people in time for a Sunday roundtable, but she called this morning and said she'd taken care of it. What was I supposed to say? I thought she ran it by you."

"She did not run it by me," I hiss. We're outside the bagel place. Eva is a few feet away chatting up the group while I smoke and bitch at Ted.

"Are you sure, Sara?"

"Of course I'm sure."

"You were pretty drunk last night."

This is true, but I'm sure I would remember agreeing to something like this. It's not the sort of thing I'd be likely to forget unless of course Eva was talking about it while I was talking about Lila's magazines. Fuck me hard with Zeitgeist's skinny-stub dick—I don't know what to say. "Well, she told me about it, but I thought she meant for the *next* Bootcamp."

Ted looks relieved. I am a lying dirtbag with possible blackout issues. No more hard liquor. No more drinking till

I'm drunk. Wine and beer only, and only with food. Ted and I join the others and walk up the street to our first shopping stop of the day. The straps of my high-heeled sandals rub against my feet and I can feel the blisters bubbling up.

By midafternoon I'm gimping behind the group like I have some kind of palsy. Women pass and either smile in empathy or sneer at my stupidity. The men—the straight men—are oblivious: they're staring at my tits, which refused to be contained by the stickiest double-sided tape and are pushing out of my clingy wrap dress. I sit down once we reach the *Snap* store. I rarely come here—it's too weird, all the staff know who I am and act skittish and extra friendly when I visit so I don't except on Bootcamp weekends and that's only because Ted reminds me that the Bootcampers always drop serious cash. It's better to endure a stop at the *Snap* store than to contend with bitchy Ted, who inevitably shows up in my office the following Monday saying something like *I have a bee in my bonnet* or *I have a bone to pick with you.* He thinks this is funny but is never actually amused if the company store wasn't on the tour.

This particular Bootcamp weekend I am delighted, ecstatic, positively *aglow* that we've stopped at the *Snap* store, as I can get off my fucking feet. I survey the shop and notice we are stocking an excellent selection of limited-edition sneakers, the sight of which make my feet throb more and I long for an axe and an epidural to numb my lower half so I won't feel the pain when I lob off my swollen, blistery feet.

We're also selling pairs of hand-knit, mismatched argyle socks and this is most helpful—I'll need something to cauterize my stumps before I shove them into a pair of three-hundred-dollar hip-hop-fantastic sneakers. I'll be like one of those ladies I see walking to the Metro station in the morning, dressed in a skirt suit with socks and sneakers, the practical pumps she'll change into at the office stuffed in the plastic Gap bag she carries. I could be one of those ladies, but better, with good clothes and expensive sneakers and hand-knit mismatched argyle socks that the Gap-bag ladies don't know they want yet but they will in about eight to twelve months. I could make myself a DO and parents everywhere would write me hateful letters because after seeing me as a *Snap* DO their kid bought in to the amputation-is-awesome hype and now there's nothing they can do to get their child's feet back. They'll never be in the Olympics unless it's the Special Olympics and that's just not the same no matter what anyone says.

I'm trying to think of the closest axe store when my cell rings. I'm disappointed when the caller ID comes up as Genevieve and not Jack and then I'm sure I'm a dirtbag whose feet deserve to be chopped off without an epidural.

"Hey, Gen. What's up?"

"You haven't called me back."

"Yeah, sorry. It's Bootcamp weekend." Gen called yesterday. I picked the message up at the bar but couldn't hear a thing. I remember this with total clarity and it's a gold-star moment on a dark and unforgiving day.

"I *know* it's Bootcamp weekend. I don't know why you need Ted there, but fine, whatever. It's work, I know. But I need to know if you're coming to the party."

"Right. The party." I have no idea what she's talking about. And why is Ted telling her I need him here? "What's the date again?"

"Next Saturday at eleven—*a.m.*"

"Of course, eleven a.m. It's not like you'd have a party at eleven *p.m.*," I say.

"We used to." Gen's voice is very small.

"Are you okay?"

"Of course. I'm fine. I'll let you go." She's snuffling, but I have to go—the group is heading out the door.

"Are you sure? We can talk later if you want."

In the background I hear Olivier shriek and I rip the phone away from my ear. After the initial shock dulls, I slowly bring it back toward my head. "I gotta go," Gen says, her voice suddenly brusque. "We'll talk soon."

At dinner I see Eva approach a stylish couple sitting a few tables over. I can't hear what she's saying, but they're all nodding and smiling. I see Eva hand them each what looks like a business card. Eva has cards? I get up and hobble over to Ted, who's currently sandwiched between Precious Finger and Zeitgeist. Precious Finger has ordered fries and mayo again and seems to be angling for a replay of last night's action with Zeitgeist, but he's having none of it and saves his lechy grin for our leggy waitress. "Eva has cards?" I whisper in Ted's ear.

"What?"

"Eva has business cards? Did you get her cards already?"

"What are you talking about, Sara?"

Maybe Ted's the one who needs to wear a helmet and live in a house with no sharp edges. "I saw Eva giving those people cards and I wanted to know if you ordered her business cards." I speak very, very slowly.

"They're *your* cards," he says. "She needed something with the *Snap* address and number so I gave her a stack of your cards so she can invite the right people to tomorrow's roundtable."

"Of course. The roundtable."

"You don't mind, do you? I'll order her cards Monday."

"Monday," I repeat after Ted.

"Are you all right? You don't look so good. Maybe you should go home and take it easy."

"We still have the gig."

"Eva and I can handle the gig."

"But she's staying at my place."

"I can give her your spare key," Ted says as he pulls his keys out of his briefcase that looks like an old-fashioned doctor's bag and dangles them in front of me.

I'm hypnotized—not by the dangling but by thoughts of a bath, my bed and a pair of ugly panties. "Only if you're sure," I say.

As amusing as it would be to watch Precious Finger chase Zeitgeist and Big Thing chase Precious Finger and the boring ones try without success to find some semblance of rhythm at tonight's gig, I've seen it before.

I didn't hear Eva come in last night and this morning it's my turn to wake her with coffee and Advil. She groans and reaches for her glasses. There are makeup smears on the pillowcase and she's not wearing her flannelette granny nightie, but a tight *Snap* T-shirt and a lacy black thong.

"Nice shirt," I say.

Eva covers her chest with her hands. "I found it in the Swag Shack," she says. "I hope you don't mind."

"Not a bit. Help yourself," I say. I'm quite sure the particular *Snap* shirt she's wearing is one of the originals. There are only a few left and they're in the locked archive room, not the Swag Shack. Then again, we did reissue them for our tenth anniversary and there's a pile of those in the Swag Shack. I shake my head. It's a *T-shirt*. I am ridiculous.

Precious Finger is the last to arrive for breakfast. Her nose is runny and she looks like she's been crying. I want to tell her that Zeitgeist isn't worth it, but decide not to. If I say that she'll start bawling and then we'll be in the bathroom and she'll tell me about riding his skinny stub and how she's never felt like this before and knows he feels the same, but he's scared. He's married, with two kids and he lives in Chicago, but it's not impossible. They have so much in common: they both work in advertising, they both love Depeche Mode, they both eat their fries with mayonnaise. I could be brutal and tell her that Zeitgeist is a prick and he only fucked her because he was drunk and she was there, but she'll say that I don't know him the way she does, that I couldn't possibly understand their connection. But she'd still want to be my friend and she'd call me and want to visit and stay at my place and talk about Zeitgeist. Sometimes it's better to hand someone a tissue and say nothing. But I have no tissues, so I bury my face in a menu even though I already know I'm having the eggs Benedict.

I lead the tour of *Snap* headquarters and the Bootcampers are suitably impressed. Eva's DOs begin to arrive for the roundtable and out of the corner of my eye I spot a girl who looks familiar: long dark hair, pretty. She's wearing a pleated miniskirt with a fitted boy's suit jacket that's been tailored and carefully deconstructed. She's wearing flat suede ankle boots and slouchy fuzzy socks. She's a DO. I lead the Bootcampers past her and I catch a glimpse of a tiny diamond stud in her nose. The girl gives me the biggest grin. It's Parrot Girl without her parrot. Eva has invited Parrot Girl to the roundtable. I hate Parrot Girl. I call over to Eva and ask to speak to her in my office. I usher the Bootcampers into the boardroom for what I call an *informal mixer* to chat with the DOs who have already arrived.

"You invited Parrot Girl to the roundtable?"

"Excuse me?"

"The fucking Parrot Girl, Eva."

"Parrot Girl's not here."

"The girl in the boy's suit jacket—that's Parrot Girl."

"No!"

"It's her, Eva."

"I saw her at the gig last night, after you left. She had a great look, and gosh, I guess I didn't notice." Eva's voice is warbly. She sounds like she's going to cry and I know I have no tissues. "Please don't be mad, Sara. I'll ask her to leave."

I sigh and fall into my fuchsia velvet chair, my anger deflated. "No, that will just make it worse. We'll do the roundtable, we'll keep it brief, we won't ask her any specific questions. Then before she leaves take her picture with the Polaroid—take Polaroids of all the DOs so it doesn't look weird—and put it on your desk so you don't forget what Parrot Girl looks like ever again. Now, I'm going to talk to Ted and fill him in."

"Let me tell him, Sara. I'm the one who messed up, it's my responsibility."

"Okay, but make it quick, and don't make him mad."

"I promise," Eva says and scurries off. I swivel in my chair and think about the whereabouts of Parrot Girl's parrot. Is it home? Alone? Does Parrot Girl have a roommate? Does she live with her parents? Does she have more than one parrot— maybe different colors for her different outfits? A gaggle, a herd, a flock, a *gang* of parrots would be good. I could get them and bring them here. No one would notice me gone, not with Miss Eva and Mushroom-Head-Dick Ted busy fel- lating the Bootcampers and the Bootcampers going down on the roundtable DOs in one naked orgy of trend and style bullshit. Precious Finger would like that; maybe she could get Zeitgeist to fuck her again.

There would be plenty of time to get Parrot Girl's gang of parrots here. I could lure them into the taxi with bits of some flavored nacho chips that I have about a trillion mini-bags of in my office that some PR company sent me last week. The chips are disgusting and my fingers are coated orange and smell like vomit after I eat them, which I frequently do simply because they're there.

I would get the parrot gang in the taxi with the disgusting flavored nacho chips then march them into my office, right past the orgy in the glass-walled conference room, right past Ted and Parrot Girl and weepy, idiot Eva whose fault this is in the first place. So after she's had some mind-blowing DO of a multiple, triple-X orgasm she can come on into my office and take that fucking responsibility she seems so eager for by lying on the floor as the parrots take turns shitting orange nacho poo all over her and imitating her pleas for mercy as she cries. I could do this and Eva would learn her lesson and then we could set the parrots free together on the roof, while I smoke.

Birthday

"Is there anything I can bring?" I ask Ted. I'm fishing for information about the mysterious 11:00 a.m. party tomorrow. I replayed Genevieve's message all week and still couldn't make out what she was talking about. I finally deleted it yesterday. If I subjected myself to Olivier's recorded screams one more time I feared I might have a seizure.

"I think Gen's got it under control. Just bring yourself—bring a date if you want to. I can't believe we're finally getting you out to the 'burbs."

"Jack's in Toronto," I say. I haven't quite come to terms with the fact that I'm breaking my steadfast no-suburbs rule for a party I know nothing about. There had better not be hats.

"Bring a non-date then. Bring Eva—or whoever. And a present would probably be good form—it's kind of ridiculous, I know. He's one, it's not like he knows what's going on. But Gen wants a big to-do, all the moms in the neighborhood throw big *to-dos*."

Olivier's birthday. Of course. He's turning one. I know

this. Or at least I know this now. I will pretend to have known this all along.

Back in my office I dial Eva's local and put her on speakerphone, which I know is obnoxious, but I've never had an assistant before and that orange button, neglected for so many years, is just begging to be pressed. "Eva, could you come in here for a sec?" Like I couldn't walk the ten feet to her desk. I swear I can feel my ass spreading wider.

"What's up?" Eva couldn't be cuter today, in her mint-green summer suit and old-fashioned silver sandals with a short square heel.

"I'm sure you have plans already, but would you like to go to a party tomorrow morning?"

"Tomorrow *morning?*"

"It's for Olivier—Ted's son. He's turning one and I know it's going to be all these Pointe-Claire mommies and their husbands and their kids and Jack's in Toronto—"

"No problem. Done. What time?"

"Eleven." I have fallen in love with Eva all over again this week. My life has never been so organized.

"Sounds perfect. What did you get him?"

"Who?"

"Olivier?"

"The baby. Right. Nothing yet. I mean, what do I get a one-year-old?"

"You wouldn't believe how many adorable baby things are out there now. You guys should really think about doing a baby-style issue."

"For *Snap?*"

"Sure. A lot of the readership must be having kids by now."

I groan and bury my head in my arms. Pull that ugly,

crystal marketing award off my shelf and give me some blunt-force trauma.

"I could help you," Eva says. "There's a great little shop in Pointe-Claire that sells wooden European toys and fifties vintage-style kids' clothes—well, they're new, repros, but they're the sweetest things. You'll wish they had them in your size."

I look down at my schlubby 501s and black Converse I'm not sure I should be wearing because Converse is owned by Nike now and Nike's not very *courant* but they're comfy and the blisters on my feet haven't yet healed. I'm quite sure that dear little fifties mini-clothes are not for me. Even for Olivier it sounds a bit gay but I have no other ideas so I tell Eva yes, I will go to this great little shop in Pointe-Claire with her and buy some retro baby sailor suit or something.

Eva snaps her fingers. "You know what we should do?"

I don't know, maybe gorge on sketchy seafood at some cheap Chinese buffet place until we're so sick and bloated with MSG there's no possible way we'll make it to the party tomorrow? I'll write Eva a hundred-dollar check if she'll dig through the tepid warming bins at the buffet to find me a handful of closed mussels I can eat to increase the odds of violent food poisoning.

"We should swing by your place, pick up some stuff, go to the kids' store and do the gift thing, then you can stay over at my house and we can just walk to the party tomorrow—it'll be fun!"

I'm not sure about this. "What about your parents?"

"Oh, they're away for the weekend. Come on, Sara. Think of it as an adventure."

"A suburban adventure," I say.

"Exactly. An *exotic* suburban adventure."

I have no plans except maybe talking to Jack on the phone and sampling CDs from the overgrown pile on my desk. And I was thinking about going for a walk to snap some DOs and DON'Ts before eating a grilled cheese sandwich at bedtime that I will be punished for with nightmares for eating so late. I guess I could go to Eva's.

Ted will kill me if I buy the gayest little summer sailor suit for Olivier—gayer than any baby sailor suit I could have possibly imagined—which means I have to and I know Genevieve will think it's darling. The one time I've seen her drunk since the baby was born she confessed she had hoped for a girl she could dress up and have tea parties with and shop the boulevards with arm in arm when she was grown. Who says she can't play dress-up and have tea parties and shop the boulevards arm in arm with her swishy sailor boy? In fact, I decide on the spot, I'm going to buy Olivier a sailor suit every year until he's, I don't know, forty, and he'll wear it because Gen and Ted will raise him with impeccable manners and I am his beloved Auntie Sara whom he'll never want to disappoint.

I decline a gift receipt when the shop girl asks if I'd like one—I can't have Ted thinking he can return it. I do, however, ask for the complementary gift-wrapping service the sign above the counter promotes and the shop girl sighs.

As we tool around the West Island in Eva's Saab, I find myself relaxed and surprised at the boutiques and the number of smartly dressed people on the streets. We buy some wine, boxes of fancy crackers and paté and Eva tells me that she's having some of her friends over for what she calls cocktail hour. "Is that okay with you?" she asks.

"It's great! Go for it!" I say this and immediately want to stick out my tongue and demand that Eva give it a harsh caning. There is no way to say *go for it* and not sound like you're pitching a campaign to the government designed to motivate kids into going outside and exercising instead of playing video games and eating cheese puffs all day and getting fatter and fatter until a TV crew from *Entertainment Tonight* has to cut through the drywall to get them out for a weepy face-to-face with D-list stomach-stapling pioneer Carnie Wilson.

Eva's parents' house is not as big as I thought it would be: a boxy two-storey of pale yellow vinyl siding, no wraparound veranda, no porch. The lawn is green and freshly shorn, the flower beds are tidy. The house is plain and unassuming, not a monster sprawl of fake Roman pillars, rock gardens and fountains or wavy terra-cotta shingles for a touch of Santa Fe.

Inside it's eggshell walls and muted colors, everything is tasteful but not untouchable. I notice a stained-glass lamp that isn't quite right. Eva's bedroom has hardwood floors and it's big, with its own en suite washroom. There's a queen-size bed covered with a patchwork quilt. I sit on the edge of the bed and can see that the stitching has been done by hand, not by machine. There's a daybed by the window, a white chest of drawers and matching vanity. Antique cologne bottles are arranged on a silver tray. Everything smells of lavender.

Eva says I can sleep in her parents' room or in the computer room that has a sofa with a fold-out bed. I opt for the computer room—sleeping in Eva's parents' bed is somehow wrong.

For dinner we eat roast chicken her mother has prepared and left in the refrigerator. Eva tells me her brother won't be home all weekend so I eat his. I didn't know Eva had a brother. I mean to ask her about him, about her family, but her mother's mashed potatoes have rendered me speechless with their deliciousness. This *is* an exotic adventure.

I take my camera out and take pictures of Eva as she arranges plates of crackers and paté. She poses like a pert fifties housewife. I help her fill decanters with gin and scotch and vodka. I make sure the ice buckets have ice. Eva empties a bottle of red wine into a carafe. She checks ornate crystal glasses for spots and I line them up according to size. "How many people are you expecting?" I ask.

"A half-dozen, maybe, but Chris said he may not be able to make it."

"Seems like a lot of work for just a few people," I say.

Eva shrugs. "Not really. We do it every week—we take turns playing host."

"Does everyone live out here?"

Eva nods and explains that almost all of her friends live at home. They'd rather do that than spend what little money they make renting some shitty basement suite in the city. Besides, she adds, their parents let them come and go as they please. I don't tell her that when I was her age living at home was unheard-of, an offense that resulted in public heckling and extreme forms of social shunning. After high school, we moved out, we found a way, we lived in shitty hovels and ate Asian insta-noodle packs every day if we had to. If you went to college or university, you maxed out your student loans, bummed cigarettes off your friends and went to preppy rich-kid parties at McGill to loot their coolers of beer that you'd smuggle out of the party and into a club in your jacket or your purse. You did not live with your parents. You did not host revolving cocktail-hour parties in their homes.

The friends arrive all at once. They have a system, the blond boy in the sweater vest tells me as he pours me a scotch. They all live close by, but whoever lives the farthest from the host's house calls on whoever lives the second-farthest, then they go together to call on the third-farthest and so on. That way they all arrive together and get to have a lovely after-dinner stroll which, Sweater Vest adds, helps keep the digestive system running as regularly as a Swiss train. He's premed, he tells me, at McGill. Wants to be a G.I. man.

I make sure I get his last name so ten years from now when I'm really old and colonoscopies are part of my regular routine, I can make sure he's not the one sticking that tube with the tiny camera up my sure-to-be size-twenty ass and giving me the news that my decrepit body is ravaged by un-treatable cancer. I'd rather hear it from a stranger.

After less than two drinks I have it all figured out. Sweater Vest carries a torch for Eva, who probably knows but chooses to ignore his unrequited love for her. He has a girl-friend, though, who dresses like Eva, but her look is off—her shoes tonight are too pointy to ever be Eva shoes and her dyed red hair is more cherry-red go-go-girl than Montreal old lady. From her frosty tone I can tell Eva Jr. doesn't like me.

Edgar is the boy in the mod sharkskin suit. According to Tiff, whose blunt black bob and wide-legged pantsuit make me think she should be carrying a cat-o'-nine-tails, Edgar is gay but tells everyone he's bi. She tells me she is bi and can tell when someone is gay. Then there's Ben, who is not gay at all—again, according to Tiff—but a man-whore whom

Eva used to date. Ben is tall. He has dark hair slicked back in a mini-pompadour. He takes off his black leather motorcycle jacket and underneath it is a tight black T-shirt and a full sleeve of tattoos. He's the only other person in the room who's wearing jeans. When he goes to the backyard to smoke, I join him.

"You're Eva's boss," he says. He reaches over to light my cigarette with a Zippo. It has a flaming-skull sticker on one side.

"You're Eva's ex-boyfriend," I say and take a drag.

"You've been talking to Tiff."

"She says you're a man-whore."

Ben smiles and winks. He's sexy. "Don't believe everything you hear, darlin'."

It goes on like this for I don't know how long. Inside, we drink and mingle, then escape to the backyard and smoke. It's not quite dark when he kisses me and I don't stop him. He follows me to the computer room with the fold-out bed. He pulls me to him and kisses me some more. He's hard and I want to fuck him but I don't, not so much because he's Eva's ex-boyfriend and twenty-four and lives with his parents, but because I don't want him to see my saggy breasts or my squishy tummy or my jiggly ass. I want him to touch me in all those places but I don't want him to see them. I twist away from him and find my camera bag. "Let's go, man-whore," I say and lead him back to the party.

Cocktail hour lasts more than an hour—it lasts more than six hours. I drink and take pictures, mostly of Ben, though I convince myself that no one notices this. I'm lying on the carpeted floor clicking away, thinking that I'm getting some great stuff. I'm *working,* I remind myself. I'm dynamic and smart, I'm into my groove—Sara B.: photographer, entrepreneur, respected *arbiter of style*.

"Sara, what are you doing?" Eva is staring down at me.

I snap her picture and everything is clear. I'm a drunk thirty-nine-year-old woman rolling around on the carpet of a house in suburban Montreal angling for crotch shots of a twenty-four-year-old Rockabilly boy whose mother I could be if I had been the one to live the after-school-special shame of teenage pregnancy, instead of that Mila girl who was in my tenth-grade math class.

"We should get you to bed." I'm flanked by Eva and Rockabilly Ben. They walk me down the hallway to the computer room. I watch as Eva and Ben remove the cushions from the sofa and pull out the hideaway bed. They smooth a fitted sheet on, then a flat sheet. Eva's tucking it in at the corners and I want to help. I say I want to help and Eva smiles but tells me to stay put. Two Rockabilly Bens blur in front of me. He pushes a pillow into a case and fluffs it. I want to help. I want to smoke. I want to fuck Ben but I want to sleep more. I think about sex and sleep and suburbs and parents and how all these kids think it's normal to be twenty-four and live with their parents.

"Where do you people have sex?"

Eva and Ben stop fussing with the linen and look at me. Ring up the neighbors, invite everyone in, stretch a glow-in-the-dark condom over my head, shut off the lights and let me suffocate, martyr myself for stupid drunk women everywhere or die as a cautionary tale.

"Just for the record, we have sex the same places you would—sometimes a couch or the floor or in a car, but mostly in our bedrooms. And yes—our parents know. If I'm dating someone for a while they don't mind if he stays over."

It takes me a moment to figure out what Eva's talking about. She's made eggs and has a selection of assorted pain medications arranged on a side plate next to a glass of pulp-free orange juice. I chase down three regular-strength Advil and a liquid-blue migraine capsule one. The juice chokes me partway down when I remember the carpet/camera roll-around and kissing Rockabilly Ben and asking the rudest question then dreaming all night about Ben wanting to play some nasty asphyxiation game with glow-in-the-dark condoms that wasn't sexy to me at all.

"I didn't mean to pry. I'm sorry," I say. "I was drunk. I was awful."

Eva shakes her head. "Don't give it another thought, Sara. Whenever I meet someone your age and I tell them I live at home, they always want to know, but they won't ask. It's annoying."

"That they want to know?"

"That they won't ask."

"So you're glad I asked?"

"Certainly. It was refreshing. And if you want Ben's number, it's not a problem."

Now it's the eggs that are choking me. "I don't want Ben's number."

I'm standing in the driveway of Eva's parents' house smoking. My head is fuzzy. My camera bag feels like it weighs a trillion pounds. I am regretting having Olivier's gay sailor suit boxed and gift-wrapped—it's adding to the weight and I'm melting in a black dress in the sun. Eva walks past me in a demure sleeveless shift and pearls. Her creamy white patent bag and shoes match her dress. She is fresh and polished. I can feel wetness spread under my arms and soak through the stretchy material of my dress. I wish I could wear sleeveless, but my upper arms are too fleshy and the skin underneath swings if I talk with my hands.

Eva walks to the end of the driveway and stops. "You coming, Sara?"

We're walking? "I wasn't sure if we were driving or—"

"It's six blocks, silly goose."

We're walking. My underarms are getting wetter and I suppose stinkier with each step but I can't stop to do a sniff test in front of Eva so I keep my arms pinned to my sides and move as slowly as possible.

"What's she like?" Eva asks. She's kind and makes no comment about my stiff arms and belabored robot walk.

"Who?"

"Ted's wife."

"Genevieve? She's great."

"She was some kind of pop singer, right?"

"In the eighties, yeah. She put out a few albums—she opened at the Forum for Roxette once."

"What happened?"

"What do you mean?"

"Well, did she just quit?"

I don't like this conversation. "She cohosted a talk show for a while."

"I kind of remember that, I think. My parents used to watch it when I was really little. She had big hair."

"It's much smaller now," I say then add, "Gen's very beautiful." I don't know why I say this. It sounds like an apology.

"How old was she when she married Ted?"

The math hurts my head. "Twenty-four," I say.

"My age. I can't imagine being married *now*."

Gen is very beautiful, even in jeans and a pink T-shirt I know retails for sixty dollars but that Ted took home from the Swag Shack for free. Her breasts are smaller than the last time I saw her. Ted mentioned that she was weening Olivier, information I had successfully blocked until now. I kiss Genevieve on both cheeks, hand her the gift and congratulate her though I'm unsure of the protocol. I know enough to know I'm supposed to congratulate a woman who's had a baby, but is it appropriate to congratulate the woman when her baby turns one? I can't very well be all, *Happy birthday, Olivier!* I could, I guess, but he wouldn't have a clue what I'm talking about and would just gurgle or drool or, worse, cry and then I would be the woman in the sweaty, stinky black dress who made the baby cry.

Gen says nothing about my maybe faux pas. I introduce her to Eva, whom she seems surprised is there. "She's my date," I say. "Ted said I could bring a date."

"Oh, dear, I hope I'm not imposing, Mrs. Wright," Eva says.

"Not at all," Gen says with a smile.

"You have a lovely home," Eva says.

"Thank you. Come, everyone's around back."

The backyard, like the house, is huge, exactly how I pictured Eva's parents' house to be. Ted leads the men around the perimeter of the lawn, stopping occasionally to point at a plant. He's carrying Olivier around like a football. The ladies are perched on the wraparound veranda sipping lemonade with napping babies slung nonchalantly over their shoulders. Like Gen they're all wearing jeans and heels and tight

T-shirts the colors of sherbet. I quickly calculate the ratio of fake breasts to real at five-to-three, with Eva, Gen and me being the three.

The women are friendly and have perfected that dewy-glow makeup that doesn't look like makeup that I can never get right. These are women, I determine, who know the tricks to using bronzer and how to blend shimmery concealer into the inside corners of their eyes to make them pop. I feel dumpy and shapeless in my stinky black dress—the dark cloud, a sulky teen. The drop-waist dress has three-quarter-length raglan sleeves and an asymmetrical hem. It was a gift from the designer, a Japanese New Yorker whose fashion star is on the rise. You can't even get this dress here. I know that these women wouldn't know that and that makes me feel better, or as superior as a hungover woman wearing a stinky black dress on a hot summer day can feel.

I listen politely as the women talk about their babies. They all have something to say about *training* their husbands to do this or that. They sit on committees with Gen or live in the neighborhood. They complain about the traffic driving into The City and swap wine recommendations that they jot in leather-covered notebooks. I'm not sure if any of them work or not or did and now don't and I couldn't care. I claim a chair in a shady spot on the veranda and my headache dulls the horror of glowy makeup and implants.

I fuss with my camera. I promised Ted I'd take some shots of Olivier. I focus on Eva, who is relaxed and mingling effortlessly with the suburban sophisticates. I snap a few pictures of her and then all the ladies want their pictures taken—solo, in pairs, as a group, with babies, without. They summon their husbands and I'm a mobile Sears Portrait

Studio, but not too mobile considering I refuse to budge from my shady veranda chair.

I'm trying to get a shot of Ted and Gen and Olivier. I release the shutter just as Eva comes into frame. Ted hands Gen the baby and slips inside the house. "I can do it," Gen calls after him.

Eva touches the top of Olivier's head. "You stay put and we'll take care of everything," she says to Gen.

The cake is dense and soggy with strawberries. I'm told it's special-ordered from a popular organic bakery. It has no icing. Gen props Olivier on her lap and Ted starts everyone off with the birthday song, first in English, then in French. I hate my singing voice so I fidget with my camera and mouth the words and hope no one notices. Gen and Ted blow out the one candle. I get the shot. My work here is done.

Eva rushes around clearing plates, refilling glasses of lemonade and cooing over babies. I motion Ted over and ask when they're going to open the presents. I want to see his face when they unwrap the gay sailor suit.

"We'll do it later—after everyone leaves," he says.

"What?"

"It's a private thing."

I stare at him unblinking, confused.

"It's not like when we were kids, Sara. There's a real movement toward not making a spectacle of opening gifts in front of the other kids."

"A *movement?*"

"It promotes competition and places too much value on material things." Ted sounds like he's memorized this from some parenting textbook. He probably has.

"He's *one.*"

"You'd be amazed how much information is imprinted before a child is two."

I'm sure he's right—I would be amazed. I would be amazed if upon hearing about this *movement* I didn't want to turn my spare room into a workshop and take two copies of whatever book this present-opening behavior modification came from and use them to build a vise that I could wedge my head in and crank tighter and tighter until my skull cracked and the wormy soft spots of my brain matter oozed out onto the author's photo and advance-praise blurbs.

Ted raises his glass of lemonade and clinks the side with a fork. Everyone stops talking. Ted's eyes are teary as he thanks all of us, the wonderful friends, for coming. He toasts his wonderful son, his wonderful wife who's a wonderful mother and it's going to be wonderful to watch her perform again. Ted raises his glass higher. *"J'taime Gen-Gen,"* he says. *"J'taime Gen-Gen!"* the Wonderful Friends say and salute Genevieve with lemonade. I'm out of lemonade, but I rattle around the ice in the bottom of my glass.

"It's exciting, isn't it, about Gen's new show?" Eva sits on the arm of my shady Adirondack chair and pours me another lemonade.

"Oh, it's exciting," I say.

"Do you think they'll have cameras at the office?"

"I'm still not clear on the details," I say, not wanting to admit that I have no details at all.

"I don't suppose so, not unless Gen comes by," Eva says.

I tune Eva out and strain to cobble together pieces of Wonderful Friends chatter. Filming starts in three weeks. In the studio, at home. *J'taime Gen-Gen:* juggling motherhood, marriage and music. Working out every day. Still have a tiny bit of tummy to lose. Gen's tummy is perfectly flat, so that last thing she said to one of her fellow sherbet-shirt Wonderful Friends is a total lie.

Ted twirls around lifting Olivier above his head, repeating *J'taime Gen-Gen, J'taime Gen-Gen,* until it's so obnoxious I want to stick out my foot and trip him so the baby goes splat and nobody's happy and twirly and making deals to star in tacky reality shows without consulting their so-called best friend anymore.

"I couldn't believe it when Ted told me. It seems like such a strange thing to do when you think about it—you're so *exposed,*" says Eva.

Ted told *Eva?* I think about changing the subject but I can't think of anything else to talk about. I try to sound casual. "When did Ted tell you?" My voice cracks. I sound like a pubescent frog.

"He mentioned something about it last week."

"He mentioned something about it last week." I mimic Eva precisely as if she were the voice on a learn-a-foreign-language cassette. I want to leave. I want to walk the freeway back to the city in my stinky black dress, laden with heavy camera gear and my punishing hangover. I try again for casual. "You know what they say—if you're not on TV these days, you don't really exist," I say. No one actually says this but me and every time I do I fancy myself quite clever.

"I like that," Eva says. "It's so true."

I wish there was a breeze and that I was wearing a white linen suit and a Panama hat and could smoke as I impart all my wisdom to my eager young student who spends afternoons sitting astride me pouring lemonade and hanging wide-eyed and rapt on my every word.

"I think that's your phone," Eva says, interrupting my vision.

I scramble through my camera bag and flip my phone open. "Hello?" There's no one there. "Hello?"

"Sara? Is that you?"

"This is Sara."

"Hello, dear. This is Esther Lewis speaking. I hope I'm not catching you at an inconvenient time."

"No. Not at all." Esther Lewis? Esther Lewis. Esther Lewis of Esther and Lila. Lila of the magazines.

"Sara, dear, I hope you don't mind me calling, but I found your card and your cellular telephone number in Lila's pocket-book and I know she had meant to give you a ring. She was looking forward to having you by for tea."

"I'd love to come by for tea!"

"Your enthusiasm is simply delightful, Sara, and I'd love to host you for tea if you'd still like to come. In fact, you could be a great help to me in regards to Lila's things."

"Lila's things?"

"Oh, dear. I'm not explaining this well, am I? Sara, I'm afraid Lila passed away three days ago."

There is nothing better than death to excuse yourself immediately from a party you don't want to be at.

Overshare

"But you hate old people," says Jack.

"I do not hate old people," I say. I hate that he knows this about me.

"You do so. They freak you out," he says.

"This is different," I say. Esther has invited me to Lila's funeral on Tuesday.

"You don't have to go."

"I think I do."

"Why? To get first dibs on those magazines?"

"No."

Jack laughs into the phone. "You're such a bitch, Sara. I love it."

"I am—" I start to protest but Jack cuts me off.

"Shit, baby. I gotta run—they need me on set. Can't wait to see you. Ciao."

I am not such a bitch. Planning to attend the funeral of an old lady I only met once, who happened to have had a mythical collection of vintage fashion magazines is not a bitchy thing to do. I am not a bitch. I know Jack likes me to be a bitch and that people say I'm a bitch, but I'm not—not really. It's Ted who's a bitch, for turning all parenting pundit and telling Eva about Gen's tacky reality show before telling me. Gen could have, should have, told me, I know, so she's a bitch, too, though not as much as her sherbet-T-shirted Wonderful Friends with their fake tits and the dewy glowing skin. And now Ted can't come in Monday because of some meeting with lawyers for Gen's show. There's paperwork, he said when he called. It's *pressing*. I'll have to oversee production of this week's issue alone tomorrow. Then Tuesday is Lila's funeral and Wednesday I'm off to see Jack in Toronto for two weeks. I feel slightly better thinking about this. I'm busy and important. I'm the girl in the movies who smokes and gets impatient with taxi drivers. I dash off to see my younger, ridiculously attractive boyfriend. I drink too much coffee and tell people what to do. I have a personal assistant whom I could yell and throw things at, but it's Eva and I'm grateful she'll put up with me. She's staying at my place while I'm gone. I'm sure she'd water plants and feed my cats if I had any. I'm a bitch with a soft head, a whore with a heart of gold.

I feel like a whore when I upload the weekend photos and see Rockabilly Ben's face in frame after frame. The shots I took rolling around on the floor are useless. This is not a surprise. But the others, the ones I shot earlier of Ben, of Eva and her friends, impress me. The kids look great. If they'd been roaming the streets of downtown I'd have certainly stopped them and asked them to pose. There's no doubt they're DOs.

I resist the instinct to delete the pictures of Gen and Ted's Wonderful Friends taken at the baby party. I crop and cut them on my computer and make a collage that has me laughing out loud. Identical bright white smiles, a row of headless fake tits, men's bald spots and khakis, big diamond rings and a close-up of a pedicured foot with blotches of sloppily applied self-tanner. The feet and the hands, I have read in women's magazines, are the hardest to get smooth and even with color.

My neck is stiff. I've been sitting for hours perfecting my scary suburban collage. Since Gen nixed our usual Sunday brunch via early-morning voice mail—too tired from Olivier's party, too many imaginary inches to whittle off her stomach—I haven't bothered to get dressed or shower. I groan and stretch and try to talk myself into going outside. Save for a shot of a lanky, tomboy skateboard chick who was behind me in line at the deli near the office the other day, I have no DOs. And I don't have a single DON'T. The DON'Ts are easier to find, but the thought of chasing down fat people with fanny packs or skinny people in pleather is paralyzing. I ignore work and continue to play with my collage. The Wonderful Friends are, without question, DON'Ts. It's more satisfying when I genuinely dislike my DON'Ts. I finish my collage and e-mail it, along with the best photos of her and her friends, to Eva. I do two sun salutations that exhaust me, then curl up on the couch for an afternoon nap.

I wake up after four to the phone ringing. I open one eye and check the call display. "Eva, hey!" I overcompensate for my drowsiness with extra perk.

"I got the pictures you sent—they're a riot. Do you need me to get releases from everyone?"

Releases? I sit up and rub my eyes. Releases for the magazine, for the photos. "Maybe hold off on that."

"There's not much time before deadline, Sara. I could get

all of my friends tonight, I think. You don't need them from the people at Ted and Gen's, do you? Since you didn't show their faces. I love the collage concept by the way."

I shuffle over to my computer. The Wonderful Friends collage is still on the screen. It's good. I cradle the phone between my shoulder and ear and click through the shots of Eva and her friends. I could collage those, too, but keep their faces, make Rockabilly Ben the biggest or second biggest next to Eva, who is a genius. I'd hug her and tell her so but she's out in Pointe-Claire. And I can't very well have her know that this whole DOs/DON'Ts collage thing is a fluke and something I did because I was lazy and didn't want to get dressed and go out on the street and take pictures, which is supposedly my job.

"On second thought, yes, get the releases from your friends. We don't need to bother with the others since they can't be readily identified." I'm all businesslike and smart. I sound like I'm wearing my glasses and know about law. "I'm working on the DOs collage now, so I should run. I appreciate your doing this on a Sunday, Eva."

"If there's anything you need don't hesitate to ask."

What I need is a massage and for Ted to pull out a bottle of vodka from his desk on Mondays after the magazine is put to bed and talk to me in his geek way about how amazing it is, everything we do, while I pace around his office-before-it-was-an-office getting hyper about clothes and music. What I need is to dish with Gen about famous French-Canadian people who are only famous in Quebec and take complicated personality tests together that always result in me being labeled some kind of narcissistic introvert and get her advice about everything that's happening in my life then not follow it and wish I had. What I need is to fuck Jack or someone but probably Jack because I'm too tired tonight to exercise the unconventional rules of our relationship and chase down what my gay friends would have, for a brief period in the nineties, called *man-pussy.*

Monday is not so bad. Production is long but nearly effortless, like I imagine it would be working on the assembly line in a doll factory. Ted calls every half hour to make sure things are running smoothly. I take the first two calls, but have Eva deal with him after that. I have other things—more *pressing* things—to consider, such as what do I wear to a funeral of a woman I met only once. The one thing I'm certain of is that I'll wear gloves so that when the old people start to touch me, and it's been my experience that old people are awfully touchy, I can sort of touch them or pat them or whatever without having to feel their loose stretch-wrap skin or the wet clamminess of their hands. At lunch I dispatch Eva to a vintage store to pick me up a pair of black, funeral-appropriate gloves. On her way out she asks if she could talk to me later about something, but won't say what. *Just an idea I have* is all she'll say.

I want Eva to have ideas, lots of ideas, mainly about making my life better. But as it turns out I don't have the time today to listen to any ideas, I'm so caught up in this funeral thing and getting the magazine off to the printer. I promise her we'll talk when she drives me to the airport on Wednesday like she offered to but now suddenly can't because of a dentist appointment she forgot about. I'm not coming in tomorrow as I've decided that a funeral is an all-day affair so I give her the spare set of keys to my apartment and make a lame joke about not getting up to any *funny business.* She

makes a sour face and tells me to give Esther her sincere con-
dolences. I feel bad and tell her to e-mail me her idea or call
me at Jack's.

"Will you be doing the DOs and DON'Ts from there?"
Eva asks.

"Not this time. I think I'll take an actual break."

"I could do them for you," she says. The sour face melts away.

"That's okay, Eva. But thanks for the offer." I smile, but it's
fakey. Eva's sour face returns. What did she think? That I was
just going to say, *Sure, Eva, you've worked here for about five fucking*
minutes and gee, it would be great if you could put together the most
important pages in the magazine for two weeks while I'm gone and
you're completely on your own. She knows that no one does the
DOs and DON'Ts but me—everyone in the city, and in the
other cities that count, knows that no one does the DOs and
DON'Ts but me. So, no, Eva, you can't *fill in* for me, neither
can Ted or Brian or any of the new people I've seen around
but haven't met yet and am not sure what they do—they can't
fill in, either. So enough with the sour face, bring back the
my-goodness-Sara-you're-my-hero face and change your last
name so people can stop asking me if you're my fucking sister
because I guess you've been calling yourself Eva B., which I
thought was cute and still do sometimes but not right now.

A minion from the art department knocks at my open office
door. I wave him in and he hands me the proofs of this week's
DOs and DON'Ts: West Island edition. Everything looks great.

Eva leans over my shoulder as I sign off on the pages. "I
still can't believe Ted's okay with this." She points to the full-
page collage of the Wonderful Friends' body parts.

"He hasn't seen it," I say. I'm sly and naughty and should
wear frilly panties and get spanked by Rockabilly Ben.

Eva's eyes bug. "Are you sure he won't mind? They're his friends."

"Don't worry about Ted. We used to do this kind of thing all the time."

We did do this kind of thing a lot. Ted wouldn't like a guy I was dating so he'd write pseudonymous rants about whatever he thought was wrong with them, like if the guy's head was too big for his body or he wore Doc Martens with shorts and wool socks or he was dumb and didn't know that to impress me he should read books, not mousse his hair, and that he should never wear plaid. I retaliated by taking pictures of the girls Ted dated who were often preppy McGill students who wore red-and-white McGill sweatshirts and leather letterman jackets and track pants and whenever they'd come by the office I'd say, "Wow! Do you go to McGill?" And these girls who were supposed to be so smart that they were double majors in math and music or linguistics and medicine wouldn't pick up on my sarcasm and say, "Oh my God, yeah, I do go to McGill!" Then I'd tell them how cool that was and ask to take their picture and they'd pose in their ugly sweatshirts and I'd make them a DON'T in the next issue and neither Ted nor I would ever have to see them again, which must have sucked for Ted because he didn't go out with very many girls.

Even Genevieve was a DON'T. Ted started dating her in secret. Ted and I were twenty-six, Gen was twenty-one, a French ex–teen pop star who wore jacquard silk dresses in jewel tones and got her picture in the party pages of local tabloids for raising money for sick kids and stray dogs. I found out they were dating after spotting a picture of them together at a benefit. I guilted Ted into bringing her around at the next possible opportunity. She smiled when I took her picture. Ted was ashen and looked as if he may throw up. He begged me not to run Gen's picture as a DON'T, but I did, despite the smile, because purple jacquard silk on a twenty-one-year-old has-been pop star was too good and the DOs and DON'Ts were my domain.

Unlike the McGill girls, Genevieve did not slink away. In fact, she was waiting for me outside the office the day the magazine came out. She tossed it at me and yelled at me in French. She cried and said she was in love with Ted and that she hated me, though with her accented English it sounded like she *ated* me. I started to laugh and she picked the magazine off the ground and threw it at me again. Then she started to laugh and we ended up at the dive bar down the street shooting pool and doing shots and talking about Ted and the guy I was seeing at the time who talked to me like he was my shrink.

Aaron—the pseudo-shrink guy—was the one who said my issue with old people came from not growing up with any living grandparents or other assorted old people around and from my mother's obsession with face creams and telling people we were sisters. And all of this manifested in my choice of career, a suggestion I argued with him on to the point of denying him sex because, I said, I didn't choose my career, it was just there. It's always a mistake to tell a man anything about your mother, especially if your mother isn't someone you talk to.

I'm not comfortable around old people. I'm not comfortable around babies, either—or cats or anyone who listens exclusively to hip-hop. I'm not comfortable at funerals, but I'm here, in a church, sitting in the back and counting down the hymns and psalms listed in the program. When the priest requests that we stand and sing, I catch a glimpse of Esther in the front row and lip-synch my way through the hymn.

Everyone at the service is old. Many of the ladies wear hats and I'm glad to see I was not alone in my decision to wear gloves, although I suspect the proper rules of etiquette may dictate that I take them off indoors. I can't make a definitive assessment about this because several of the old ladies have taken theirs off, but not all. I leave them on knowing that the service will eventually be over and then the old people will get touchy.

There's more singing and praying and then people talk about Lila and a chorus of sniffles rises up from the pews. I wish Jack were with me, tall and handsome in a black suit, or Eva or Gen or Ted or even Rockabilly Ben. I'm maudlin now and convinced I'm the loneliest girl in the world. I sacrifice myself to self-pity and join the chorus of sniffles. My vintage black satin clutch wiggles beside me. My phone is on vibrate and is in a state of arrest.

I don't go to the burial. I tell Esther I have some urgent work to attend to, by which I mean I need a drink and to check my voice mail and buy the sympathy card I forgot to get yesterday. I promise her I'll see her at the reception, which of course I will because it's at her and Lila's apartment—Esther's apartment now, I guess. "I'll see you soon, dear. I'm so pleased you came," Esther says. She touches my gloved hand and I barely flinch.

I opt for vodka over wine—as a legitimate mourner, drinking hard liquor midday is permitted if not required.

I peel off my gloves and dial up my voice mail. I have fourteen new messages: first Eva in a panic saying Ted wants to talk to me *now;* then Ted saying he wants to talk to me *now;* Ted again; Genevieve cursing, *How could you?*; Ted; Ted; Ted;

Eva again; a filthy message from Jack describing what he wants me to do to him when we get to his place tomorrow. I replay this one three times and save it. There's another message from Ted and another and another, then Eva and finally the shoe repair guy informing me that the boots I took in to be resoled are ready for pickup.

I order another vodka and suck it back before calling Eva.

"Oh my gosh, Sara, Ted's really, really mad about the DON'Ts."

"He'll get over it," I say, buoyed by the vodka hitting my system.

"Is that her?" I can hear Ted in the background. "Give me the phone. Sara? What the hell were you thinking? Do you have any idea what you've done?"

"Fucking relax, Ted. It's funny."

"It is not fucking funny, Sara, it's *embarrassing*."

"Oh, please. No one can even tell who they are—they can't be *readily identified*."

"That's hardly the point. These are our friends."

"*Your* friends," I correct him.

"Yes, *my* friends, Sara. You should have run this by me. Gen is devastated. She won't even go to the market she's so afraid she might run in to someone."

"Oh, fuck me, Ted." I'm getting riled and people are looking at me. I cup my hand over the mouthpiece. "We used to do shit like this all the time."

"Yeah, about a million years ago! And this isn't the same thing at all."

"It's exactly the same."

"No, Sara, *you're* exactly the same—the rest of us have grown up."

"Fuck you, Ted." I press the end button on my phone and turn it off. I order a double. Ted's words swim through the vodka. I push my sunglasses onto my face but the tears stream down past the frames. The waitress approaches me and asks if I'm okay. "I just came from a funeral," I say.

"I'm so sorry," she says and leaves me to drink in peace.

People are leaving by the time I make it to Lila's reception. I try to slink in unnoticed, but Esther waves and walks across the room to greet me. She takes both my hands in hers and I shrivel into myself. I must have forgotten the gloves at the bar and I still don't have a sympathy card. Esther escorts me to the kitchen, where I load up a plate with deviled eggs and pieces of quartered tuna sandwiches on white bread. I wolf down the tuna first thinking that if I eat enough I may die of mercury poisoning. This is a serious concern according to Gen, who read an article about it or saw something on TV and once said I had a death wish after she watched me eat eight pieces of yellowtail sashimi and Gen's one of the grown-ups so she would know these things. My eyes well again with tears. Esther pours me a scotch and steers me into the living room. I sit on the sofa across from a high-end entertainment center that seems out of place against the flowery wallpaper. There are three remotes sitting atop the television and I wonder if I could inconspicuously grab them and take them to the bathroom and empty out the batteries and swallow them and all their mercury goodness to speed up the process I've started with the tuna.

Esther pats my knee. I'm crying again. "Lila had a lovely life, dear," she says and offers me a monogrammed cloth handkerchief.

I wipe my dripping nose. I dab at my eyes and mascara stains the white material. "Thanks."

I stare at the handkerchief balled up in my hand, unsure of where to put it or what to do. "You can keep it," Esther says. "I have boxes of them."

I change my mind about the battery swallowing—it wouldn't be fair to Esther to die in her bathroom on the day of her best friend's funeral.

"Now you just stay put, dear." Esther pats my knee again. "I'll get you another drink and just holler if you need anything else. Things will wind down soon and we'll have a chance to talk."

I do as I'm told and as the guests leave I begin to notice the wonderland of the apartment. Much of the wall space is covered with framed black-and-white photographs and signed fashion illustrations, though from where I sit I can't see by whom. There are two columns of bookshelves, cabinets filled with ancient Barbies and porcelain curios. An enormous oval mirror in a baroque gold gilt frame hangs in the small foyer. I'm sitting on the couch on the far wall directly facing it. I catch bits of my reflection poking out around the others, who are standing and talking in the middle of the room. Finally it's just me staring back at myself. Esther calls my name from the kitchen and asks if I like cognac. I like everything. "On occasion," I say in my best polite grown-up voice.

"Well, dear, this is certainly an occasion," Esther says. "Follow me."

She's carrying an expensive-looking bottle and two glasses. I trail her into a bedroom off the living room. It's Lila's room. I sip the cognac and Esther motions to me to take a seat on the bed. The room is big with a wall of built-in shelving that stretches to the ceiling. There are magazines, hundreds of them, probably thousands. Esther steps on a footstool and reaches up, pulling down a stack of large-format magazines. Each are tucked into plastic sleeves. "Lila spent a week last year fitting every one of them into these bags—some kind of special plastic, so they won't deteriorate." Esther shakes her head but her smile is wide. "I told her she was crazy, but she wasn't hearing any of it." She hands me the pile of magazines and I can't help but squeal. I set my cognac on the bedside table and sort through the stack, making sure I'm seeing what I think I am.

"Those were her favorites," Esther says. "I'll admit they are quite pretty."

I count them off in my head—all twelve issues of *Flair* magazine. I have three beat-up copies I paid too much for at a shop in New York, but these are pristine, their die-cut covers sharp and perfectly preserved. These are not simply magazines or collectibles, but art. Fashion designers and artists and writers scour vintage ephemera stores and haunt online auction sites for copies of *Flair*. Completing your *Flair* collection is a rite of passage for all the stylish style-makers.

"From what I understand there were only a dozen issues published," Esther says.

I run my hand over the cover of the Paris theme issue from April 1950. I don't dare remove it from the special plastic.

"Go on," Esther says. "Open them up. Let's have a look."

"We shouldn't," I say.

Esther laughs. "Why not? Lila's not going to rise from the dead and strike us down. Besides, they're yours—and anything else in here you find to your liking."

I scan the shelves—it's all to my liking. "I couldn't," I say.

I'd need to get Eva to help me load it all in her car. It would take at least three trips. I could rent a van for a day. I try to calculate how much it's all worth. I wish I could bang these thoughts out of my mind on the heavy wooden headboard without causing a scene.

I wonder if magazines are insurable and it strikes me that I am a woman who preys on grieving old ladies. I'm a *Crime Stoppers* reenactment in the making. I'm an evil Poe raven feasting on a spilled basket of onion rings to-go outside a highway truck stop. I'm a bitch and a fraud. I'm a terrible friend and a fucked-up baby who wants her gums rubbed with gallons of whiskey to put her to sleep. I'm crying on a dead woman's bed.

I find the monogrammed handkerchief Esther gave me earlier. It's hardened with salt and snot and it's rough on my eyes.

"Sara, dear, what is it?"

"It's…it's nothing—everything." I have reached full blubber. I bury my face in my hands but I can't breathe. I inhale as deeply as I can through my nose. Mucous floods my throat and I start to choke and cough. Esther picks a box of disposable tissues off Lila's dresser. No more monogrammed hankies for me. I clear my throat and a lump forces its way into my mouth. It's viscous—not liquid, not solid and it's tender like an organ. There is no delicate way to do this and the viscous organ lump has filled my mouth to the point that there's no room to speak. I pull several tissues from the square floral box and cover my lips. I open my mouth and the lump oozes out past my teeth. I resist the urge to look at the thing, to find some science store on the way home and stop to buy a microscope and a lab coat and goggles and spend hours mar-veling at the lump like it's the world's fattest man making a guest appearance at the Ripley's Believe It Or Not! Museum on the Embarcadero in San Francisco. I quickly ball the lump up in the tissues and drop it onto my lap.

I tell Esther everything, about Ted and Gen and their baby and their Wonderful Friends, about Eva and Parrot Girl and Beefy Cartoon Pants Man. I tell her about Jack and about Rockabilly Ben—there's not much to say about him, but I find myself liking to say his name.

My insides are raw, I can feel them red and knotted and angry, and the blood is thick and can only seep slowly from the wounds I can't see. The pain is strangling, not at my neck, but all over. My mouth is surprisingly loose. It's the only way to release the pain, untangle the knots, and I've lost any control, any filters, and my thoughts push out of my mouth in such heavy heaves words trip on my breath. I may be making no sense. I may be speaking tenth-grade Spanish or reciting bits of a particularly hilarious story Ted and I came across in *Penthouse Forum* shortly after we'd taken *Snap* weekly and there were never enough hours and it was endless fun thinking of ways to stay alert as we worked through the night.

We'd read this piece over and over to each other and would stay awake every time, always laughing, as it involved a three-some with a double-amputee. *She was literally spinning on my dick like a record on a turntable.* I know the whole story by heart and so does Ted, or he did back when he was fun. I hope I'm not saying things like that to Esther but I could be. I know I've told her about Zeitgeist and Precious Finger and the fucking and the fries and mayo. I know I've said *fuck me* and *fuck Ted* and *fuck Gen* and even *fuck baby Olivier,* for which, if it was ever in question, I am without a doubt going to hell if sometime soon I start to believe in God and Satan and heaven and hell and die of unnatural causes because I don't think it's natural not to have a soul. I say this and Esther assures me I do, but she doesn't know me. She tells me it's going to be all right again and again. It's a hypnotic mantra and I almost believe her until the tears come again.

I refuse to have my body confront me a second time with a viscous phlegm ball so I shut my eyes tight until the tears have squeezed out. When I open them again and I look Esther straight in the eyes, which is hard since I'm drunk and my eyes are puffy slits, and unfocused, I tell her I've made my career by mocking people. I tell her I have no conscience— how can I? I've been doing this for more than fifteen years. It's not a skill, it's a personality trait. Esther isn't buying it and continues to speak so softly and calmly and slowly in a way that sounds like she actually cares so it makes me want to smother her with her dead friend's pillow, right there on the bed. She doesn't understand, I can't put it any plainer.

I tell Esther I'm a bitch and a brat, a hypercritical, judgmental fuck, void of empathy or sympathy. I tell her how it's all been a fluke, a lucky break so undeserved. I do nothing good, I feel nothing good and sometimes just nothing at all. If I had to choose between Jack and my fuchsia swivel chair, I'd pick the chair. Esther's still sitting beside me, still telling me it's going to be all right.

I tell her I don't care who's a DO and who's a DON'T— I expect this to shock her, my biggest reveal—but the moment I say it aloud I want to crawl out of the room, down the steps and into the night. I'll travel through alleyways and low-traffic side streets, I'll forage behind Dumpsters and befriend raccoons. I'll learn their ways and their customs. A young girl will find me and coax me to her backyard, where she'll feed me berries from the trees and leftover steak she smuggles out of the house. We'll be secret friends and I'll never have to talk because she'll think I'm a raccoon. But this will not have a happy ending. The girl will grow up and she'll tell someone—a boyfriend—about me and he'll tell someone else and soon there's a documentary crew and a book deal and a reporter from *Vanity Fair* living with me in the corner of the girl's backyard. It's no longer quiet and I have no choice but to speak just to tell them to all to shut up. Then the girl figures out that I'm not a raccoon and we're no longer friends.

"It wouldn't be any easier to be a raccoon," I say. I'm past the point of caring what Esther, or anyone, thinks. She laughs and curls an arm around my shoulder. She's surprisingly strong. I want to push her arm off, ask her what the hell she wants from me, pull her Montreal red hair out of her head in clumps until her scalp is patchy and bleeding. I shirk away from her. Esther drops her arm and I glare into nothing.

She sighs and pours me another cognac. "You remind me so much of Lila."

Mignonne

I wake up fully dressed in Lila's bed. My eyes are sealed with a thick layer of crust and it hurts to open them. I've cried and then slept with my contacts in. I look at the clock on the bedside table. It's not digital and it takes me a moment to remember how to tell time. It's ten—no, eleven. My flight is in an hour. I have to go. I have to go *now*.

Esther is puttering in the kitchen. There's a place set at the table, but there's no time to eat or chat or play tea party. "I have to go," I say.

"Now, don't you go rushing off, dear. Take your time. There's a bottle of aspirin in the medicine cupboard."

"You don't understand. I have to be at the airport—I'm flying to Toronto in an hour."

"Oh, my. That is going to be tight. We'd better get a move on. I'll drive you."

"I need to go home—my things…"

"No time for that. You hop in the shower and I'll take care of the rest."

My hair is loose and wet. My eyes sting and I have no

makeup except lipstick in my black satin clutch. Esther knocks on the bathroom door. She turns the handle and extends her arm inside. She holds out a dress on a hanger. "This should fit," she says and clicks the door shut.

I don't have time to consider the dress. It's black and shiny cotton and miraculously, it fits. It's sleeveless but I try not to think about that. I know it's Lila's and do my best to block that out, too. It's a short flight. I have a few things at Jack's; anything else I can pick up at the *Snap* store on Queen Street.

Esther hands me a short beaded cardigan—the kind Eva wears—and I shrug it on over the dress, relieved that my wobbly upper arms are covered. I force my feet into the pair of pointy snakeskin heels Esther has laid out. They're a half size too big, but I can walk and they don't pinch my toes. Two brown leather suitcases and a matching carry-on bag stand in the entrance. "Take these," Esther says. A corner of the cardigan is folded into my neck. Esther pulls it out. "That's better. Now you are dressed to travel."

Esther speeds to the airport. I take my sunglasses out of my black clutch and check my wallet for cash. There's no time for drawn-out thank-yous and goodbyes. Esther pops the trunk of her old Mercedes and I haul the luggage out. The heavier suitcase causes me to stand lopsided. I promise to call when I'm back. She tells me to take care of myself, that a nice warm cup of tea will be waiting upon my return. She wishes me a safe flight and I rush through the sliding doors.

I am the person on the plane whom the other passengers hate. I'm last on and breathless and even though there's ten minutes before scheduled takeoff time, I sense they're a hostile bunch who blame me for not getting them there faster.

The flight isn't packed. There's an empty seat between me

and a bald man in a suit. He's scowling at the financial section of the newspaper. There will be no small talk.

Once the seat belt sign pings off I unzip the brown leather carry-on Esther packed and start rooting through it. There's a makeup bag with an unopened jar of a pricey Swiss wrinkles-away face cream, a stick of creamy concealer—a cheap drugstore brand—and a red Chanel lipstick that's never been used. There's a mirrored compact with a translucent pressed powder by a cult beauty brand from Sweden, a pot of rouge, Maybelline mascara and a miniature spritzer of Jean Paul Gaultier eau de toilette. I release the tray from the back of the seat in front of me and spread out the tubes and bottles. I hold the compact mirror in one hand and start work on my face. I swear I can feel the expensive Swiss face cream repairing my haggard skin, and the cheap concealer is a miracle— how could I not have known about this?

Satisfied that I look somewhat presentable, or at least not so gruesome as to frighten Jack at the airport, I replace the makeup, clip the tray back into place and dig back into the brown leather carry-on.

Esther has packed a pink suede pencil case with pens, multicolored fine-tip markers and a package of ultralight cigarettes. There's a worn, illustrated copy of *Alice in Wonderland* and a two-week-old issue of *Us Weekly* that I read at my desk on a particularly uninspired day. But it's four thick notebooks that take up most of the space and weigh the bag down. I wrestle them out. The pages of the first notebook are unlined and crammed with sketches and notes, photographs and newspaper clippings. The second is the same, as is the third. The fourth is blank. I return to the first and open it to a random page. There's a sepia-toned photo of a woman in a beautifully tailored black dress with a jagged neckline sitting on a stiff-backed chair. Her dark hair is up. She looks to be in her late twenties but it's hard to tell. She doesn't like the photographer or perhaps having her photo taken at all. I know this look from my work. She's smiling but her eyes are pensive if not a bit sad and that gives everything about her away.

Beneath the photo in a swirly hand is written *Portrait of a Lady Undone, 1958*. I look closer—it must be Lila, but what the caption means is a mystery, nothing else on the page offers so much as a hint, not the drawings of black dresses, not the ad for fine uncultured pearls, nor the detailed recipe for Hungarian mushroom soup.

"What the hell *is* all this stuff?"

"I have no idea," I say. I've laid the two brown leather suitcases out on Jack's bed and am unpacking. I hang up three black cotton dresses, all different from the one I'm wearing. There's a fancier dress, too, the one from the photo in the notebook with the jagged neckline. It's creased from packing so I dart to the bathroom and hang it on the hook on the back of the door. I pull the shower curtain closed and blast the hot water—the steam will lift the wrinkles out. I find a strand of pearls in a velvet box. I can tell by the clasp that they're very old; the color and the way they're knotted makes me think they're real. In another velvet box there's a gold necklace with a red jewel cut in the shape of a teardrop. There are earrings to match—the kind that you fasten to the earlobes by screwing them on. Maybe it's time to rethink not wearing jewelry. There's a black lightweight suit with a sleeveless shell, cropped jacket and a choice of pencil skirt or wide-legged sailor-style pants. There's a shoulder bag and an evening bag, a pair of patent ballet flats and low-heeled sandals. At the bottom of the second suitcase are the twelve issues of *Flair*. No wonder it was so heavy.

I'm going to have to figure out what to do about my glasses. Jack wears a prescription slightly lesser in strength and has about ten pairs so I can make do that way if I have to. I have a duplicate set of toiletries here—shampoo, body cream, contact lens solution, that milky facial cleanser from France I like. All the things that take up too much space and weigh down your carry-on when you're off to visit your long-distance boyfriend. But I'm going to have to nip out and buy underwear. Jack can come along—he'll like that.

"She just gave you all that stuff? That's kinda weird. Are you sure she's, you know, okay, up here?" Jack taps his head.

"She's not sick or anything—I don't think so." It hadn't occurred to me that Esther might be actually demented or senile and that's why she's giving a stranger her dead friend's things, but I can't think about that right now because I have to think about shopping.

We're walking to a lingerie store in Yorkville, which means uncomfortable lacy thongs and embellished super-lift bras for the next two weeks. I won't complain. Jack says he's buying and he's bounding along Bloor Street like a puppy. He talks like he can't get the words out fast enough, telling me about the drama of the music video he shot last week and the technical challenges of the one he's booked to shoot starting Monday. "There's *a lot* of prep," he says and I take this to mean that he's not going to be around much for the next week. I'm not disappointed. I don't really care.

Jack picks out bras and thongs and I try them on. Everything is red or black or red-and-black and it's all either totally sheer or lace. He keeps asking how I'm doing in the dressing room and I know he wants me to invite him to take a look. The curt Russian saleswoman is monitoring us with a strict eye. There is nothing I can do about this and wouldn't even if I could. The thought of standing in tarty lingerie under white lights with Jack trying to fuck me in front of a three-way mirror makes me recoil, and recoiling does nothing for my jiggly stomach. I'll let Jack think that denying him a peek is part of our game. It's the same every time. I put him off and put him off and I let him believe it's all part of some sexy control game. I don't tell him that a little shopping, a pint or two at the bar, snacks and a glass of wine at his place is what I'm going to need before I'm ready to let him on me or in me. He'll do everything I say and I'll still keep my bra on and insist the lights are out.

We finish shopping, have drinks, then drinks and snacks. I think of Rockabilly Ben the whole time Jack is fucking me. This makes me feel guilty and slutty but it also makes it hot. I remind myself that thinking of Rockabilly Ben while Jack's cock is inside me is in no way a violation of our unconventional relationship rules and promptly grant myself absolution and permission for another glass of wine. Jack, however, has other ideas. He arranges himself so we're facing each other, noses almost touching.

"I've been thinking," he says. His voice is slow and syrupy. This is my cue to flee, but I'm wearing only a bra. And I can't leave Lila's stuff behind, especially if Esther does turn out to be demented and her old-people friends hunt me down at night wearing masks and cloaks and carrying torches and demanding the return of Lila's things. I close my eyes and hope

I look dreamy, not stressed. Men always do this. They say they're cool, they're great with the perma-casual unconventional long-distance relationship. They don't want to get married, they don't want to have kids. And then they do, then it's all let's-take-it-to-the-next-level and I'm forced to play the villain, the soulless girl with the frozen heart.

"I've been thinking that we should do something together—a project. I've been e-mailing with Ted about maybe working with you guys on some videos or an online show."

Get me some *Cosmo* and some *Glamour* magazines. Tear out the pages that purport to tell readers *what he's thinking* and wrap me up tight. Blindfold me, gag me, douse me with gasoline. Invite Jack and Ted and every ex-boyfriend I've had. Invite Eva and Esther and Rockabilly Ben. I insist—I demand—that Gen bring the baby and her Wonderful Friends. Let Parrot Girl light the first match. "You've been e-mailing with Ted?"

"We've been bouncing some ideas back and forth. Oh—I had a couple messages from him this morning. He said to tell you he wants you to call him."

"I'm sure he does."

"Of course he does," Jack says. He kisses me. My eyes are still closed. My sarcasm has gone undetected. "So you'll think about it?"

"What?"

"Working together?"

"Yeah, sure. I guess I could give it some thought."

"Awesome. What time is it?"

I open my eyes and glance at the clock. "Five to six."

"Shit. We'd better get moving."

"Are we going somewhere?"

"Dinner."

I shower and change into the Lila dress with the jagged neckline. I take out my contacts and borrow Jack's glasses, a pair with chunky black plastic frames. The glasses are wide on the bridge of my nose and keep slipping down. If I keep my head tilted the smallest bit up they'll stay put. And I'll have to remember not to squint.

I use Lila's makeup and wear the pearls. As I'm stuffing toilet paper into the toes of the patent ballet flats to prevent the shoes from flapping when I walk I realize my birth control pills are in my medicine cabinet at home next to the economy-size bottle of Advil.

I drop the toilet seat cover and sit. I could call Eva and have her courier the pills to me overnight. I could find a clinic in the morning and get some more. I could ask Jack to wear condoms for the next two weeks or fuss with sponges and spermicide or not fuck him at all. I could absolutely not give a shit because I'm thirty-nine years old and as anyone who's caught even a moment of a daytime talk show knows, I'm most likely a barren crone.

I choose to absolutely not give a shit and if by some preposterous fluke I do get pregnant, I'll carry the mutant two-headed, harelipped baby with Down's syndrome and no hands, then drop it off at Jack's. Maybe he can e-mail Ted for parenting advice or make a video for the sappy French ballad Genevieve will write in honor of my fluke, abandoned, mutant baby.

I'm in no mood for this dinner and Jack is vague about the details. I sit in the taxi with my arms crossed. I press my body against the door and look out the window, away from Jack. I'm resentful for the imaginary pregnancy that's his fault and huffy because I will forever have to shoulder the guilt of not having the strength or humanity to raise the mutant baby myself.

We jerk-and-stop through traffic to a loft somewhere way down Queen Street West. "It's just a group of creative couples who get together for dinner once a month."

"*Creative couples?* Sounds fun." I'll bet they're those people who talk about how they don't watch TV and then after two drinks you overhear them lamenting the cancellation of *Everybody Loves Raymond*.

"It really does, doesn't it?" Again, my sarcasm moves through Jack unnoticed. "I've wanted to go for ages—it's an awesome networking opportunity, but it's couples only."

"*Creative* couples."

"Exactly."

A woman with long curly hair greets us. She hugs Jack and he hands her a bottle of wine. "This must be the famous Sara B.," she says. She looks at my hair. She looks at my dress and shoes. She smiles and I know I've passed her entrance exam. "I'm Michelle," she says. I shake her hand. "I was delighted when Jack said you two would be able to make it." A man with a shaved head and slim black jeans approaches. He puts his arm around Michelle's waist. "Dave, you know Jack. And this is his artner, Sara B. Sara's one of the founders of *Snap*—right?"

"Right."

"I'm Dave." He shakes my hand.

Michelle gives me a tour of the loft. She's a sculptor, Dave's a painter, they have two kids who are staying at Michelle's sister's house overnight. I don't care. I recognize Dave's work—he's good and his pieces are expensive. He shows in

New York. The creative couples are gathered on angular sofas and around the island kitchen. I count ten people, twelve including Jack and myself. Michelle points to each person like she's a first-grade teacher doing roll call. "That's Susie and her artner, Charles. That's Steven and over there—that's his artner, Geoff. That's Carol—I think I saw her artner, Travis, sneak off to the bathroom. And that's Rachel and her artner, Paul. Rachel's writing a story for *Toronto Citylife* about our dinners."

I stare at Michelle. "I'm sorry?"

"Rachel's writing a story for *Toronto Citylife* about our dinners." Michelle speaks slower this time.

"No. I got that. *Artner?*"

Michelle laughs. "It's clever, isn't it? Julia and Ryan came up with it—they're in L.A. this week. If you're here next month you'll meet them."

I am somewhat stunned by my hangover, by Ted and Genevieve's anger, by Esther, by the suitcases full of a dead woman's things and by my imaginary mutant baby. But I am clear about this: I will not be here next month, I will not be meeting Julia and Ryan, I am not anyone's *artner*.

There is no meat at dinner. I haven't touched the mock salt-and-pepper squid or the mock Szechwan beef but am confident in the fact that the only thing worse than an artner dinner is a vegan artner dinner cooked by a woman who truly believes that tofu tastes like meat and says so.

"The first time I made this sweet-and-sour tofu pork—this is so funny—Dave spit it out on the plate. He was convinced that it was *real meat*. Can you imagine! But it *is* very authentic, isn't it?"

The artners agree. I push a soggy piece of fake meat something-or-other around on my plate. Jack frowns at me from across the table—artners do not sit together at artner dinners, they're separated to achieve maximum social networking potential as I learned from Michelle when I mistakenly tried to take a seat beside Jack.

Jack points to my full plate indicating he wants me to eat. *Fuck you.* I mouth the words at him. The social networking at the table has reached a fever pitch. Someone makes a toast to tofu chef Michelle. I raise my glass along with the others but would like nothing more than to bind each pair of artners together with ropes of messy animal intestines that they have to gnaw through to escape then slap their smug faces with slabs of raw veal until they cry. I'll hook up one of Jack's video cameras, maybe a webcam or two, and lock them in the loft indefinitely with no food but the slapping veal. After days, a week at the longest, they'll give in to the inevitable and cook up the veal, but it's maggoty and rank so they fight over what to do next even though they all know what they'll have to do. I'll get Jack to stream the video live to the *Snap* Web site and everyone on earth will watch as the captive vegetarian artners turn cannibal, dismembering each other piece by piece—it's Michelle's arm for lunch, Steven's left leg for dinner. And soon they're limbless, just a pile of talking torsos huddled together in a puddle of urine and sticky feces. People will watch, the artners will die and someone will sue us for something. Jack will blame himself and I'll be there to remind him, as I bounce on my knee our mutant baby who, it turned out, I couldn't give up, that he was the one so keen on us working together, on *Snap* having an online show.

I wander around the loft after dinner looking at art and pictures, guzzling wine and avoiding Rachel the writer, who is asking people questions and taking notes while her artner,

Paul, scampers about taking photographs of everyone with a vintage Polaroid Land Camera. Eventually, Rachel and Paul catch me coming out of the bathroom and pounce.

"Do you mind if I ask you a few questions about tonight, Sara? Your initial impressions of the artners concept since you're a newbie, how these get-togethers can benefit both your personal and professional life—that sort of thing. And maybe Paul could get a picture?" Rachel has a piece of tofu stuck between her front teeth. She stands poised with her pen ready.

"Do you have to use my real name?" I ask.

Rachel seems taken aback by this. "I'd like to—I'm using everyone else's."

I lean in close to Rachel. My voice is hushed. "It's just that this night has been such a moving experience. I'm at a critical juncture in my life and, well, I shouldn't be telling you this, not unless you promise not to use my real name—"

Rachel's eyes flicker with excitement. A confession is second only to swag on the official list of journalist turn-ons. "Sure, anything you want."

"I don't want to be a downer, but I've been having a tough time lately and this artners thing is what I need to get my life back on track. The camaraderie, the conversation, the networking opportunities—I don't feel so alone anymore. I mean, I was going to kill myself tonight, but then Jack brought me here and now I feel so connected, not just to Jack, but to the whole artners community."

"That's pretty powerful stuff," Rachel says, closing her notepad. She wishes me luck on my *journey* and Paul moves in to take my picture.

I bring my hand up to my face. "I really don't like having my picture taken." This is not a lie. "Here. Let me see that."

I hold out my hand and Paul reluctantly surrenders his camera. I hold it at arm's length and point it at my face. I stare into the lens and press the shutter button. The camera whirs and spits the photo out. I thank Paul and give him back his camera. I tuck the Polaroid in Lila's evening bag and from across the room announce to Jack that we're leaving.

Jack is blabbing on the way home about Geoff, who's a film producer. Jack's taking a meeting with him after his latest music video wraps. Geoff told Jack it's time to take it to the next level, to get out of the music video ghetto and move up to features. He's holding Geoff's business card and stroking it like it's pussy.

I let Jack fuck me and for a change he doesn't pet me and call me darling and tell me how beautiful I am and how much he loves me. He just fucks me, and hard—no foreplay. He pins my arms above my head with his hands and doesn't look me in the eye and I like it. I know he's not fucking me. He's fucking Geoff's card, the networking *artners,* some vision of a feature film, a brick of extra-firm tofu. This is fine, preferable, really. He grunts a good-night and gives me a lazy kiss between my shoulder blades, above the band of my ruffly underwire balconette bra. As soon as he starts to snore I inch away from him, out of the bed and onto the floor.

I grope around in the dark for one of Jack's T-shirts and the brown leather carry-on. I wriggle into the first shirt I find then I stand up and feel around the floor with my feet for the bag and stub my right baby toe on the sharp edge of the white laminate chest of drawers I've always hated. A little yelp escapes from my mouth. Jack tosses under the sheets but doesn't wake up. Jack's semen is running down my thighs. With any luck our imaginary mutant baby is expelled with the ooze.

I locate the bag and creep out into the living room where I take a roll of Scotch tape from Jack's desk drawer. I sit on the floor and pull out Lila's notebooks. I find the blank one and open it to the first page. Lila's black evening bag is lying on the coffee table and I slide out the Polaroid I took of myself at the party. I tape the picture into the notebook and with a Sharpie write *Artners Dinner* on the strip of white space below the photo in a fat loopy hand that makes me think of optimistic ten-year-old girls who have flat chests and dream about unicorns. I scrutinize my face. The edges are soft, but that's from holding the camera too close with an unsteady hand. A grin saturates my face, but my eyes are tired and sad, a portrait of another lady undone.

Icon

Jack has work and places to be. I putter and I try, unsuccessfully, to sleep. I ignore Eva's phone messages and Ted's and don't bother to check my e-mail. I wear Lila's dresses and spend at least an hour every day on my hair and makeup, something I didn't do even as a teenager. Sometimes I go to the store for cigarettes or wine, but mostly I stay in Jack's apartment and pore over Lila's notebooks and try to untangle her life.

Lila had very specific ideas about things: fingernails are red or plain and buffed with a layer of clear polish; dresses are black—always; when cooking at home, one-pot meals trump elaborate dinners with several courses; men are insufferable, women are worse; being a tree is better than being human. She hated squirrels and drew several versions of a voluminous fur cape made of squirrel pelts, heads still attached. She wrote at length about trapping versus shooting the squirrels that ran rampant in her neighborhood; she had no qualms about guns but was unsure of what the most effective method of killing the trapped squirrels might be. *POISON???* she wrote in capital letters.

Lila eavesdropped on conversations and recorded snippets

of dialogue in her notebooks—a married couple talking about the weather, a man in a park laying out his career options to a bewildered dog, a young mother at the supermarket scolding her toddler for snatching a lemon from the bottom of the pile causing hundreds of lemons to tumble to the floor. Her writing about people was devoid of emotion or empathy, the photographs pasted into the notebooks were all of herself.

She made shopping lists and wrote detailed instructions about her beauty regime—weekly baths in buttermilk and baby oil, petroleum jelly hands in rubber gloves for an hour each night, facial tightening exercises. In the mornings after Jack's gone to work I open the notebook to that page and spend thirty minutes in the bathroom contorting my face to match Lila's step-by-step photographs and tell myself it works. I do it again when I'm bored and can't sleep.

It's noon by the time I've done my facial tightening exercises, gotten dressed and done my hair and makeup. Today I have resolved to go out to buy a pound of ground beef and a box of Velveeta cheese for the casserole I'm making for dinner. I found the recipe in one of Lila's notebooks. She scribbled a star beside it and the page is dotted with grease stains and this is enough to convince me of its tastiness. It's Wednesday. Jack calls as I'm almost out the door and says the video will wrap by seven, eight at the latest, and that I should come meet him for drinks with the band and the crew at nine at a pub on Gloucester. He calls me *baby* and *sugar*. I don't tell him I'm making casserole.

I pass the market deciding I'll go for an extra-long walk and pick up the ground beef and Velveeta on the way back. Lila had strong feelings about walking—she wrote that walking at a brisk pace for one hour every day kept the legs shapely and the buttocks high. She recommended that one squeeze their buttocks and stomach as they walked and drew a picture of the ideal walking posture: tilted slightly back, feet before shoulders, eyes forward not down. She also noted that a lady wearing heeled shoes should be sure to walk heel-toe, never toe-heel, as the former will make walking effortless while the latter will cause nothing but pinched toes, bunions and blistered feet. I run through Lila's directions in my head: shoulders back, feet forward, bum and tummy in, then heel-toe, heel-toe, heel-toe. I get the rhythm and am astonished by how simple it is. I'm gliding, I'm giddy, shoes clickety-clicking against the pavement. I want to poster the city and share my news, bestow my newfound heel-walking know-how upon lesser women. I see myself on talk shows, laughing and graceful, demonstrating my moves and garnering thunderous applause. But my goodwill vanishes as my clickety-click is silenced by the squish of fresh dog shit. I will keep the secret of walking in heels to myself.

The sky is overcast, but by the time I hit Queen Street, the sun has broken through and the black Lila dress I'm wearing sucks in the heat and the smell of the dog shit on my shoe wafts up around me, making me gag.

I'm closer to the *Snap* store than I am to Jack's so I stop in to use the bathroom and clean the dog shit off my shoe. We have three stores: the one in Montreal, this one in Toronto and another in New York. We sell T-shirts and sneakers, accessories and music, books and expensive Japanese toys. I rarely visit the stores except when I'm feeling especially slothful and in need of a fresh batch of DOs and DON'Ts— I'm guaranteed to find both hanging around a *Snap* store.

I don't recognize either of the staff behind the counter. The girl has choppy hair with extra-long pointy bangs and a phone pressed to her ear; the guy is her doppelganger: same hair, but no phone. They're poking each other, pointing and giggling as I make my way toward them. My face burns. There's a display of plastic figurines from Japan at the till, a set of limited-edition characters with round heads, mix-and-match animal bodies and snap-on hair. I reach for one of the figurines and pop off its hair and its bunny-body. I roll the head around in my hand and remember a story a cousin of Ted's told us as teenagers, about skinning an animal with a golf ball. He explained how he'd make an incision, slide the golf ball under the skin, then place his hand on top of the fur and roll the ball to separate the skin from the body. He told us that once the skin is loose it should slide right off and it's ready to be dried or taxidermied. I squeeze the round toy head in my hand. I'd skin the girl first, then the guy. I'd do it carefully, hiding the precise incisions in their ass cracks. The faces would be tricky—working the toy head around the eyes without any tearing could be difficult, and the girl's nose is very small— but the results would be spectacular and *multipurpose* and Ted would like that. We could use the skins to dress mannequins, have an art opening with wine. I could style and shoot them as DOs then as DON'Ts. They could be mascots and hipster talismans, the new star faces of a perennial Halloween.

"Aren't those wicked?" the girl asks me.

I look down at the toy head in my hand and quickly set it down. "Wicked. Yes. Indeed." *Indeed?* I want to slice open my ass and roll the toy head around until my skin is falling off and it's easy to step out of. I could do it here at the store. We could print up handbills and posters, it could be an event— performance art—the kind of thing people talk about forever and lie and say they were there even though they were across town eating barbecued pork chops at a picnic table in their parents' suburban backyard.

The Hipster Twins nudge each other and look past me. They're barely able to contain their laughter. Their faces are bright with gleeful contempt and I relax knowing it's not directed at me. I look across my shoulder pretending to pick a thread off the sleeve of Lila's dress and freeze when I see him, but it's too late.

"Sara B.! My God! How the fuck are you?" Alex strangles me in an awkward embrace. The Hipster Twins are quiet.

"Alex, hey," I say as I pull away from him. His hair is bleached platinum and thinning and his face is deeply lined. I count two, no, three holes in his nose where he once wore thick rings. His breath is bad and his crushed velvet pants are too tight. A small, spongy belly hangs over his belt exposing a sliver of flesh and the hair that peeks out from the neck of his shirt is gray. He's got to be fifty. I stare at him, not knowing what to say. I want to clean the dog shit off my shoes and run.

"It's so weird to run in to you—I was just talking about you the other day and saying to Jamie…twenty-six, so hot, long story, you don't want to know. So I was telling Jamie about how insane we used to get and, oh my God, the parties and you'd wear that big black wig and we'd be doing piles of blow in the DJ booth, and that time we had the doll-burning party and the sprinklers went off in that warehouse and the cops came? I was just talking about you!"

Alex puts his hands on my waist and jumps up and down. The Hipster Twins gawk. "That was some party indeed," I say. *Indeed? Again?*

"Listen. I've got to scram, but I'm doing a party on Friday.

You have to, have to come." Alex reaches into the leather messenger bag that's slung across his chest and pulls out a square of pink paper. *Midsummer's Night Dreamz*. Fantasy costumes, DJ Miss Alex, two-for-one highballs before ten.

"Wow. I really wish I could, but I'm going back to Montreal tomorrow." I am a liar, worse than the ones who would say they saw my self-skinning performance art live but were in reality pork-chop-eating suburban gluttons.

I can read the disappointment in Alex's face. He stuffs the pink paper back in his bag. "Sure. Well, maybe next time. Give me a call when you're coming to town. Same number."

"Definitely."

"Well, *ta,* then!" Alex says. He blows me a halfhearted kiss on his way out the door.

I turn my attention back to the Hipster Twins. "I need to use your bathroom," I say with what I hope is some authority.

"You're Sara B.," says the Boy Twin, holding out a limp hand.

"This is, like, amazing," say the Girl Twin. "You're, like, amazing."

"The bathroom?"

"Yeah, sure. Okay, of course." The Boy Twin is still holding my hand and yanks me past the counter and down a short hallway to the bathroom. I'm afraid he's going to follow me in, hold my hand while I pee and try to get the dog shit off my shoe. I consider this. I'm not keen on him watching me pee, but I'm sure all I would have to do is ask and he'd gladly clean my shoe; he'd probably keep the paper towel, ask me to sign it, sniff it when he's stoned or feeling low.

I shake the Boy Twin off and step into the bathroom. "Let us know if you need anything," the Girl Twin calls out.

"Will do." I stand still and listen for the sound of footsteps walking away. Nothing. I turn the water on. The Hipster Twins are waiting. I take off my shoe and scrape the dog shit off with wet paper towels, which leave behind a pulpy residue and I hope I haven't ruined Lila's shoes. I find my shopping list in my wallet and make a note to pick up black shoe polish at the market, along with the ground beef and Velveeta.

I keep the water running as I gather my dress up and sit on the toilet to pee. The Twins are waiting. I try not to think about them or about Alex or about the fact that I'm unsure whether I asked the Twins to use *their* bathroom or *the* bathroom when it's technically *my* bathroom, mine and Ted's. There's a copy of the latest *Snap* on the back of the toilet. I flip through it, hoping it will distract me enough to be able to pee. I skim a semifunny piece on mimes and an interview with a porn star notorious for having sex with six guys at once—two oral, two vaginal, two anal, all simultaneously— and am finally able to pee. But then see Eva and I stop, every- thing stops. *Eva B.'s Life of Style,* the piece reads. It's two pages, color, the DOs and DON'Ts pages, *my* two pages. But there's Eva—Eva at home, Eva entertaining, Eva at brunch, Eva at a club. It's a diary of snapshots with pithy captions. There's an editor's note written by Ted welcoming the new column. I close the magazine then open it again. I look closer at the photos. At brunch Eva's flanked by Tiff and Rocka- billy Ben. There's another girl facing away from the camera. I take off Jack's glasses and hold the magazine right up to my face and squint until I'm convinced it's Parrot Girl.

I sit, frozen, with the magazine in my hands for I don't know how long. My brain is loud with flashes set to a heavy backbeat: Eva laughing at brunch with Parrot Girl, at the office twirling in my fuchsia chair; Ted and his *it's embarrass-*

*ing*s and *you're exactly the same*s; Jack and his fucking artners; Lila and Esther and their red-colored hair; Genevieve singing "J'taime My Baby Tonight" as Olivier screeches; the Hipster Twins laughing at Alex—poor Alex. They all laugh and talk and sing over each other, crashing against my skull. The Girl Twin is wearing a shrunken pink T-shirt with a black silk-screened skull. It's not very original. I'll make her a DON'T. I need to find Alex. His number is not in my current address book or the one before, but the one before that, the bulky one I rarely used that Ted gave me that had sections to keep track of birthdays and anniversaries and pockets to keep important receipts. It's in the back of a drawer in my desk at the office. I have to call Eva. I don't want to call Eva. I want to kill Eva. I'm wearing a dead woman's dress.

"Is everything all right in there?" The Boy Twin.

"It's fine. I'm fine." My throat is dry and my voice comes out scratchy. I'm sweaty and my head is pounding. I push Jack's glasses back onto my face but my eyes won't focus, they're turned inside-out, watching the strobe show in my brain. I can't shut it off or turn the volume down. My ears are ringing. I slide off the toilet and onto the floor. I reach my arms out in front of me and crouch in a resting pose I learned in a yoga class I went to with Gen. I breathe in through my nose and out through my mouth. I turn my head and see shadows move in the crack at the bottom of the door. There are whispers but the water is still running and I can't make out what they're saying. The Twins are waiting. I have to buy black shoe polish and ground beef and Velveeta at the market. I'm making casserole and meeting Jack. I have to find Alex and ask him if he's happy.

"Are you sure you're okay?" The Boy Twin has his arm

around me and helps me down the short hallway and into the showroom.

"Here, have some of this." The Girl Twin shoves a can of energy drink at me. It's sweet and disgusting, but I'm parched so I swallow it in three gulps. I steady myself against the counter and separate myself from the Boy Twin. The Girl Twin is suddenly beside me with a Polaroid camera. "Do you think maybe I could get a picture with you?" she asks. Her voice is timid and she blinks a lot when she talks.

I shrug. "Sure. But only if I can borrow the camera and whatever film you've got."

The Twins look at each other, unsure of what to say. "I guess that would be all right," the Boy Twin says.

"I mean, it's the store's camera, so technically I guess it's *your* camera," the Girl Twin says.

"Just like the bathroom," I say.

"What?" the Twins respond in unison.

"Never mind."

The Boy Twin takes a picture of me with the Girl Twin then the Girl Twin takes a picture of me with the Boy Twin. I take the camera from the Girl Twin, point it at my face and shoot. I drop the camera and the photo into my bag, not bothering to wait for the picture to emerge. The Girl Twin hands me several boxes of Polaroid pack film. I grab a copy of the current *Snap* from the stand by the door and leave without saying goodbye.

The heat outside is oppressive. Everyone looks like they're walking in slow motion. My feet race to catch up with my speeding brain. The heavy backbeats have been replaced with up-tempo pop with no lyrics, sunny coffee-shop Muzak. My dog-shit-free heels clickety-click in time with the song in my head. Gen and Ted jive while Olivier sits gurgling happily on a blanket. Eva and Parrot Girl eat chips and guacamole. They're wearing leis. Esther is there and Lila is alive—they're wearing sleeveless minidresses with big Hawaiian prints and their arms are perfectly toned. The Hipster Twins are carving slices off a roast pig on a spit that looks so delicious even the vegan artners can't resist. Rockabilly Ben swims naked in a pool. Alex sits in a cabana chopping rails of coke and regaling a posse of teenage boys with tales of early-nineties debauchery. Jack eats casserole straight out of the baking dish. He calls me *baby* and *darling* and he kisses my hand. His lips leave a faint imprint of sauce. I run along the grass and dive headfirst into the pool. I touch the bottom then swim to the surface. I stretch out my body and float on my back. People are talking but my ears are underwater and I can't hear a word.

The other shoppers at the market force me to break my rhythm and my methodic clickety-click, which infuriates me and annihilates the pleasantries of my nightmare backyard luau in favor of a tacky low-budget game show called *Fast Food* where the contestants are held at gunpoint as they do their shopping. There is no time for browsing or reading of labels, calculating the value of this can of deadly mercury-filled tuna over that can, or searching through pockets to find that goddamn coupon or asking the cashier if you can write a fucking check when the line behind you is twenty-deep. There is no time for such fuss. Contestants shop fast for what they need, the good ones have a list and a plan and they pay in cash. The shopper to finish in the shortest time wins a toaster oven and gets to shoot the slow shoppers in the head at close range. There's a studio audience and everybody cheers when the last coupon-clipping check-writer is killed after pleading for his life and wetting himself.

Three full episodes of *Fast Food* play in my head before I make it to the cashier with my black shoe polish, ground beef and Velveeta. The clerk looks at the ceiling as she asks me how I'm doing, if I have any coupons or some kind of *club card*. She scans the tin of shoe polish, the pound of ground beef, the Velveeta—the Velveeta won't scan. The cashier sighs and glides the bar code over the scanner again—and again. The Velveeta won't scan. She keys in the UPC number by hand. The Velveeta won't register. She picks up the phone on her till. "Price check on four," she says, her voice broadcast throughout the store. The people in line behind me huff as if somehow I've willed the Velveeta not to scan, its code not to register. I think about abandoning the Velveeta, fleeing before the cabal of shoppers behind me overcomes me and suffocates me with a makeshift hood of plastic, not paper, bags. But I cannot leave, I am committed to making this casserole. I could use cheddar, Jack has cheddar in his fridge. But Lila's recipe calls for Velveeta and Lila's recipe has a star beside it.

A young man with a spotty face and deep wet circles under his arms approaches the cashier. He sighs loudly and takes the Velveeta away and everyone in line behind me huffs again and I'm sure they're going to lynch me. I pull the camera out of my bag and hand it to the cashier. "Would you mind taking my picture?"

In Jack's kitchen I gather all the ingredients and arrange them neatly on the counter, like they do on cooking shows. I brown the ground beef with the onion and some mush-rooms and spices. I cook the egg noodles at the same time. I'm very efficient in my dress and heels. I stir a can of tomato soup into the beef mixture and then the Velveeta. Once the noodles are cooked, I add those, too, and pour it all into a casserole dish I'm surprised Jack has. I cover it and put it in the fridge.

I pour red wine into one of those stemless glasses that are deceiving in the volume they hold and take out the Polaroids of myself. I write *Snap Store, Toronto* on one, *Fast Food* on the other and tape them on the pages after the *Artners Dinner* photograph in the notebook that was Lila's and blank. I smooth out the latest *Snap* and turn to Eva's *Life of Style* spread. I cut out the brunch picture, the one with Eva and Tiff, Rocka-billy Ben and the girl looking away, who I'm convinced is Parrot Girl, and tape it into the notebook. Then I copy Lila's casserole recipe out word-for-word.

The phone rings. Caller ID tells me it's Jack calling from his cell. There's a note by the phone that says *Sara—call Ted and Eva!* I crumple it up and toss it in the garbage. Jack talks fast and in fragments, the way he always does after a shoot. He speaks too loudly after too many hours of blaring playback of whatever song he's making a video for. I hold the phone away from my ear and page through the phone book until I find Alex's number and write it in the notebook underneath the casserole recipe. Jack keeps talking. They're wrapping early, something about the drummer walking out, enough footage, deal with it in post, drinks at the pub, upstairs on Gloucester, you know the one, the pub, upstairs, on Glouces-ter, come on, you know, yeah, see you there, baby.

Jack isn't at the pub when I arrive, but Alex is. He stands and waves me over and I wish he'd sit down because people are looking. He's wearing a silky shirt and a black vest with shiny silver buttons, his pants are brocade and as tight as the crushed velvet pair I saw him in earlier. I paste on a smile and tell myself this is not a mistake, Alex is an old friend, when he lived in Montreal we used to talk every day, he bought me drinks when I was twenty and had no money, he told me when my hair was all wrong.

"I was so glad that you called!"

"Me, too." I remember the time my boyfriend dumped me for a man and Alex poured a pitcher of beer over his head. I remember all the blow-job tips he gave me and I really am, genuinely, happy to see him. It's sad when people lose touch.

"So tell me everything—work is good? The boy is good? There is a boy, right?"

"Jack. He's meeting us here."

Alex claps his hands. "Yay!"

As if on cue, Jack walks in followed by a dozen others. There are two women: Renee, the makeup artist Jack uses, whom I've met, and Lucy Sparkle, the lead singer of the New York electro-goth band Jack is shooting the video for, whom I haven't met but I've heard only has anal sex with her actor boyfriend because she once got pregnant and had an abortion, this according to a friend of a friend in Manhattan. I shake Lucy's hand. She's wearing lipstick the color of eggplant and looks appropriately dour.

Jack gives me a quick kiss and introductions are made all around. "And this is my old friend Alex," I say with maybe a hint of defiance. Alex stands and curtseys. Jack shoots me a puzzled look that I choose to ignore.

Several drinks in and I'm crossing and recrossing my legs. I've been drinking beer and I have to pee, but I can't leave the table because I need to monitor what Alex is saying because he keeps going off about this time we did this and that time we did that and I'm mortified, although everyone else—including Jack—seems to find these tales of my aberrant youth riveting. I shift and grimace until I can't take it anymore and I dash to the bathroom and get in and out as quickly as possible. I don't have the patience for the push-button hand-dryer so I wipe my wet palms on Lila's dress on my way back to the table where Alex is recounting my brief fling with lesbianism—if a drunken tongue kiss in a club with a hot Swedish girl can be considered lesbianism. I switch from beer to wine.

I should be happy that no one is laughing at Alex or calling him a queeny old hag even though he is and all of his stories are about a million years old. I should be happy that he's happy being a queeny old hag with old stories. I should be happy that when he lived in Montreal and was the belle of the ball he took me under his wing and taught me about hair and music and blow jobs, but I am not happy at all. How can he just sit there being so fucking happy and old and in those brocade pants? Didn't he know that the Hipster Twins were laughing at him today? Couldn't he tell I was lying when I said I was leaving tomorrow? Doesn't he know that I invited him out because I feel sorry for him? Can't he just tell me why he's happy—how he can be so shameless and oblivious and happy—and leave me alone with these people who would never talk to him if he weren't my guest?

I'll bet Alex won't tell me his happy secret even if I ask nicely—I imagine it's the only thing he has of any value, though some of his records might fetch a nice price considering the current market for eighties vinyl. I wish I had a tiny tape recorder. Ted gave me one once to record the interviews I did for *Snap* when I used to do interviews. I used it once then buried it in the back of my desk. Notes were easier and besides most of the people I interviewed were in bands or fashion and so drunk and stoned that anything I wrote was often at least close to what they meant and most of the time I made them sound better, smarter, cooler than they really were. But the tiny tape recorder would be easier than the notes I'm scribbling on the small pad I've dug out of my purse. My pen moves furtively, my hands under the table. I can't see what I'm writing and Alex is talking too fast and I fear I'm missing the clues that he's dropping, the hidden hints to his happy secret.

My hand cramps at a crucial point in the conversation—Alex is talking about the time we went to Maine and couldn't find a place to eat where the fish wasn't fried—and my pen drops to the floor. "Fuck!" I drop to my knees and feel around the sticky tiles until my hands are filthy and I find the pen. I hit my head on the underside of the table as I try to stand and my wineglass topples over, spilling cheap Merlot down the back of Lila's dress. "Fuck!"

Jack bends down and helps me up. Everyone stares. A flash goes off in my eyes and I'm blind. Alex breaks the silence with laughter and everyone joins in. My vision returns and I see Alex setting the camera and the undeveloped photo on top of my open purse. "I couldn't resist," he says with a satisfied smile. That I'm humiliated, filthy and sticky makes him happy, he's practically erupting in cheer. His secret to happiness is revealed. I won't need my notes.

I order another glass of wine to replace the one that's drying on my back. Jack leans over. "Maybe you should take it easy, baby," he says.

"Fuck off," I snarl at him.

The chatter around the table dies until dour Lucy Sparkle, who allegedly uses anal sex as birth control, speaks up. "Hey, Sara, Jack says you can hook me up with Gen-Gen."

"What?"

"Gen-Gen—Genevieve whatever—the French chick. We want to cover 'J'taime My Baby Tonight.' We do it live and it's fucking awesome."

"I'll bet."

"Didn't I read she's doing a TV thing?" Alex chimes in.

"And making a new album." Jack talks like he's the fucking authority on Gen but the only reason he knows anything about her at all is because of me.

"Oh my God. Sara—you have to hook us up. It would be wicked to work with her," says Lucy.

"Wicked." I pretend to agree, but what I'm really thinking about is how you'd get two big cocks up Lucy's teensy little ass like that porn star who's interviewed in the new *Snap*. "Has anyone seen the new *Snap*?" I ask and look accusingly at Lucy. She's got a confused face on but I think she knows what I mean.

"I was reading it today on set," says Renee the makeup artist. I love Renee. "Loved that new column with all the pictures—is that Eva B. your sister?"

I hate Renee. "She's my assistant," I say, doing my best to keep my voice even.

"Well, it's great. Her look is so *fresh*."

Fuck off, Renee. You're not looking so fresh with your messy ponytail and your vintage Polo rugby shirt that's probably a boy's size twelve from the eighties that on second thought might not be a bad look—it might be a DO—but I just can't tell. I have to go. I tell Jack that I have to go and he tells me to relax. I pull on his sleeve and tell him I have to go *now* and he tells me to chill.

"I do not want to chill, I want to *go*."

Alex lets out a whoop. "Oooh, you'd better go, Jack. You don't want to set this one off."

"Shut up, Alex," I say.

"Uh-oh—she's in a mood," Alex says in a singsong voice. I will kill him. No, I'll make him kill himself, bite his own penis off right here on the table and bleed out while we watch and order more drinks—that, I'd stick around for. Alex was always bragging about how he was so flexible, that he could suck his own cock, get him high on coke or poppers and he'd show you. I think about grey pubic hair and then I really have to go. I stand up and straighten my dress. The stream of wine down my back is dry and stiff. I grab my bag. I think of Lila and what she would do. She would walk feetfirst, shoulders back and clickety-click out of there. She wouldn't have been in a grubby pub—she would be designing dresses and eating casserole and reading her fashion magazines while enjoying a civilized drink and transcribing the pathetic ramblings of the kind of people who frequent grubby pubs.

I navigate the stairs with some difficulty, but make it to the bottom without falling. I stumble my way to Yonge Street and flag a taxi. I'm close to sleep by the time we pull up in front of Jack's building.

I unzip Lila's dress as soon as I've dead-bolted the door. I pour the last half of the red wine from earlier into the stemless glass on the desk and drag myself to the kitchen. I turn the oven on and take the casserole out of the fridge. I wash my face clean and shower. I redo my makeup and put on a different dress. I set the table and light candles. I empty a bag of mixed greens into a bowl and toss it in store-bought vinaigrette. I hear Jack's key in the door just as the timer on the stove beeps.

I'm wearing oven mitts and holding the baking dish. "I made casserole," I say brightly, holding it out for Jack to see. Orange pockets of Velveeta bubble up through the browned top.

"I don't want casserole," Jack says. His voice is flat.

"But I made it for you."

"I don't want casserole, Sara. I'm going to bed."

I set the baking dish down on the stove and strip off the oven mitts. I toss back the last of my wine and follow Jack into the bedroom, trying not to cry.

He moves away from me when I move close. The lights are out and I'm naked—I've even taken my bra off. Jack is wearing boxers and a T-shirt. I press my breasts up against his back and he moves away from me again. I slide an arm around him and slide my hand inside his underwear. His cock gets hard in my hand and he groans and rolls onto his back. I straddle him and fuck him relentlessly until my inner thighs are chafed and he comes inside me.

Whore

Jack doesn't try to talk me out of it when I tell him I'm going home three days early. I want my bed, my pillows and my ugly stretched-out underwear. Jack's in a rush to get to the edit suite and the taxi I called will be here any minute, but I stop what I'm doing and push Jack back on the couch. I open his pants and hike up Lila's dress. He feigns disapproval, but his cock is hard and by the time I get him inside me he's moaning and bucking his hips. I bear down on him and think about Gen and Ted and Eva and *Snap* and that things aren't really so bad—I just have to deal with it, be professional, wear my glasses and one of Lila's suits. Jack comes just as my taxi honks outside. I climb off him and adjust my dress. Jack mentions that he'll be in Montreal next week, to talk with Ted and me about the *Snap* video, TV, online whatever. There are no sentimental goodbyes.

The flight is full and I'm stuck in a middle seat between a businessman who doesn't look up from the *Fortune* magazine he's reading as I squeeze by, and a woman whose immediate eye contact and chipper *hello* tell me she's a chatterer.

"Business or pleasure?" Chatty asks.

I'm bent over trying to pull one of Lila's *Flair* magazines from the brown leather carry-on without elbowing either Chatty or the businessman, but it's impossible so I stick my hand in Lila's purse and feel around until I find my notepad and a pen. "What?"

"Your trip to Montreal—business or pleasure?"

"I live there." I flip past pages of illegible notes. A Polaroid picture sticks out of the pad. I flip it right-side up and gape in horror. My eyes burn bright red, my mouth is slack and Jack's glasses balance on the tip of my nose. My hair is disheveled and my shoulders are curled. I'm a softheaded hunchback with cleavage and my face looks so old. I shove the picture back in my bag.

"You're a lucky one—I'd love to live in Montreal. There's so much *culture*. It's so *European*."

"Mmm," I say and start making a list of vegetables to buy. I'm going to eat healthier, cook more at home.

Chatty goes on about Montreal and her trip—it's business, she's a *life coach* and she's written a book about women and work and *choices* and all I want to do is finish making my list of vegetables. She finally takes a breath as I write *bok choy* and I think she's done with me, but she's not. "So, what do you do?"

"I'm a photographer." I say this out of habit and with no enthusiasm.

"That sounds exciting."

"Actually, I'm the co-founder of *Snap*—it's a weekly magazine, and we do a lot of *consulting*." I have no idea why I say this.

"I know it," Chatty says. "You do all that cool youth-culture pop-culture trend stuff."

"Yup."

"I'd love to interview you for my next book—it's stories about successful women entrepreneurs." Chatty pulls a slim leather case from the inside pocket of her suit jacket and produces a business card. "Seriously. Call me. I'm in town until Saturday. I know you're probably *obscenely* busy but maybe you could find a window? I'm staying at the Queen Elizabeth."

"Maybe." I take her card. *Ellen Franklin, Franklin Enterprises, Toronto.* And in script lettering at the bottom of the card: *Because life is all about options.*

After we deplane I try to lose Chatty Ellen Franklin by taking out my cell phone and pretending to check my messages even though the phone has been dead for more than a week, its charger plugged into the wall by my bed at home. I race through the terminal doing my best imitation of someone determined and important, the dead phone pressed to my ear. But Chatty Ellen Franklin catches up to me at baggage claim so I nip outside to smoke.

Chatty Ellen Franklin smokes, too. This is unexpected and elevates her a smidgen above her previous ranking as airline irritant. We smoke and make the requisite small talk about how awful smoking is and about how neither one of us really smokes that much, mostly when we're stressed or when we drink, which for me is pretty much all the time but I don't tell Chatty Ellen Franklin that.

We get our bags and I agree to share a taxi, not so much because Chatty Ellen Franklin has won me over with her perma-smile and motivational lingo but because I'm too ex-hausted to make an excuse not to and she thinks I'm a suc-cessful entrepreneur who should be in a book.

As we make our way into the city I learn that Chatty Ellen

Franklin is all about women helping women. She speaks to women's organizations and networking groups about making the best choices for themselves—*because life is all about options*—and about encouraging other women to do the same. "It never ceases to shock me how it's often *women* who keep other *women* down when we should be supporting each other. If a woman is unhappy with her choices she doesn't want the women around her to be happy with theirs—you must have run in to this on your way up."

I push the power window button up and down, up and down until I catch the driver glaring at me in the rearview mirror and stop. "Not that much—I've always worked mainly with men," I say.

"Ah," says Chatty Ellen Franklin, like this one statement has profound meaning. "But you have girlfriends? We see the same kind of judgment and competition in friendships, as well."

"I can see where you're coming from," I say in the most noncommittal way. I could explain how I've alienated my best girlfriend by mocking her Wonderful Friends, how I want to quash my assistant like a pesky bug because she's got this great *Life of Style*. I could explain my deep-seated loathing of Parrot Girl and how the only call I want to return is Esther's—if she calls—and why I'm wearing a dead woman's dress. I could try to explain but I don't, of course, because I can't explain it at all.

Chatty Ellen Franklin is dropped off first at the Queen Elizabeth Hotel with her bags and her life with its limitless options. I tell her I'll call the same way a guy does after a drunken one-night stand and so-so sex. I think about my vegetable list and resolve to be nicer to Eva and to call Gen after I've sucked back a bottle of wine and when I know Ted won't be home.

* * *

I'm not sure whether I should knock. But then I think, it's my place and that would be kind of ridiculous. There's music playing so I know Eva's there. I turn my key and tiptoe inside, which is as ridiculous as knocking.

There's no one in the kitchen or the living room, but I can see one of Eva's vintage sweaters tossed over the back of a chair and an open bottle of sparkling water on the coffee table. It's a bright and sunny Sunday afternoon but the shades are drawn and the windows shut. The door to the guest room is closed. I hear Eva talking but can't make out what she's saying. She must be on the phone. I pull up the shades and open the windows. I pour myself a glass of sparkling water and take a seat on the sofa. As I shuffle through a stack of mail I hear Eva giggle. I collect the magazines and newspaper sections that are strewn around the room and arrange them in a pile and I hear Eva moan. I'm about to rush into the guest room to make sure she hasn't hurt herself when she moans again, louder this time, and lets loose a string of demands to fuck her, fuck her harder, fuck her *cunt*.

I stand in the middle of the living room, unmoving. *Eva said* cunt. I notice a pair of men's shoes beside my peacock-feather-print wing chair and an expensive-looking briefcase that's not dissimilar to an old-fashioned doctor's bag and that's when I know that Eva's in my guest room moaning and demanding that Ted fuck her cunt with his mushroom-head dick.

I can't leave. But I don't want to stay. I want to hijack Eva's car and bolt out to Pointe-Claire and get Gen and Olivier and drive them to a safe house that serves Cobb salads and has a round-the-clock spa, a place where suburban women go when they discover that their husbands are cheating on them with fake redheads who are all *golly-gee* and manners on the surface, but are in fact more *fuck my cunt*. But I don't leave. I stand, paralyzed, thinking that someone should publish an etiquette book that's actually useful, one that would tell people like me what to do in situations like this.

Ted walks out of the guest room and things are suddenly much worse. He doesn't see me and he's not wearing any pants. I don't want to look but I do—his mushroom-head cock swings as he makes his way to the bathroom. And he's humming. It's all too much. As my ass thuds into my peacock-print wing chair, Ted yelps, startled. It could be a scene in a movie if I hadn't opened the shades and the hiss of air being pushed out of the chair cushion wasn't audible. Plus I should be smoking and from where I'm sitting I can't reach my cigarettes.

"Sara!"

"Hey, Ted." I don't turn to face him. One look at that mushroom-head cock today was enough. I remember that when I was a child and I asked my mother how, if a woman had boy and girl twin babies, the mother could tell which was which. My mother said that the boy twin would have a *ding-dong* between his legs and the girl twin wouldn't. The Hipster Twins from the *Snap* store in Toronto pop into my head, naked and identical except for the flaccid, pasty *ding-dong* between the Boy Twin's legs. My chest heaves. I feel sick.

"Sara, I—"

I hold a hand above my head. "Don't."

"Shit!" It's Eva, standing in the guest room doorway. She's wearing my black silk robe, the one that matches the lace-trimmed chemise. Eva's too short to be wearing it and it drags on the floor.

"Hello, Eva." I say this slowly. I motion them over to the

sofa. "Come, sit." I stand as they sit. When I stick my arm out toward them to grab my cigarettes they both jerk back. It's a movie, maybe a sitcom. No, definitely a movie of the week, a cautionary tale with Gen cast as the wronged wife, the woman in peril. The cast will be culled exclusively from actors who starred on nineties' teenage soaps.

"Please, Sara, don't tell Gen. I don't know what I was thinking." Ted is holding my favorite throw pillow over his mushroom-head cock and now I'm going to have to burn it. "Please, Sara. It didn't mean anything."

Eva glares at Ted. "Since it *didn't mean anything* it won't matter if Gen finds out." She's practically spitting.

"That's not what I mean, Eva, come on." Ted turns to me. "It just happened." He looks like he's going to cry. He should cry. In the movie of the week he would cry.

I take a deep drag and wave my cigarette at them as I blow smoke rings. "You should go." They look at each other. "*Both* of you."

Ted starts to protest and Eva talks over him. They jockey for position, raise their voices to be heard and all I hear is noise. They each want the chance to *explain* but I tell them to leave. I have a headache and I need a drink.

I may have cut my time in Toronto short but as far as I'm concerned I'm still on vacation and can't be expected in the office until Thursday. That should give Ted enough time to deal with Eva and tell Gen or not and figure out that it's best if he never brings it up to me again.

My first instinct is to tell Gen. She'd want to know. Or maybe not. I want her to know but I don't want to be the one to tell her. Maybe she already knows, maybe they have an *arrangement,* though that's unlikely considering Gen's view on my arrangement with Jack. I've slept with married men whose wives didn't know and no one got hurt, except on occasion me if it went on for too long and I started to believe that I loved him and he loved me and that somehow someday we would be together. Gen slept with a married guy once, I'm sure she told me this in the early intense days of our friendship when if Gen wasn't with Ted she was with me, drinking wine and spilling all of the secrets she didn't tell Ted. And Eva—maybe it was just once, maybe she made a mistake. But, no, Eva said *cunt* and that tells me this was not a one-time thing.

I rewind the past month, try to recall every time I was with Ted and Eva together at the office, at lunch, Trend Mecca Bootcamp Weekend. Oh, God. Bootcamp weekend. Oh my God. Ted was there—he was never there before. I left early. Oh my God. I took Eva to their house for Olivier's birthday. I aided and abetted. I was drunk and stupid and it didn't occur to me that anyone other than Gen—and even this I find endlessly appalling—would want to fuck Ted and his mushroom-head dick. It's not that he's bad-looking or dumb or boring, but he's *Ted.* And I am an unwitting accomplice, an accessory after the fact. But it's not my fault, it's none of my business, I can't get involved.

"Oh, my. That is a sticky one, dear," says Esther when I tell her about Ted and Eva and Gen and how I thought about telling Gen but decided I should stay out of it.

We're walking to a bar Esther knows near her place. After Ted and Eva left I called Esther and suggested a drink. Walking to have a drink is much healthier than pouring a bottle of wine down my throat alone, at home, with the telephone in dangerously close proximity. My cell phone is still dead and the voice-mail box on my home phone is full. I erased none of the angry messages from Gen or Ted or the panicked ones from Eva or the ones from Diane who used to work at *Snap* wanting to know if I could be a judge on the TV show she produces called *Stylemaker.* I will erase none of these messages so no one can leave a new one.

Esther doesn't move very fast and I'm finding it hard to keep my pace slow to match hers. We stop at a corner and wait for the red light to change even though there's no traffic coming in any direction. There's a boarded-up shop—Esther says it used to be a tailor's shop—that's postered and graffittied with a giant For Sale sign that looks like it's weathered more than one winter. Someone has spray-painted *Satin Rules* in red block letters on a slab of plywood that's been nailed over one of the building's windows.

"Oh, dear," Esther says, noticing this.

"I think they meant *Satan* rules," I say.

"Either way, the message is quite effective."

At this I laugh. "Indeed."

The bar is in the next block beside a small bookstore-cum-café called Connections. A sign indicates that part-time help is wanted and that healing stones are sold inside. The main display, however, is a tower of books, its author's photo smiling out at us fifty-fold. It's Chatty Ellen Franklin and her book, *The Infinite Woman.* In smaller type below the title it reads *Because Life Is All About Options* and there's a tiny trademark sign beside the slogan in the upper right-hand corner.

"I met her." I point at the display.

"She looks very nice," Esther says.

"She wants to interview me for her next book about successful women entrepreneurs."

"That's fantastic! We'll have to order a glass of champagne to celebrate!"

"I haven't said I'd do it or anything."

"Don't be silly, Sara. Now, come on, we're almost there."

I should have worn something else. The men at the bar are in jackets, the women all wear dresses or skirts. I'm wearing my grubby 501s and a T-shirt silk screened with a snake smoking a cigarette. Everyone looks like they've come from church. I wish I was wearing one of Lila's dresses, but I was unsure of whether wearing her clothes around her best friend would be too weird. But she was the one who gave them to me in the first place, though it's unclear if I should give anything back. This collides with the Ted-Gen-Eva-cunt dilemma in my head and I decide to order an overpriced bottle of champagne to celebrate my successful entrepreneur status rather than a couple of piddly extra-overpriced single glasses.

The bar itself is not especially distinctive, but it's elegant and old with dark woods, candlelight and purplish-burgundy velvet banquettes the color of Esther's hair. The bar is called George's and according to Esther it's run by the original George's son, George, who greets us personally and takes our order for champagne.

"And what are you ladies celebrating this evening?" George Jr. asks.

"Sara here is going to be in a book about successful women entrepreneurs," Esther says.

I blush and rip a strip off a cocktail napkin. "We'll see. Nothing's confirmed."

"What kind of *successful woman entrepreneur* are you?" I look up briefly. George Jr. is smiling down at me. He's holding a pitcher of ice water. He's cute and looks vaguely familiar. I rip another strip off the napkin.

"Sara is one of the owners of that lively little magazine *Snap* and the stores, too. And she does a lot of *consulting*," Esther answers for me again.

"It's a lot of fun," I say. I am an idiot with a bulbous soft head because that's not what I mean at all. What I meant to say is that I loathe my job, it's inane and boring and I'm not even good at it anymore and my business partner is cheating on his wife with my assistant, who will bewitch you with her quaint suburban ways and her *golly-gee* manners and then steal your pages and your non–last name and demand that you fuck her cunt. I rip another strip from the napkin then crumple it up.

George Jr. snaps his fingers. "You're that girl who does the DOs and DON'Ts."

"That's me." I look up at him. His smile has disappeared.

"I was a one of your victims," he says.

"Excuse me?"

"A DON'T. I was one of your DON'Ts."

"No!" Esther chimes in. "I don't believe it."

I don't want to believe it. I don't want to remember, but then I do. I remember having him sign the release. He was wearing a black suit with white socks. It was a few years ago. I was doing a DOs and DON'Ts dedicated entirely to hosiery. I wish more than anything else I had that bottle of champagne in front of me so I could swill it back in continuous gulps until the chill and the bubbles locked my head in a spinning brain-freeze that with any luck would obliterate the memory of every DON'T.

"Sorry about that," I say. I am really, truly, sorry.

"Oh, it's all in fun, George," Esther says.

"I know," George says. "It's silly."

It's silly.

"But I never wore white socks with a dark suit again." He manages a weak smile. "I'll send Carol over with your champagne—good luck with your *successful entrepreneur* interview."

"Thanks." He turns to go. "Just a sec." I root through my bag to find the Polaroid I didn't bother returning to the Hipster Twins. "Would you mind taking my picture?"

George eyes me warily. "Is this a joke?"

"No joke. Please?"

"Okay." George takes the camera. "Say cheese." I don't smile. The flash goes off. I may have blinked. The spiffily dressed customers turn to look. There's nothing to see.

George hands me the camera back. "Thanks."

"No problem."

Esther wants to talk about my trip to Toronto and how wonderfully romantic my time with Jack must have been. I want to talk about Lila and her magazines, but mostly about her notebooks and if I might be able to take a look at more of them, if there are any. Neither of us brings up George Jr. and he doesn't return to our table.

I tell Esther about the artners dinner and toss in a tidbit about Jack buying me piles of frilly expensive lingerie at that store in Yorkville. I mention that I reconnected with a dear old friend and checked in on the *Snap* store. I tell her I made a casserole from a recipe in one of Lila's notebooks but leave out the part about how I ate it alone, in microwaved chunks, for four days and Jack didn't try it once.

"That casserole was always a favorite of Lila's—served it

every second week. For all her flights of fancy and her closets full of dresses, she could be quite practical—and frugal. I've never met a woman who could squeeze so much style from a penny. I'll have to give you the rest of the notebooks."

"Are you sure?" I hope I don't sound too eager. "I could just borrow them if you want them back."

"Don't be silly."

It's silly. What I do is silly. George Jr.'s words still ring in my head.

Esther lifts the champagne bottle from the standing ice bucket beside the table. I reach across to help her but she shoos my hand away, insisting on pouring the drinks herself. The veins in her hands bulge and I look the other way.

The champagne has me craving scotch, or at least a giant goblet of wine, but Esther doesn't offer and I'm too self-conscious to ask. We're back at her place and she's pulling several volumes of Lila's notebooks from a shelf in her bedroom. She hands me six. "I don't want to give you everything at once because then you won't have to come and visit," she says in the flippant voice people only use when they're trying to cover their sadness.

"I'd visit anyway," I say and I mean it. I pat Esther's shoulder. I can feel a bone jutting under her sweater set. I quickly snap my hand away and hope Esther doesn't notice. I wish I hadn't left the black vintage gloves Eva found for me at the bar the day of Lila's funeral.

I tell Esther I'll find a taxi. It's still light outside and I walk down the street, past *Satin Rules.* I'm lugging another of Lila's bags—an oversize black leather tote—filled with six of her notebooks. I stop in front of Connections bookstore-café and, fueled by champagne, I go in and buy a copy of Chatty Ellen Franklin's book, *The Infinite Woman*. The clerk rings through the purchase and I steel myself for a raised eyebrow or mocking look. But instead the clerk smiles, puts the book in a paper bag stamped with the store's logo and tells me to have a pleasant evening.

Outside, I attempt to shove the Connections bag into Lila's tote, but it won't easily fit, so I open it wide as I walk and try to make space.

"Dirty magazine?"

"Huh?" I look up and it's George Jr. standing outside his bar. He points to the Connections bag I'm desperately trying to push inside Lila's tote. "Just a book."

"Here." George Jr. grabs the Connections bag from me. I want to grab it back, tell him I'm only shopping at Connections and buying Chatty Ellen Franklin's book as a gift for a friend, as part of a joke, for something I'm doing for *Snap*. "Hold it open," he says, gesturing toward the tote. I manage to separate two of the notebooks and George Jr. wedges the Connections bag between them.

"Thanks."

"No problem."

"Hey, look. I'm really sorry about the DON'T thing."

"It's okay."

"No, it's not and I am really sorry."

George Jr. smiles, sincerely I think, and rolls his eyes. "It's silly."

It's silly, it's silly, it's so very, very silly. Maybe that's what I should tell Chatty Ellen Franklin when she interviews me if she interviews me. Everything I do, it's all so silly, silly, silly.

I stop at the *depanneur* near my apartment and pick up a bottle of cheap French red. I ignore my phone and my computer and crack open one of Lila's notebooks. This one is older than the others I've seen but only by months, maybe a year; in several of the photos she wears the black dress with the jagged neckline. I skim through before scrutinizing the details. There are formal photos, of her and a man. There are letters from a man written in black ink addressed to *Darling* and signed *With Love*. A strip of photographs slips out onto my lap, the glue that secured it to the page long, dry and brittle. It's Lila and a man—but not the man in the formal photographs—heads pushed together, pulling faces in a photo booth.

All the malls have photo booths, even ones that will print the pictures of you and your friends on tiny stickers. This was popular several years ago. I wrote about it in *Snap* and made the corporate cool hunters who paid us too much money to tell them about such things squeeze into a photo sticker booth to have their personal portrait taken with borders of hearts and flowers or big-eyed anime characters or Hello Kitty. If I asked him I'm sure Jack would go to a photo booth with me, push his head into mine and pull faces. I'm short of breath and claustrophobic thinking about it. He'd probably show off our adorable photo-stickers at an artners dinner and then all the artners would want to do it and Michelle and Dave would buy a photo booth for their loft with the commission fee of one of Dave's paintings and all the vegan artners could take turns posing and one-upping each other.

The man in the formal photographs is Luc and he was Lila's husband. The *Darling* man in the photo booth is Stephen and he was Lila's lover. There are more letters, written hurriedly, assuring Lila of the fantastical life they will have together one day and they are always signed *With Love*. Lila pasted the envelopes into the notebook, Stephen's letters tucked inside.

Some pages have three or four, glued amid theater ticket stubs and postcards from Vermont and Lake George. There are cryptic notes, sketches of black dresses, bits of poetry, an occasional recipe but no white space. I read until there's no more wine and the pages of letters abruptly stop. There were a dozen sheets left blank at the end of the book. I flip through the rest in the pile Esther gave me—neither Stephen nor Luc are mentioned again.

I can't sleep so I put on one of Lila's dresses. It smells of smoke and sweat, but I'll take it to the dry cleaner tomorrow. I take out my notebook and paste into it the awful picture Alex took of me, then the one I asked George Jr. to take. I try to think of something smart to write on the pages. I check my bag for any interesting scraps on which I may have written something profound but find only receipts for cigarettes and liquor and one from the market in Toronto where I bought the ground beef and Velveeta. So I draw a picture of a dress I imagine Lila would wear then I write *Satin Rules* in big cursive letters and laugh.

Snap

At least Eva isn't sitting at her desk outside my office screaming for Ted to fuck her cunt, but why she's here at all is a
mystery—Ted has had plenty of time to get rid of her. But
Eva is smiley and chirpy in her vintage sweater and orthopedic shoes and her Montreal red hair. She hands me a stack of
messages and a proof copy of next week's issue. "Oh, and I'll
be out tomorrow morning. We have to shoot the pictures for
my column," she informs me before heading back to her
desk. She's humming again.

I growl and skulk into my office where I discover more
than one thousand e-mails in my in-box, six bankers boxes
filled with swag and a copy of Chatty Ellen Franklin's book
on my desk, complete with a personal note, her cell number
and the room she's staying in at the Queen Elizabeth. I swivel
my chair until it's directly in line with the open door of my
office. Eva's back is to me and in perfect position. I lift Chatty
Ellen Franklin's book up and take aim, but before I let go, in-
tending to hurl it at Eva's head, Ted appears in the doorway
and I bonk myself on the head with the book as casually as I

can, as if I were conducting some sort of test or checking to see if my head was hollow.

"Whatcha got there?" Ted asks. He closes the door.

"Book."

"Nice."

"Why is she here?"

"Eva?"

"Of course Eva. Or were you waiting for me to do it?"

"I don't think we should fire her. She's too valuable."

"She's my *assistant*. I'll get another one."

"Sara, her column is really taking off and Jack I and have been talking about her doing some work on the *Snap TV* project. Didn't you read any of my e-mails? Listen to my phone messages? Didn't you talk to Jack?"

"He mentioned that you might want to talk to me."

"Jesus, Sara."

"I was on *vacation*."

"Yeah, freaking out the kids who work at the Toronto store and, what, telling some journalist that you were going to kill yourself until you got invited to an artners dinner?"

"That was a joke." How does Ted know these things? "How do you know about artners?"

"Gen and I have been to a couple of dinners." His voice is quiet now.

"Lucky you."

"It's good for networking."

Fuck me—people have artners dinners here, too? "Okay, Ted, whatever. How *is* Gen?"

"She's fine," he says quickly. "She doesn't know. She doesn't need to know."

"Really."

"It's not going to happen again. I've talked to Eva—we're all business. She understands."

"She's a *cunt*."

"Just leave it alone, Sara. Don't turn this into one of your dramas."

I spend the morning fuming and scrolling through two weeks of three-way e-mails between Ted, Jack and Eva, all of which have been copied to me. Eva: we need more of an online presence, it'll make *Snap* more accessible; Jack: give people more of a chance to be involved; Eva: exactly. Let people be involved with the shows, let them interact with the brand, be part of it not just dictated to; Ted: make it more democratic?; Eva: and younger; Jack: this could work; Eva: let everyone in on it—you know what they say, if you're not on TV these days, you don't really exist; Ted: I like it, I like it a lot.

I like the idea of sawing off Eva's fingertips with an extra-sharp serrated bread knife. There would be no more e-mails, no more *Life of Style* for Eva B., no more hijacking of my one original smarty-pants bite of nouveau philosophy. I dig around in my desk drawers knowing I won't find an extra-sharp serrated bread knife, but I do find a rusty letter opener that's shaped like a cross and has a skull for a handle. I carve tiny lines into the plastic of my phone that won't stop ringing until I look up and see Genevieve heading straight for my door.

"Sara speaking," I say into the phone. I didn't check the caller ID and am suddenly consumed with fear—it could be anyone.

But it's Diane. "You're one tough lady to get hold of."

"I know, I know. I've been away."

"Listen. I don't have a lot of time here, but I need the biggest favor. I need a guest judge for tomorrow. We tape at three. I can have you out by five."

"I don't know...." Diane produces *Stylemaker*, a television show in which twelve high-strung, fashion-obsessed contestants live together and compete with each other in style challenges and try not to get eliminated and be labeled a *fashion faux pas* by judges who are usually fashion magazine editors and second-tier former models. The last one standing is crowned The Stylemaker and wins money and prizes and gets to go on early-morning TV shows across the country and tell people what to wear. It's very popular.

"Come on, Sara. It'll be fun—painless."

"I guess if you're not on TV these days, you don't really exist, right?" Gen is standing in my doorway. Her breasts are huge.

"So you'll do it?"

"E-mail me the details." I sign off with Diane and hang up the phone. Gen barrels toward me and kisses me on both cheeks. Her breasts are huge.

"We must make a pact—no more fights!"

"I'm sorry, Gen. It was supposed to be funny." Her breasts are huge.

Gen waves a hand in front of her face. "Let's forget about it and go for lunch. We never go for lunch anymore."

I glance over at Eva's desk. She's not there. "I know. It's been forever. Let's go right now."

Gen unlocks her black SUV with the beep of a remote and I open the door. "Just throw that stuff into the back," Gen says, indicating the papers on the passenger seat. On top of the pile there's a greeting card that reads *Congratulations on the Twins* and has a drawing of a smiling woman with huge breasts like Gen's, except the drawing of the woman on the card is a cartoon.

I'm not feeling well and wonder if someone in the kitchen at the restaurant can make me some plain toast or if there's one of those two-cracker packs of saltines I could have. But I doubt it—the menu is gorgonzola-fish-tartar-quail everything. I order a ginger ale that comes in a small tumbler filled with so much ice that half of the two gulps of soda that fit in the glass dribble down my chin.

"Are you okay?" Gen asks.

"I'm just feeling a little queasy."

"You're not sick, are you?" She sounds genuinely alarmed.

"I don't think so. Maybe just fighting something off." I order the plainest salad and isolate the flat toasted garlic-herb croutons and nibble on them. I stare at the mixed greens and roasted red peppers, the shavings of chèvre, but eat none of it. Staring at the salad makes me feel flush and sick but I don't know where to look other than at the salad because if I look Gen in the eye I'll want to tell her about Ted and Eva—or not want to, which may be worse—and if I look below her neck it's all huge breasts and I have no cartoony greeting card in my purse.

Gen tells me about her show—shooting starts in a week. I tell her that I met Lucy Sparkle and that her electro-goth band is interested in doing something with her. I'm momentarily proud that I remember this but then Gen tells me Jack already e-mailed Ted about it and passed the message along to her and now her manager is looking into it. Gen has a manager and huge breasts.

I survive lunch but am sure I'm going to vomit as Gen's SUV lurches through midafternoon traffic. I power down the window and stick my head halfway out.

Gen pulls into the *Snap* parking lot. I thank her for lunch, pull the handle and push my weight against the door. "Aren't you going to say anything?" Gen asks. I open my mouth but nothing comes out. "You, of all people, Sara. I know you know—you won't even look at me for God's sake!" She wags a finger in my face.

She knows about Eva, she doesn't care, it's all very progressive. My stomach settles. I can breathe and look her in the eye. She sticks her chest out. But she's talking about her huge breasts. "You can touch them. Everyone wants to touch them."

I feel sick again. "No. Thanks. I'm good."

"It's just that after Olivier they were so saggy and stretched—"

"You don't need to explain," I say.

"They feel totally normal if you touch them like this." She takes my hand and places it firmly on the front of one of her huge breasts. "Or like this." Gen moves my hand under her huge breast and lifts it. "It's only when you touch them from the top that you can tell." She guides my hand to the top of her huge breast and presses it down. It's very firm, like a ball, and too round.

"Wow," I say, because I can't think of anything else. I step out of the car, feeling very nauseous. Then I see Eva walk by, bouncy in her orthopedics and smirking, and this makes things worse.

"Having fun, ladies?"

"Hey, Eva!" says Gen. "I've been meaning to call you and thank you for the card—it's hilarious."

"I thought you'd get a kick out of it," Eva says.

I crouch on the gravel beside Gen's SUV and throw up.

I am pregnant. I know this because I spend the rest of the afternoon with my office door closed logging on to every pregnancy Web site I can find. I lurk on a forum for newly pregnant women with morning sickness. They describe in detail the dizziness (yes), the bloating (yes), the fatigue (yes) and the vomiting (obviously), but are so chipper about it I have to flee and search instead for abortion clinics and information pages about fetal alcohol syndrome. I read about how some cases of fetal alcohol syndrome don't always manifest as physical handicaps, but as behavioral and psychiatric problems like sociopathy. I've dated at least three men I'm positive were sociopaths, so I figure I could deal with a kid sociopath and this would be a preferred option to the mutant baby I'd be so repulsed by and guilt-ridden about that I'd have no choice but to drop the two-headed, harelipped creature with Down's syndrome and no hands on Jack's doorstep. But then there's always the chance that the baby could be a mutant *and* a sociopath. That would be no good. There has to be a test for that. There's a test for everything. I do a search for prenatal tests but immediately clear my screen and my search history when Eva knocks lightly and opens my door without waiting for me to say it's okay to come in.

"Ellen Franklin is here to see you."

Chatty Ellen Franklin is better than the thought of a nine-inch needle poking into my belly. I reach over and grab the copy of her book from the top of the swag box I threw it on this morning and put it back on my desk. "Send her in."

"I apologize for dropping in like this—I just finished doing a seminar not that far away and thought I'd take the chance and see if you were up for a drink."

My stomach turns over at the thought of my usual red wine, but something cold, like a vodka and soda, has a refreshing appeal. Maybe a vodka and ginger ale would be better. Most of the baby damage happens in the first weeks after conception so the mutant sociopath baby that there's no way I can have is in all likelihood already a mutant sociopath so another drink isn't going to make any difference now. I agree to go with Ellen to the lounge at the Beaver Club at her hotel, where we can drink in dim lighting surrounded by business-men with expense accounts and eat bowls of nuts that according to a TV newsmagazine special investigation I saw we shouldn't eat because public nut bowls are rife with germs and microscopic creepy-crawlies. But we have to stop first at a drugstore to get a pair of pressure bracelets that the least chipper of the chipper women on the morning sickness Web forum swears are the only thing that help her nausea. I don't say goodbye to Eva or to Ted.

The pressure bracelets look like sweatbands and are made of white terry cloth with a raised bead on each that pushes on the inside of my wrists and is supposed to make me feel better. I'm an asshole and tell Chatty Ellen Franklin that terry cloth sweatbands are a DO as per the eighties-Olivia-Newton-John-sings-"Physical" revival. I also tell her I have an inner ear problem that sometimes makes me dizzy and sick and affects my balance. I could have bought a pregnancy test while I was at the drugstore, but why bother when it's going to tell me something I already know. People always say that women just know when they're pregnant.

"I know how busy you must be, but have you had a chance to give any thought to letting me interview you for my book?"

"I'm not sure—I don't think I'd have much to say."

"I can't believe that. You founded such an influential and unique business—I'm sure you have great stories."

"Cofounded," I correct her.

"Of course. Look, I don't want to pester you and if it's no, it's no, but, Sara, sharing your experience could be so valuable." Ellen leans forward. "Off the record?" I'm pretty sure I'm not the one interviewing her, but yeah, okay, whatever. I nod. "Most of the women I interview are very corporate, MBA-types. It would be great to include someone more creative. There are only so many times I can hear about the *management track,* being *on the same page* or how they've given *one hundred and ten percent* to get where they are before I want to drip hot oil into my ears and slice off every navy blue button on every navy-blue-suited woman." She reaches into her purse, pulls out a Swiss Army knife, waves it around and laughs. Our waiter, who has noticed our empty drink glasses, looks nervous. I order another vodka and ginger ale and decide I like Ellen Franklin.

Four drinks in I like Ellen Franklin better than Eva or Ted, definitely better than Gen's implants. I like her better than Jack—what do I tell Jack about the mutant baby growing inside me?—and the Hipster Twins, the artners, queeny Alex and Parrot Girl, which goes without saying because I *hate* her. I like Esther, but she's so old and I wish she wouldn't touch me. I think I like Rockabilly Ben but that could just be because he's young and fuckable and Eva's ex-boyfriend. I have a drawer stuffed with business cards people have given me who want to have lunch or a drink or hang out or hook up. My personal address book is full of names of people who I call sometimes when I'm drinking wine alone and feeling social but not enough to make the effort to go out. This usually happens in the winter. Sometimes the people in the address book call me for a restaurant suggestion or shopping advice; they ask me to meet up with them, invite me to come over and see the kid, meet the fiancé, tour the new house but

I mostly don't because I'm sick, I'm working, I already have plans to knock a few back, read tabloids and smoke.

Ellen Franklin is a very good listener. When I tell her about Eva's affair with Ted she shakes her head. "You wouldn't believe how many young women there are like that—they try to tell me these relationships *empower* them and at the same time they don't understand why the more senior women won't help them move up. It's the sense of entitlement that makes my head spin. These girls really think that the perfect man, the perfect job, the perfect life is going to fall from the sky."

Ellen is riled. She talks about Entitlement Girls like there is nothing worse in the world. Then I tell her about Gen and her Wonderful Friends and her new huge breasts and Ellen becomes positively incensed and it's very satisfying.

"How are we supposed to support each other if these girls are off sleeping with other women's husbands and the women who could be acting as mentors are too put off by the entitlement issue to want to help at all? And the stay-at-home moms are warring with the working moms and all of them are trying to look like teenagers with their fake tits and lips and poison in their faces. It's a big fucking mess." Ellen takes a sip of her wine. I nod silently and think about how Ellen really needs some soft layers in her strict bob—it would be more flattering to her face—and she should ditch the expensive-looking mauve pantsuit in favor of something not young, but less old. "And as long as it stays a big fucking mess my bank account is going to be very, very happy."

"What?" I heard her words but they didn't register. I'm not a very good listener—I'm a mutant-baby-maker with no friends.

"Let's just say that the big fucking mess women have made for themselves is very good business for me."

I raise my glass. "Cheers."

It's after midnight when I arrive home. I move the heap of Lila's dresses that I forgot to take to the dry cleaner today and flop into my favorite chair. I'll have Eva take the clothes in tomorrow, see how that fits with her *Life of Style*.

I think I have a life coach but I'm not sure. Ellen marked up the copy of *The Infinite Woman* that she'd left for me at the office. She said that in particular I should read the chapters *Stuck* and *Getting Unstuck*. I guess she thinks I'm stuck. I scan the first page of *Stuck* but my head is cloudy so I skip ahead and find a quiz that's supposed to tell me what I'm good at.

I'm an independent thinker who's best suited to working alone or with a small group of like-minded people. I'm creative and would rather give direction than take it, though I may have issues with delegation. I am an introvert by nature. I may have a tendency to be overly critical of myself and of others. My standards are high, apparently, but obviously not too high because I'm drinking a bottle of nine-dollar wine with a twist-off cap. I may be impulsive and exercise poor judgment on occasion. I may be reactionary and avoid confrontation. I'm likely to place more value on working at something I enjoy than on making money. Working for or running a small business in a creative field may be the ideal career path.

I stumble over to my desk and log on to my e-mail and find a copy of the latest financial statement Ted sent me. *Snap* hasn't been a small business for a long time. We own property and stores, we sell ads and companies back up dump trucks of money to our door so we'll tell them what's cool-hot-hip-*phat-sick-rad*. Ted's a suburban dad who's fucking my assistant's cunt. I haven't shot one DO or one DON'T for next week's issue and I couldn't care.

I'm spinning—even my desk chair is too high off the floor. I slide onto the rug and pull the wastepaper basket beside me and throw up into it—pieces of nuts covered in vile elastic red goo. My chest is tight. I can barely breathe. My lower abdomen cramps. I make it to the bathroom but just in time. The stink of diarrhea makes me vomit again. I light a candle, I draw a bath. My breathing is choppy and I think I should get a paper bag but I don't have one. I empty cotton balls out of a bag onto the bathroom counter and affix it over my mouth. I breathe in deeply once and out and then it occurs to me that the bag is plastic and I'm going to suffocate and for a moment this doesn't seem like such a bad thing at all. But I put the bag down and climb into the bath counting slowly in my head, trying to regulate my breath. I wash myself with a ginger scrub and my breath returns to normal. I think my breasts are sore, but my whole body is sore and I try to measure the soreness levels in different places by poking myself hard in the thigh, the arm, the breast. My stomach churns and makes an inimitable sound. The mutant baby is not happy.

I have options. I can call in sick and stay in bed. I can take a handful of Advil with coffee, put my sunglasses on and go to work. These are not the options that Ellen probably had in mind when she told me I have options or when she had printed *Because life is all about options* on her business card.

I compromise and take the morning off, sending Ted an e-mail saying I'm out scouting for DOs and DON'Ts. I lie in bed but now lying down makes me feel sicker than standing up so I take the Advil and drink the coffee. I want to wear my contacts but they sting every time I try to put them in so I'm stuck with glasses and big baggy eyes everyone can see. I put on the terry cloth pressure bands and head out into the sun.

It's especially muggy and on especially muggy days it's easy to find DON'Ts. People have frizzy hair, everyone is grumpy, women wearing makeup find it halfway down their face in minutes and most people smell, which I've often wished would register in the photos because it would up their DON'T factor that much more. No one cares what they're wearing; it's one of those days that cool and comfortable trumps style. I'm no exception in my white cotton dress that's cute on a hanger but I know makes me look big and disgusting and my size-ten ass at least a fourteen. But I'm the one taking the pictures, not posing for them, and I really couldn't give a fuck what anyone thinks because I'm hungover with no sunglasses and I'm laden down with a purse and camera gear and a laundry bag and a mutant baby who doesn't drink red.

I decide to devote this week's DON'Ts to shirtless guys after snapping two on my way to the dry cleaner. Eva should be doing this but she's not because no matter how much pleasure it would bring me I cannot ask her to take in my dry cleaning without confirming that I'm a smarmy dirtbag cliché, which I am but I don't need Eva to know this.

I walk in the muggy heat looking for shirtless guys. I find two more and then just as I'm close to Connections bookstore-café I see the ultimate DON'T: a pasty shirtless man wearing nothing but a red Speedo and flip-flops carrying a laptop bag. I'm excited in the way I used to get when I spotted a spectacular DON'T. This guy is amazing, he's perfect, I love him. I ask him to move down the block a bit, so he's standing in front of the boarded-up tailor's shop with the *Satin Rules* graffiti. He poses and ignores my no-smile rule. "I'm a big DON'T, right?" I make a *mmm* sound and the Speedo Man laughs. "It's great—I love it!" This guy is a rarity, he really doesn't give a fuck. This guy knows what's going on. This guy needs a shady tree and a Wi-Fi connection, not a life coach. This guy is so much my hero I want to make him a DO.

I am going to Connections to return the copy of Ellen's book that I bought but turned out not to need because of the free copy she gave me. I'm not doing this because I'm cheap, but because if I don't then I'll be the girl with two copies of *The Infinite Woman* in her apartment and as much as I like Ellen, I can't be that girl. If they won't refund my money maybe I can get coffee credit.

"Good book?" It's George Jr. of George's bar, the DON'T who wore white socks with a black suit and thinks my work is silly.

The clerk informs me that I can't get coffee credit, only book credit, and holds up *The Infinite Woman,* scanning the barcode and frowning in a way that doesn't strike me as appropriate for someone who works in a store that sells healing stones. I wish she'd put the book down or under the counter. "Oh, hey," I say to George.

"You're an *Infinite Woman,* huh?"

"No. I'm just—I'm just returning it."

"Being an *Infinite Woman* is no fun?"

"No. I mean, it is. It's my friend's book. She wrote it."

"So you're returning your friend's book?"

"She gave me a copy but I already had one but I hadn't been into my office and didn't know it was there so I bought one and, well, I don't need two." I'm feeling sick again and softheaded. I wonder if the mutant baby will know it's soft-headed or think it's normal and that its head—or two heads—is the same as everyone else's. I think it would be better not to know.

"Ah. It all makes sense now."

"It does?"

"Not really."

We stand in silence. George Jr. sips his coffee. I glance at my imaginary watch. "I should get going."

"Off to find more DON'Ts?"

"I already have." I start to tell him about Speedo Man, but stop abruptly in the middle of the story. I sound too enthused. George was a DON'T. I'm an insensitive bitch. I feel really sick now, like a wave of crap and puke is going to explode out of me at any moment. No one wants that. Maybe I need a healing stone. George asks me if I'd like to have lunch at the bar. I do not need lunch. I need a toilet and then to get to work. I need to find some DOs. I need to have a fucking abortion. I do not need lunch. "Sorry. Can't" is all I can manage to say before I'm out the door charging down the street toward Esther's place and praying she's home.

There is nothing I can do about the smell. I puke and shit and flush the mess down Esther's toilet. I wipe the flip side of the seat and the rim of the toilet to make sure I haven't left any physical evidence and flush again. I look for matches or a can of aerosol air freshener but find nothing. There's perfume in Lila's room on her dresser but there's no way I'll be able to sneak out of the bathroom and back in again without Esther noticing. I do find a container of Cornsilk face powder, the kind that comes with the big puff. I pat the puff in the powder and wave it around the small room. It smells somewhat better but the powder is yellowish and fine and covers every surface and looks like dusty grime. I find a cloth and do my best to clean it off. Then it's the breathing again and this time I feel like I'm choking. I'm sweating and manic, I hurt all over and I want to scream but my voice is locked. I force myself upright and open the bathroom door. Esther is setting out a plate of biscuits on the coffee table.

"Sara, dear. What is it? Oh my goodness, you look terribly ill."

I try to speak but can only wheeze in gasps. Esther helps me into Lila's room and onto the bed. She fetches me a glass of water, which I manage to drink without drowning. She puts her hand on my back. I wince and she takes it away. Her face is close to mine and I can see every line, the slackness of her skin, the way her eyelids hang down, obscuring her lashes.

I don't know at first where I am. I sit up and bring my hand to my face; my glasses are still on. It's Lila's room and I'm lying on her bed, my white dress bunched around my hips. I can hear Esther talking in the other room. "I understand," she's saying, "but she's very sick."

"Esther," I call out in a creaky voice.

"Just a moment. I think I hear her." Esther taps on the door frame. She has my cell phone and is covering the mouthpiece. "It's someone named Diane, about a television show?"

I reach out and Esther hands the phone to me. "Shit, Diane."

"It's three-thirty, Sara. Where are you?"

"I'll be there in twenty minutes." *Stylemaker.* I'm supposed to be at the studio being a judge. "I promise. I'm sick. I'm sorry."

"Just get here as fast as you can," Diane says and clicks off.

"Shit," I say.

"I hope you don't mind that I answered your phone, Sara. It kept ringing and ringing and I was afraid it would wake you, so I've taken some messages—from Ted and one from Gene-vieve and two from Ellen Franklin."

"No. That's great, Esther." I stand up and am so dizzy I sit right back down. "I've got to get to the studio. My friend Diane...I said I'd be a judge on her show...."

"You should be in bed, my dear."

"I have to go...."

"Then I'm going with you." Esther is at Lila's closet pulling out black dresses and tossing them onto the bed. She holds up two—one in each hand. "Which one do you like better?"

I point to the shift with the three-quarter sleeves. It's hot and muggy, but I refuse to go sleeveless on television. And the studio will be air-conditioned.

"Thank you so much, Esther." I'm dressed and we're driving to the studio. I comb my hair and put red lipstick on without using a mirror and hope I don't look too deranged.

"You can stop thanking me and just tell me what's going on. Is it that sticky situation with your friend Ted and your assistant?"

"No. Yes. Partly. I just—" Oh great. Now I'm going to cry.

"What is it?"

"I just can't do it anymore."

Esther is quiet. She lights up a cigarette. "Then don't."

I have to do this. It shouldn't be hard. All I have to do is sit in a swivel chair and not swivel as per the instructions of the director, who I can tell is pissed with me for being late—and make comments about the contestants' personal style. Only three of the original ten remain—two women and a man. Their challenge for this episode was to hit the streets and find the biggest fashion DON'T they could. Then someone rounded up the three chosen DON'Ts, got them to sign releases, probably told them they were going to be on TV and TV is awesome and brought them to the studio, where they sat in a room with a one-way mirror like you see on those detective dramas and at focus groups and made them watch while the contestants pointed out all of their style shortcomings to the three regular judges.

I watch this on tape as a woman—who I can tell is also pissed at me for being late—does my hair and makeup. The contestants are imperious and smug as they point out the flaws of their DON'Ts on photographs that have been blown up and placed on easels. Then I watch the reactions of the DON'Ts. There are tears. Sequestered behind the mirrored glass they look simultaneously furious and broken. The footage is unedited so I see the producers calming them down, coaxing them and baiting them with interview questions. *How do you feel about what you just heard?*

Then it's back to the contestants and the reveal of the twist: *your DON'Ts are here and your challenge today is to make them over into your personal image!*

The DON'Ts walk onto the stage to join their respective contestants. Offstage, Diane urges them to stand a little closer to their photo blow-up. It's ugly and intense and I understand why the show is so popular.

They don't show me the tapes of the makeovers-in-progress. There's no time, Diane says. "It'll be better this way," she adds. "You'll be coming at it really fresh—no biases or preference for one contestant over another." I don't tell her that I hate them all.

With my makeup done, it's judgment time. The first contestant, Marie, trots onto the stage from behind a curtain which has a larger-than-life projection of her DON'T *before* photo. Marie faces us, gives some bullshit wordy definition of her personal style and how she really, really liked imposing her look on her DON'T but she doesn't say *imposing*. The DON'T comes out and the two women hug and the DON'T looks like a fatter, weirder version of Marie. She can't walk in her heels and I want to jump onstage and show her how, but I don't because she looks happy and Diane would kill me if I did. So I ask a couple of questions and make some doodles on a pink index card that a production assistant gave me to score the contestants.

Next up is Yves, who's made over Marc, who looks surprisingly hot—better than Yves—now that his baby-blue jeans and chambray denim shirt have been replaced with rock-star black and he's had a haircut. Yves is ecstatic and nearly drooling over his creation as he gushes about his look, his style. I write *blow job* on a pink index card because Yves is looking at Marc like he'd drop to his knees and give him one in a second if Marc—who strikes me as very straight— would let him and I find this endearing.

Finally, there's Heather and Amy. Heather is striking with razor-cut blond hair to her shoulders, a heart-shaped face and perfect bow-tie pixie mouth that would not be conducive to blow jobs. Amy has a similarly shaped face and mouth and with her hair colored and dressed in a dress that's short and angular and very modern mod, she could pass for Heather's sister. It's impressive, but Amy is clearly uncomfortable and Heather is clearly a bullying bitch. When I ask Amy if she's happy with her makeover she says, "It's not really my style," which prompts Heather to explode.

"It's *my* style. You have *no* style." I wonder if they'll edit that out.

The contestants and their DON'Ts huddle backstage and get interviewed again by producers as we debate who should win and who should be eliminated. I immediately say Marie wins, Heather goes, Yves stays. The other judges look at me like I'm insane. It's a toss-up, they all agree, as to whether Yves or Marie goes.

"But Amy was miserable up there," I say.

One of the judges looks confused. "That's Heather's DON'T," says another, clarifying.

"This isn't about making people happy, it's about *personal style*," says the first judge.

"It's about bullshit," I say and all three of the resident judges gasp. The male judge, who's the fashion director at a national magazine better known for its recipes than its fashion-forward thinking, clutches at his throat, aghast. He's wearing an ascot. I am quickly outnumbered, outvoted and ignored. Heather wins, Marie goes, Yves stays to compete in the final episode. We tape the announcement, I say goodbye to Diane and am done.

Esther is waiting for me in the lobby. Diane wouldn't let her in the studio. The season has started airing and she can't have word leaking out about who makes the finals. "She's *seventy-five*," I said to Diane, but there was no convincing her.

"How are you feeling, dear?"

"Dirty," I say. Esther looks unsure as to how to respond. "Never mind. It's over."

"We should get you to a doctor. You're still looking peaked."

"I'll be okay. I just need to get some sleep." I'm feeling

worn and achy and the nausea still comes in waves, but it's better. I think I can breathe. I want to go home.

Before Esther drops me off she has me promise I'll go to the doctor on Monday or to the hospital tonight if I have to. She asks me to call her in the morning to tell her how I'm feeling and invites me for tea if I'm up for it and says that she'll come over to my place and bring me whatever I need if I'm not.

The phone is ringing as I walk in the door and I run to pick it up more out of habit than any actual desire to talk to anyone. Gen once told me that pregnant women can be very moody and scattered. I pick up. It's Ted wanting to know where I was today, what's going on, why Esther answered my cell when he called earlier. I am limp, my exhaustion a full-body sensation.

"I was sick and then I had that taping for *Stylemaker*."

"What taping?"

"Diane asked me to be a guest judge on the show—it was awful. Look, can we talk tomorrow?"

"You're a judge on fucking *Stylemaker*?" Ted spits the words out slowly.

"Yeah."

"Jesus, Sara. Don't you think you should have talked to me first? We have to make these decisions together. What's Diane's cell number? I'll call her and tell her it's a no-go."

"It's already taped."

"Then they'll have to retape. We can't have you on that thing—it would be diluting the brand."

"Don't talk to me about *diluting the brand*. You're the one who wants *Snap TV* and to make everything all *people power*."

"We have to move the brand forward—but not by going on fucking *Stylemaker*."

"We don't *have* to do anything."

"We need to have a meeting."

"I don't want to have a meeting."

"What *do* you want, Sara?"

"I want out." This escapes from my mouth before I have a chance to stop it.

"Out of what, exactly?"

My breath gets short. I should say I need a vacation, a leave. I could say I want to work on the *Snap* online-TV-whatever stuff with Jack. I should tell Ted I need time to think, but I don't. "I want out—of all of it."

"Think about what you're saying, Sara. This is *our* company, this is *our* vision."

"We never had a vision, Ted, we just thought pictures of people in bad outfits were funny."

"Don't devalue what we've built." Ted sounds defensive. "What are you going to *do?* Work at an agency? Pay people like us to tell you what's good? It's not going to get any better than this, Sara. You can't just walk away."

"I have to."

"Can we please have a meeting to discuss this?"

"I can't." I find my purse and take out the Polaroid camera.

"Is this about Eva? Because that's over, it's done, it was a mistake. It's completely over. I told Gen."

"It's not about Eva." I lie on the living room floor and hold the camera above my face. I can't believe he told Gen. I'll have to call her back.

"Fine, then. Let me know what your plans are for your shares."

"I will." I press the shutter and the flash goes off, blinding me momentarily.

"Are you at least going to finish next week's issue?"

"I can't." I crawl over to the coffee table and open my notebook to a blank page.

"Fuck, Sara." He sounds more exasperated than angry.

"I'm sorry, Ted. I really am." I fan my face with the Polaroid until the picture starts to come through.

Movie

Ted called Jack and Jack calls me freaked out and fucked up and I'm calming *him* down. He's teetering on hysterical, telling me I'm having a meltdown. I light a cigarette and flip through one of Lila's *Flair* magazines. "I am not having a meltdown," I say, blowing smoke into the mouthpiece of the phone, wishing it was Jack's face.

"You need to think about this, Sara."

"I've thought about it."

"You're not thinking clearly. Are you drunk?"

"Fuck you. I'm not drunk." I pick myself up off the floor and go to the kitchen to fetch a bottle of wine.

"So what are you going to do?"

"Have a drink?" I think I'm funny.

"Seriously, Sara. What are you going to do?"

"I don't know. I'll figure it out."

"What about me?"

"What about you?"

"We had *plans.*"

I have no idea what Jack is talking about. My heart jumps.

Could he know about our mutant baby? Maybe we're one of those couples who can read each other's thoughts; maybe he's feeling sick. He could have phantom morning sickness—I think I've heard about this. We could, we should, be part of a study at a university about psychic couples but we'd have to be called Jane Deer and John Doe because I don't want to be harassed by nutters calling up day and night wanting relationship advice once word of our remarkable connection gets out. And we wouldn't get married, so there'd be the name thing to deal with. The mutant baby would be called Baby Deer-Doe in the university study and in the press, and no one would know it's a mutant baby and if we ever went on a talk show we wouldn't take the baby but we would wear bad wigs and sunglasses and the producers would have to alter our voices with a computer so we sounded like generic robots.

"What about *Snap TV*?" Jack asks.

"Sounds like it's a go," I say, trying to sound flippant and airy. I have no special powers. Jack is not phantom sick, phantom pregnant. I take a big sip of wine, not bothering to wait for it to breathe, which according to wine people I've met is something you really should do and is not some affected wine-people bullshit.

"This is putting me in a really uncomfortable situation." The mutant baby screams inside me as red wine splashes all over its two squinty faces. "I thought we were going to work on this together and now if you leave *Snap*…"

"I've left *Snap*."

"Ted says you just need a break."

"Ted is fucking around on his wife." This has nothing to do with anything but it's the easiest thing to say.

"And you're fucking with *me*. What the hell am I supposed

to do now? I'm supposed to be coming out there on Sunday. I thought we were supposed to be working together. We talked about this when you were here."

"We didn't talk about it—I said I'd think about it. And it doesn't matter—just do it with Ted."

"Ted says everything is up in the air until you guys work this out. I have a *plane ticket*." And I have a mutant baby inside of me growing two heads and not enough toes. I pace in front of my living room window. The sky is dark, threatening rain. "What do you want me to do?"

"Do what you want," I say. The wine is numbing.

"Can't you see how this affects me?" He's whining now.

"This isn't about you."

"Because it's all about you. It's always about you." Jack's voice cracks. I stifle a laugh. Thunder crashes outside and I'm sure we're in a movie. Jack's the victim and I'm the broad, a great dame like Marlene Dietrich who says snappy things and wears men's suits. I put out my cigarette and light another. The movie is black-and-white, all shot in the rain.

"I'm really tired. Can we talk about this tomorrow?" I fake a yawn. So much for snappy.

"I need to know what you want me to do."

"I don't care what you do." I'm bored, tactless, wrong and a bitch.

"Fuck you, Sara." There's a click and dead air.

"Hello?" He's gone. I'm elated and light even in my mutant-baby pregnancy bloat.

I drink wine and call Gen on her cell. The thunderstorm has begun and my movie has changed. It's color and affirming, about the power of female friendship in the face of patriarchal adversity. I'm the quirky one who ditches her job and her boyfriend; she's the beautiful one who leaves her cheating husband. We have a slumber party—we need to have a slumber party now, tonight, I'll invite her over, I'll insist she come, as soon as she picks up—and hatch a plan, something kooky and unexpected. We open a business or put on a show. We do something daring or go on the road. Gen's phone rings to voice mail and I leave message, saying it's urgent, it's imperative that she call me right back. I use the word *pronto* and silently blame it on the wine and the stress and mutant Baby Deer-Doe.

I take the phone into the bathroom and check my messages while I pee. I've dealt with Ted and with Jack, there's nothing to fear. I skip through them, fast-forwarding, deleting, pleased with myself, my new life and the affirming chick-flick I'll make with Gen. This is what I needed. Ellen was right—life really is all about options.

There's a message from Gen and I can tell immediately that she's upset. I listen once then play it back. I dial her number and it's voice mail again. I leave a message. A clap of thunder booms outside. The air is dense and wet. I'm sweaty and breathing hard. I listen to Gen's message over and over. I fill her voice-mail box with messages. I plead, I'm angry, I need to make her understand that I didn't want her to get hurt, I wanted to stay out of it, that Ted fucking Eva was none of my business, that she needed to hear it from Ted and not from me. *If you were my friend you would have told me.* That's what she said. *I can't believe you knew and you didn't tell me.* I wipe myself and there's blood on the toilet paper: my period.

I walk in the rain without an umbrella. It's warm and I'm soaked and it doesn't matter. I could pee as I walk and no one would notice. The chick-flick is in turnaround. I can only make sad epics now, ones with sweeping scores and characters that are unrepentant smokers.

The rain is coming down so hard I can't keep a cigarette lit. My mouth tastes bad and I wish I had some gum. My abdomen contracts in dull cramps. I'm only half-drunk, but my brain is so heavy I'm surprised my neck doesn't snap under its weight.

I have options. I hate Ted for telling Genevieve that I knew about him and Eva, but I can either sell my half of the company to him or to someone else. This really isn't much of a choice because I don't know anybody else and can't fathom calling the agencies and people we've worked with and say, hey, can I sell you my half of the company? I can have my office boxed up and delivered to me at home or I can do it myself. I can keep trying to call Gen or I can stop. I can buy tampons made of recycled paper or continue using the environmentally unfriendly but easier-to-use ones with the plastic applicator I have stashed in my bathroom closet. These are my options.

"I think I quit my job." I duck under the canopy of a defunct shop. I have to talk loudly into my cell phone for Ellen to hear me over the rain and rumbling thunder. It's her last night in town and she's at a dinner-drinks meeting but says she'll come over after. She says she'll bring some wine. She says it'll be fun and I should be excited—I get to do something new, I'm free to do anything I've ever wanted. She urges me to think about the boundless opportunities.

I buy a bottle of champagne on my way home. It's not very good, but it was the only one at the store that was chilled and ready-to-drink. The bubbles fizz up into my face as I take a sip. I strip off my wet clothes and change into a vintage dress that I've never worn but suspect that Lila would have if it were black and not daffodil-yellow with a green-leaf print. My Lila clothes are still at the cleaners.

I drink champagne and page through Lila's notebooks, reading and rereading her notes and letters, looking for clues. I'm Nancy Drew, Harriet the Spy, I'm a girl detective, a chain-smoking, heavy-drinking, trash-talking private eye who dresses like a real lady and who all the boys want to fuck. But she never mixes business with pleasure. She has morals and standards, she lives by a *code*. She's a loner and mysterious but not in a serial-killer way. She's harmless, but she's been hurt. She cares about her clients, she solves every case with flourish and aplomb. She doesn't give interviews, she doesn't talk about her past. She's a hero to wronged wives and the parents of runaway teens. She's passionate and determined. She takes the cases no one else will touch. People say she's *feisty*.

I reach for my notebook and put Lila's aside. I make notes and write the opening scene. This is my movie—it's a mystery, it could be a thriller, it's certainly a blockbuster, it might be a *franchise*. I wake my computer and start to transcribe what I've written in my notebook but I need some inspiration and order six screenwriting books online and make a playlist of songs that I'll insist be on the movie's soundtrack. It will have to be a double album and we'll release it on vinyl, too, in a limited edition, each record numbered and the songs remixed by famous DJs.

The music sounds tinny coming out of my computer speakers. I sit very close and turn the volume up to its maximum. I sing along and think I don't sound terrible. I play the chorus of my new favorite song back again and sing until I'm sure my voice is blending seamlessly with the lead singer who, once he hears about how his band's music provided key inspiration to such a successful film, will invite me to sing the song with him onstage at an outdoor festival. And I'll play guitar and everyone will be surprised and someone will write about this in a magazine profile about me. I make a note on a Post-it to get a voice coach and sign up for guitar lessons.

I kill an hour answering imaginary questions from a contributing editor of *Vanity Fair* who's writing a feature story about me and my movie and my life. I wasn't going to sit for an interview at first but was eventually persuaded after reading some of the writer's work. In every piece she'd write about how good her subjects looked, how their skin glowed and *without a stitch of makeup,* though I'm unconvinced that makeup is measured in stitches. So I agree to talk to her. When she asks me about my high-profile friendship with a particular Hollywood star known for his roguish behavior I blush and play coy. When she asks me about my days at *Snap* I smile and speak fondly of the experience and even of Ted. And when she asks me about how it feels to be looked up to by so many young women I tell her how flattering it is and that I take being a role model exceptionally seriously.

Ellen is right—opportunities abound. I can make movies, take guitar lessons, be a role model for young women. I can be a successful screenwriter and I can sleep with roguish movie stars. I can travel and design handbags that sell out in Japan. I can have another glass of champagne and wait for Ellen.

Lila's notebooks are spread out on the living room floor. There's a stack of Polaroids on the coffee table. Several letters on my computer keyboard are stuck together. I take a sniff. It's white wine. There are pages in my notebook filled with bullet points about Lila; there's a list of songs I want to learn to play on guitar. In unfamiliar handwriting—it must be Ellen's—there's the name and phone number of a well-known literary agent.

I unzip the back of my yellow vintage dress and head for the bathroom. It's past noon. There's no sign of Ellen. As I peel off my dress I notice a stain of menstrual blood on the back. My inner thighs are wet and red—I'm leaking. I change my tampon and step into the shower to scrub myself clean.

I have one message, but it's not from Gen. It's Ellen; she's at the airport. She thanks me for my hospitality and moans about her hangover. She says she'll call me and we'll do the interview for her book over the phone. She says to call her agent but to wait until Tuesday so she'll have the time to talk to her first, to tell her all about me and my book idea. "It's gonna be great," she says. "I just know it."

What's gonna be great is getting a jumbo bottle of extra-strength Advil down my throat with about a gallon of coffee, but I'm out of Advil and too impatient to brew coffee myself. As revolting as I feel I look, I head out into the sun.

It's Saturday afternoon and navigating my way to the counter at the café on the corner proves an obstacle course and an exercise in forced manners. It's stroller gridlock; all the suburban mommies are running their city errands. They wear heels and tight, expensive jeans. I look among them for Gen, but of course she's not there. She's probably crying in her walk-in closet, cursing me and throwing Ted's clothes in a garbage bag that she'll drop off at the Salvation Army. I'd climb into a garbage bag and gladly throw myself into the donations bin at the Sally Ann. I'd smell like mothballs and no one would be quite sure how to price me and I'd live in fear of being bought by some perv when all I'd really want is to go home with a nice little girl and play dolly dress-up. But before donating myself to charity I have to buy a new keyboard for my computer and I should pick up my dry cleaning and then there's that book I need to write that I can't remember anything about though I like the idea of recasting myself as a bestselling author. Everyone knows screenwriters get treated like shit and I'd likely have a better chance of sleeping with a roguish movie star as an author because Hollywood people are impressed—if not intimidated—by creative intellect and there is no doubt that if I write this book I will be regarded as nothing less than a *creative intellectual.*

I walk into a drugstore to buy the Advil, a liter bottle of lemon-sweetened iced tea and a new keyboard because drugstores today sell home electronics and patio furniture. I queue up to pay and wonder whether my book is supposed to be fiction or nonfiction.

The woman in line in front of me is wearing the worst possible thing. First, it's a Lycra dress, which is never good, especially if you're wearing a lumpy bra, which she is. Second, it's neon pink with cutouts that expose her shoulders. Third, she has it cinched with a three-inch elastic belt with a giant butterfly clasp that her stomach spills over. She's a spectacular DON'T and I reach for my camera, which I didn't bring, and suddenly I'm weak and hot. My breathing gets hard and the pink-dress woman glances over a bare shoulder at me with an expression more of disgust than concern. I can't breathe properly through my nose because it's stuffed with gooey snot the way it always is after a night of too many drinks, so I'm forced to breathe through my mouth and this is not attractive and the more I think about it and try to control it the more laborious my breathing becomes. People are looking at me and it's freaking me out. I tell someone I have asthma and have forgotten my puffer. This seems to appease them and the pink-dress DON'T lets me cut in front of her.

What have I done? What have I done? What have I done? What have I done? This pounds through my head as I walk—it's a recorded loop set to an annoying and infectious beat that I just can't shake. *What have I done? What have I done? What have I done? What have I done?*

I flag a taxi. It's effortless, like it is for those smiley girls-on-the-go in tampon commercials. I check my bag to make sure I have a handful, which I do, and ask the driver to take me to Pointe-Claire. I don't know the exact address but I think I remember how to get there. I wash three Advil—no, four—down with the iced tea and wait for the pain in my head to subside, which I'm sure it will by the time I make it to Ted and Gen's. Or is it just Gen's now? Ted may have fucked Eva, but he's too guilty to screw Gen out of the house, if she even wants it, that is. I don't know if I would. I think I might want something new, plus it would be best to be the one to walk out and give the big fuck-you to the asshole who fucked you over. Maybe Gen's not going to be there and instead I'll find Ted, drunk on cheap cans of beer, answering the door in his boxers, his eyes red from crying and consumption. I won't offer him even one of my Advil.

I instruct the driver to go up the main street and then turn so we drive past Eva's parents' house. From there I know it's six blocks, a left and two rights. This may not be the most efficient way to get there, but it works and the driver doesn't complain: the fare comes to over forty dollars.

I ring the doorbell and practice my face—looking down, sad, sheepish, ashamed and upset. The box with my new keyboard is long and awkward under my arm and just as the door opens I drop it. "Fuck!" I scramble to the ground to pick it up only to find a bemused-looking Ted staring at me.

"Always graceful," he says. He doesn't seem drunk and he's fully clothed. He looks tired but not a mess.

"Can you just tell me where Gen is?" I'm not here to talk to Ted.

"She's upstairs with Olivier."

Gen is here. Gen is here? Ted is here. "Can I talk to her?" I shouldn't have to ask permission to speak to my best friend.

Ted steps outside and closes the front door. "She doesn't want to talk to you, Sara."

"But, what? She'll talk to *you?* I'm not the one who cheated on her—that would be you."

"I know, and we're working through this. But she thinks you betrayed her."

"By not telling her you were fucking Eva?" This is insanity. *This* is what I should be writing the book about and pitching to Ellen's agent.

"She's pretty upset. She says she can't trust you anymore."

"But she can trust *you?*"

"We're working on it. We're *married*. You wouldn't understand."

"I don't want to understand."

"You should go. I don't want to upset her any more than she already is."

"Of course you don't." My voice drips with sarcasm. Ted watches me balance the keyboard box under my arm and hoist my bag to a secure spot on my shoulder.

"I'm sorry," he says. I see now that his eyes are rimmed red.

"So am I." There's nothing else to say so I go. I avoid walking by Eva's parents' house but find my way back to the main street all the while keeping an eye out for a taxi. I'm no longer a smiley girl-on-the-go in a tampon commercial but a puffy, sweaty mess of a woman carrying a box with a new keyboard and fighting a nasty hangover headache. And there are no taxis—no taxis at all.

"Hey, sexy. I thought it was you." It's Ben, Rockabilly Ben, Eva's ex-boyfriend Ben who kissed me the night of her cocktail party.

"Not too sexy today, I'm afraid."

"You're lookin' good to me." The stupidity of his words evaporate when he looks at me. "What're you doing around here? I thought you were allergic to the suburbs."

"I am." I play with one of my short ponytails.

"You must be traumatized."

"I am." I'm flirting. I can't help it.

"I guess I'm going to have to buy you a drink."

"I guess so."

"There's a pub about two blocks from here." Rockabilly Ben moves closer to me. He lights a cigarette and my impulse is to ask him to put it out—people are staring. Street smoking makes suburbanites hostile. A woman walks by us and lets out a loud—I'm guessing fake—cough. Rockabilly Ben is oblivious.

"I have a better idea," I say. "Do you have a car?"

I wait for Rockabilly Ben at the end of the driveway of his parents' house as he fetches the car and says whatever a twenty-four-year-old man who still lives with his parents says when he's heading into the city with a thirty-nine-year-old unemployed woman who's lost her best friend and has a great idea for a book but no idea what it is.

He drives a black SUV that I suspect is his mother's because there's a customer loyalty punch card from a tea-to-go shop I noticed on the main street and Rockabilly Ben doesn't strike me as a tea drinker or the kind of guy who would use a customer loyalty punch card unless it was for cigarettes and buy-five-get-the-next-one-free smoking incentives are surely illegal. Ben tells me how sexy I am at least a half-dozen times and this makes me feel good and turned on through the fog of my hangover. He may well be saying I'm sexy, I'm sexy, I'm sexy because he doesn't know what else to say, but I choose to believe he says it because I am sexy. I make a point of filling in the conversation gaps with rants about Ted and Gen. Rockabilly Ben agrees that Gen shouldn't punish me for what her husband did. Neither one of us mentions Eva.

My apartment smells like stale smoke, liquor and some sickly scented spray air freshener that's supposed to replace all those bad smells with the fresh scent of early-morning dew but doesn't. Rockabilly Ben says nothing about this. He finds his way to the kitchen where, surprisingly, there's an unopened bottle of French red on the counter and he opens it. He doesn't take off his shoes. As soon as a whiff of wine hits my nose I involuntarily gag. I pour a glass of water to chase down the wine and keep me from puking.

Ben kisses me hard and tells me he wants to fuck me, that he wanted to fuck me that night at Eva's. I giggle and purr and touch his chest through his T-shirt. He takes my hand and leads me to the living room. He sits on the couch and pulls me to him but won't let me sit. I stand in front of him and he touches my breasts. He runs his hand over my belly and I flinch. It's soft and pudgy and I don't want him to know that. I try to guide his hands but he pushes them away He pops the button on the front of my jeans and slides his fingers down. I squirm and jump back. My period. Fuck.

"I can't," I say.

"Yes, you can." He holds my legs between his and pins my hands behind my back.

"I have my period."

He laughs. "And that means I can't fuck you?"

I start to explain that usually, in my experience, it's the guys that you're having a long-term relationship with, the guys that you live with who think they might change your mind about never wanting to get married and having kids who will fuck you on your period. Ben rolls his eyes and growls, "I'm not one of those guys."

He's not. I like this and he fucks me after I go to the bathroom to pull out my tampon. He tells me to strip, after which he keeps my hands pinned behind my back. He shoves a cushion under my hips and fucks me on the living room floor while I bleed and come three times. He flips me onto my back and positions my feet over his shoulders. I'm spread and open, bloody and wet. He grabs the Polaroid from the coffee table and the flash hits my eyes just as I'm about to come again. We take a wine break and move to the bedroom and he fucks me some more until I feel raw and swollen and sore. He holds me down, restrains my body with his, he teases me and fucks me relentlessly until there's blood all over the sheets and we're both spent.

He asks me to set the alarm for 4:00 a.m. He has to be back in Pointe-Claire early, for work. I do as I'm told and fall asleep.

★ ★ ★

The bleating of the alarm startles me. I roll over and there's
Ben, sitting up, pulling on his black jeans. I want him to fuck
me again. I tell him this and he screws up his face. "Can't.
Gotta go to work."

"Maybe later, then?" I say, too eagerly. I prop myself up
on an elbow and arrange the sheets so they're covering my
breasts and most of the bloody mess underneath.

"Sure. Yeah, maybe. Look, Sara—I gotta run." He looks
at the clock.

"I know. Work. What kind of work do you have to do this
early on a Sunday?"

"It's a publishing thing."

"Publishing thing?"

"It's just a part-time thing until my band gets going again—
we're looking for a new drummer."

"That's tough."

"Tell me about it."

"So what's the publishing job?"

"It's just temporary." He finds his wallet in his back pocket,
pulls out a card and drops it on the bed. "I'm late—I gotta
go. It was great running in to you."

"Yeah, you, too," I say as he walks out of the bedroom. *Ben
Miller, Independent Adult Carrier Contractor.* The front door
opens then clicks shut. I look at the card again and decipher
the language. Rockabilly Ben is a paperboy—a paperboy with
a business card.

Kick back the covers and assess the damage. Menstrual
blood stains the sheets in Rorschach blobs. One resembles a
two-headed baby and this makes me laugh. I would have
made a terrible mother.

Lila

What have I done? What have I done? The chant starts again but it's worse this time—this time I know the answer. *What have I done?* I've quit my job, I've left my boyfriend, I've lost my best friend, I've fucked a paperboy and I still haven't picked up my dry cleaning. Jesus. I've fucked a paperboy. This is what I've done.

I had options, I know this, I read it in Ellen Franklin's book, which is really quite good and smart and I'm thinking that maybe I shouldn't have returned that extra copy I had because I could have sent it to Gen and she might see past this *married* thing and see that there's more than Ted and her reality show and her house in the suburbs—there's me and it's not too late to make that chick-flick. I had options and I chose to fuck a paperboy. The saddest thing is I'd do it again and have spent the morning masturbating in my bloodstained bed to thoughts of Rockabilly Ben holding me down and fucking me hard.

After noon I resolve to get out of bed and do something— anything. I change the bedsheets, I shower, I am clean but feel anything but as I stand in the center of the living room surveying the damage. Two-day-old wine bottles, ashtrays on overflow, stacks of Polaroids and open notebooks remind me of Ellen and that tomorrow is Monday and that I'm supposed to call her agent Tuesday and give her the rundown of my fabulous book idea. More pressing, however, are the red spots on the rug from the menstrual fucking, though on close inspection I'm sure I could get away with telling people it's wine. And there's the Polaroid that Ben took, a close-up of my face right before I came. The picture is fuzzy and I'm slack-jawed, my eyes half-closed. I look pained. I shove the picture into my notebook upside-down between two random pages.

I've quit my job, I've left my boyfriend, I've lost my best friend, I've fucked a paperboy and I'm dizzy and short of breath but there's no mutant baby to blame.

I gather my things: Lila's notebooks, my notebook, a box of tampons, Ellen's book, the Polaroid camera and a makeup bag. I check my wallet for the dry-cleaning ticket. I find it and my breathing steadies. I fucked a paperboy. I have to go.

I call Esther on my cell in the taxi on my way to her place. She asks me how I'm feeling and I tell her not so good and she insists I come over right away. I feel like an asshole and a baby. I offer Esther money—I can pay her to let me stay for a few days, to clear my head. She refuses the offer and makes me tea, which makes me feel small and useless. I can't think of anything to give her in exchange for her kindness. But I can't think about her kindness for too long because I'll start crying and want to hurl myself into a four-liter box of wine. I tell Esther about Jack and Gen and my job and my alleged book. I leave out the part about Rockabilly Ben.

Esther finds a pair of short-sleeved black cotton pajamas in a drawer in Lila's room and then I'm wearing the dead woman's clothes again and things seem better and like I could sleep for a thousand years.

I wake up in Lila's bed. I'm sore all over and my eyes are sticky. Esther stands in the doorway with a cup of what I'm hoping is coffee, not tea. "We have an appointment in an hour," she says. "Help yourself to anything in the closet." She hands me the mug. It's coffee. I want to give Esther a reward, an international prize.

"What kind of appointment?" I ask.

"Doctor, then lawyer. You need to get your affairs in order, my dear."

I don't have affairs—I have unconventional relationships. Ted has affairs. Cunts like Eva have affairs. But I know what Esther means and I'm too tired for clever wordplay.

The doctor is old, probably as old as Esther, and his hands are clammy and look like raw chicken skin. He asks me questions about exercise and smoking and eating and drinking. I say I walk a lot and that I only smoke when I drink and I lie when I say I don't drink much. He asks about the regularity and flow of my periods, he listens to my heart and asks me to breathe deeply in and out while he listens to my back with a cold stethoscope. He orders blood work and gives me a sterile plastic cup with an orange lid to pee in and deliver to the lab when I go in for the blood tests. He asks me many questions about stress and takes my blood pressure, which is a bit high but not particularly worrisome. He says I'm having anxiety attacks. He says I'm a good candidate for generalized anxiety disorder but can't be sure so he refers me to a psychologist and prescribes me Ativan, which I know is a tranquilizer, to calm me down. He tells me to take the medication on an *as needed* basis, which I interpret to mean *pretty much all the time.* He tells me not to drive when I'm on it; he says not to drink. He tells me to come back for a refill if the problem persists, which I know I'll tell him it does even if it doesn't. Before I leave he reminds me to be sure to call the therapist.

I'm disappointed that the pills are so small and that the doctor has only prescribed me thirty. We stop at the pharmacy and wait until the annoyingly thorough pharmacist rattles off every possible side effect one by one in the slowest voice ever, pausing between each *dry mouth* and *drowsiness* for me to signal that I understand with an *uh-huh* or nod of my head. Esther drives me to the lab for my blood work. I tell her I can do it tomorrow, but she won't hear of it. "If you wait until tomorrow it'll never get done," she says, so I pout the whole time in the waiting room, brooding and silent, reading three-month-old copies of *People* with the crossword puzzles done in ink with incorrect answers. Hilary Duff did not star on *Full House.*

The Ativan kicks in by the time I'm sitting in a chair in a tiny room with a strip of elastic around my upper arm and a needle shoved in my vein. The drug makes me mellow and calm but I can't look at the needle. I wonder which I would be worse at: being an intravenous drug user or the mother of a two-headed mutant baby. Thoughts of the two-headed mutant baby prompt me to think of Jack, who may be, could be, might be in town now. I hope he works things out with Ted and *Snap* and I feel bad for not feeling more, but maybe that's the one side effect the pharmacist failed to mention.

At lunch I want to order wine, which I think is perfectly reasonable since it's after noon and I'm eating—and I'm not alone. It's social. I'm a social drinker—this is what I told the doctor and now this information is official because it's doc-umented in a file in the office of an old doctor in Montreal with clammy hands that look like raw chicken skin. I skip past the poultry selections on the menu and order a spinach salad with bacon and chopped hard-boiled eggs. Gen ate this kind of thing a lot after Olivier was born, when she was avoiding carbohydrates. Esther orders a toasted turkey sandwich—no wine, only mineral water, and I change my order to the same.

I tell Esther about Ellen's agent and my genius book idea that I can't recall. I feel no shame explaining this to Esther. She's seen me fucked up and babbling, crying and incoherently drunk and the Ativan numbs me enough to be able to talk about my idiocy without worrying about tears or pride. When I tell her I blacked out she doesn't seem surprised.

"There are notes, but I can't make sense of them," I say.

"You could call Ellen—fish around about the book. Ask her for advice on talking to her agent. Tell her you're nervous."

This could work. I want to hug Esther, but of course I don't. The drugs have me loose and slumped in my chair and I'm content to watch the waitresses smile and take orders, and listen to the people at the table behind us laugh and wonder what could possibly make them so happy.

The lawyer's name is Susan and she's the daughter of a friend of Esther's. She's forty—Esther told me this on the ride over—with severe hair and a no-nonsense manner. There are three pictures on her desk: one of her wearing sunglasses and a giant backpack and grinning at the peak of a big, impressive mountain; one of her huddled over a table of umbrella drinks with a group of women in leis; and a professionally shot picture of Susan and two German shepherds. No husband, no kids—we're not that different, I suppose, except for the mountain climbing and Hawaiian getaways and the dogs and the fact that I'm sitting stoned on prescription drugs in her office wearing a dead woman's dress and trying to forget that I fucked a paperboy and she's a grown-up sitting behind a mahogany desk asking me questions about my business that I can't answer. I swear I see an actual sneer when I shrug and say *I'm not sure* for the trillionth time. I sign the papers where Susan tells me to and her assistant takes my credit card information and now Susan is my lawyer. She shakes my hand and says she'll write a letter requesting full disclosure of *Snap*'s finances and have the documents couriered to her for review. I think she hates me but I couldn't care.

Once I'm back at Esther's I'm feeling very *proactive.* Ted was always feeling *proactive* and encouraging me to be *proactive,* too, or at least not mock him endlessly about using the term *proactive.* He'd be proud of me now, taking matters into my own hands, calling Ellen Franklin, seizing the fucking day like a teenage Ethan Hawke in *Dead Poets Society.* Ted would be proud—he might be—but now I'm the shrew with a mountain-climbing lawyer on retainer. My anxiety returns with a familiar thud—a fat man is sitting on my chest and it's hard to breathe. I set down the phone halfway through dialing Ellen and pop another Ativan into my mouth before trying again.

"Heeey, Ellen. It's Sara." *Do I sound stoned?*

"Hey, Sara. I was just thinking about you. I talked to my agent this afternoon and she's really keen to talk to you. She said Ballast Books is looking for new titles for its *Ordinary Lives* series. She thinks it could be a good fit—just pitch her tomorrow and whip up a proposal she can shop."

Sure. I'll whip something up. "Sure. I'll whip something up," I say.

"And don't forget you're mine on Friday night."

"Friday…" *Friday?*

"The interview for my book."

"That's *this* Friday, right." *It could have been next Friday, the one after that, some Friday next year. This is not impossible.*

"I'll call you at seven—and no cocktails until after we're done." Ellen says this playfully, but I know she's not kidding. I pull the quilt covering Lila's bed up over my head as if it's going to shield me from the reality that Ellen knows I'm a fucked-up lush.

"I'm not sure if I'll be home, so I'll call you." *I never want to go home to the smell of cigarettes and wine and paperboy fucking and the dirty sheets in the hamper and the stains on the living room rug.*

"And where might you be? Something you're not telling me?" *Yeah, that I never want to go home to the smell of cigarettes and wine and paperboy fucking and the dirty sheets in the hamper and the stains on the living room rug.*

Ellen would understand about Rockabilly Ben; she'd probably laugh and ask for details. I'll tell her another time. "Nothing too exciting—I'm staying at Esther's."

"Lila research. Smart. You're barely out of *Snap* and you've dived headfirst into something new. Your focus amazes me, Sara."

My eyes are at half-mast but I press on. Maybe my focus is amazing. I'm sitting in the den off Esther's living room, which is really more of a nook, tapping away at Esther's antiquated PC, trying to gather information about Ballast Books and this *Ordinary Lives* series Ellen was talking about. Ballast Books publishes those books about regular people that everyone's always surprised are so interesting. *Because everyone has a story.* That's their slogan. It takes me an hour to navigate the pub-lisher's Web site to learn this. Esther has a dial-up modem and after an hour of waiting for pages to load and for *graphics that cannot be displayed* I'm fraught and wired and I call the phone company and order Esther a high-speed Internet connection for the new Mac that I've arranged to have delivered tomorrow. And there's not enough Ativan in the world to stop me from helping myself to a glass of wine as Esther putters in the kitchen. She's making Lila's casserole for dinner.

Do I ask Esther if I can write a book about Lila? Do I tell her? This is not something I know how to do so I fumble and choke on my babble until Esther stops me. "Sara, dear. Whatever are you getting yourself so worked up about?"

"I'm writing a book about Lila—I want to write a book about Lila."

Esther sets down her fork. "I see. And this is the book you're going to be talking to your friend Ellen's agent about tomorrow?"

I nod. "I remember now. The notes make sense. You see, there's this series of books called *Ordinary Lives,* and it's very successful, but the whole point is that these 'ordinary lives' aren't ordinary at all, and obviously Lila's life was anything but ordinary so Ellen thinks it would be a good fit, and I have some of her notebooks already and maybe you could help fill in the blanks for me?"

"It's an interesting idea. I have no doubt that Lila would have loved it. It's an awfully ambitious project, Sara. Are you sure you're up for it?"

I have no fucking idea. "I think so. It might be good for me— for my focus."

"Well, then. We'd better get straight to work after dinner." Esther lays out Lila's notebooks chronologically—all of them, including ones I haven't seen before—on the floor in Lila's bedroom, in front of the shelves of vintage magazines that get me more flustered and lusty than I ever was for Jack. We start from the beginning; the first notebook begins shortly after Lila married—at twenty, Esther says. There are pictures of an apartment, a man, the same man she's posed with in the picture where she wears the dress with the jagged neckline and looks so unhappy, *Portrait of a Lady Undone.* "That's Luc," Esther says. "Lila's husband. He was very dashing from what I heard—certainly handsome."

"What happened?" I ask, picking up the next notebook in line. I'm anxious to move ahead, to know it all. The photographs are black-and-white, taken in the fifties and yellowed around the edges. Many of the square black corners pasted into the books to keep the pictures in place have dried up and fall into my hands every time I hold one of the notebooks upright, so I stop and splay out on the floor and open the pages carefully and one by one.

Esther reaches over me and grabs the third book, the one with the *Portrait of a Lady Undone* and the photo booth pictures and the casserole recipe. "She fell in love with another man— Stephen." I remember the letters he wrote her, the way he always called her *darling.* "Luc found out and it was quite a scandal. He tried to reason with her, but Lila would have none of it and she left him. They were divorced—nobody got divorced back then—and she moved in with Stephen. I met her around that time, when I was working at the English library in Westmount. She'd come in to read the magazines she couldn't afford to buy, although she always scraped together enough to pick up *Harper's Bazaar* and *Vogue.* Stephen was a writer and didn't make much money. He wrote paperbacks that you could only order from the ads in men's magazines while he worked on his novel."

"He wrote porn?"

Esther laughs. "I'm sure it would be considered very tame today, but back then the books were mailed in plain paper wrappers. Once I got to know Lila she'd bring copies to me at the library and I'd read them under the checkout counter. Some racy stuff. There was even one about bondage. I still have them in a box in my closet if you want to take a look. Lila would have killed me if she'd known I'd kept them."

"Why?"

Esther closes the notebook, sets it down and sighs. "Stephen didn't turn out to be the man she thought he was. They had so many plans—to travel, to start a magazine together. Lila wanted to design dresses, Stephen was going to finish his 'real' novel. Lila wanted to host fabulous parties and do all the things they talked about, but a few months after Lila moved in Stephen started to talk about getting married, having kids and all the things Lila could have had with Luc but didn't want. Stephen started to complain about their cramped apartment. He started writing for an advertising agency and gave up the paperbacks. He started wearing a suit and talking about moving to Pointe-Claire. Lila was horrified. She felt he'd conned her by pretending to be someone he wasn't, so she left."

"What was the final straw?"

"He told her to grow up."

My laugh comes out like more of a snort. "I've heard that one."

"Lila didn't have many friends and when she left Stephen I don't think she really had anywhere to go. She started spending every day at the library and I noticed that she'd wear the same dress sometimes two or three days in a row. She was always clean and beautifully turned out, but it was odd. I have no idea where she was staying—she never told me. But one day I invited her over for a drink after the library closed and we ended up blind-drunk and she stayed, well, until we bought this place in nineteen sixty-five." Esther smiles at something only she can see in her head. "I'll never forget that day I went with her to Stephen's to collect her things. She was so matter-of-fact about it, efficient. Stephen was crying, begging her to change her mind and she told him to *fuck off*. I'd never heard a woman talk like that before."

"What happened to Stephen?"

"He got married and moved to Pointe-Claire—right down the street from Luc and his second wife as it would turn out. Had two kids, stayed in advertising as far as I know."

"And Lila was okay with this?"

"She was and she wasn't. She'd always say that she was, you'd never hear her say otherwise. But the truth is often in what people don't say. She designed her dresses and she'd put together fashion photo shoots for the newspaper. Men were constantly ringing her up for dates but after Stephen she wasn't interested in seeing anyone seriously. She believed all men were looking for was a wife for them and a mother for their kids and she didn't want that, but I think she resented the way married people with kids were always accepted and invited to everything. Lila's choices scared people, so she kept to herself most of the time. She lived by a strict personal code—she had very strong opinions about what was appropriate and what was not, whether it be about clothes or food or socializing."

"I've read some of her rules. They're pretty smart. And the how-to-walk-in-heels instructions are genius. She *should* have had a magazine."

"She got close, once, to securing the financing, but the deal fell through when she wouldn't sleep with the financier."

I roll my eyes. "That's such a cliché."

"She wasn't the same after that. She went on designing her dresses, and there was a point in the late sixties that one of her pieces was featured in *Chatelaine* and a movie star, some American girl, I can't remember her name—was photographed wearing another one of Lila's dresses. That was all very exciting and she had lots of orders and had some meetings in New York, but nothing ever came of that and I think she lost her spirit. Once she knew that she wouldn't have a magazine or be a famous designer—the things she dreamed about for so long—she changed. I don't think she regretted not having a family, but she was lonely."

"I'm lonely." My voice is barely a whisper.

"Me, too." Esther nods. "I think that's the hardest thing to say."

By 6:00 a.m. the sun is up and Lila is no longer a mystery. She's a woman who almost did so many things. I jot down a few points in my notebook that I want to be sure to bring up when I talk to Ellen's agent. I don't need to sleep, I don't think I can. I start to write, make an outline. Esther went to bed around four. She was so stiff from sitting on the floor in Lila's bedroom she could hardly stand. I helped her up and walked her to her bed, guiding her through the living room and down the hall, keeping my eyes ahead and away from the liver spots on her hands.

I don't need a pill; I don't want a drink. I'll write this book, this book about Lila, and people will get to know her and it will be about the way it is if you're a woman and you don't want a husband and kids, but it won't be a downer, some story that the daytime talk shows pick up that prompts more single self-loathing and unnecessary hysteria. No, it will be a cele-bration about choices, but not in a two-bit schlocky way, and I won't gloss over the hard parts. It'll be Lila's story, but bigger, contemporary, a reasonable alternative to lobotomizing one-self with a stiletto heel after too many reruns of *Sex and the City* and books with pink covers illustrated with retro-style drawings of girls flagging taxis and drinking colorful cock-tails. It has to be real, raw, funny, smart. There will be sidebars with Lila's advice on manners and makeup and of course walking in heels. There will be casserole at the launch party. Lila's story is my book and I won't sell the movie rights, not unless it's just right and I'm writing the screenplay and some-where in the contract it says that no matter what, the Lila char-acter can't get married and have kids and live happily ever after. This is no romantic comedy.

I have a coffee and smoke three cigarettes in a row while I wait for the clock to turn nine. I snap a quick shot of my face with the Polaroid—a portrait of the author before. I wait four more minutes and then I call. Ellen's agent's name is Teresa and she talks very fast, though with the coffee and nicotine kicking in, I'm matching her speed with my pitch that I get right into after we've said our good-mornings and how-are-yous like we are the best of old friends.

Teresa says *uh-huh* a lot as I race through Lila's story and I'm not sure when or where to stop because I haven't figured that part out so I get into the stuff about the sidebars and having some reproductions of her sketches and wouldn't it be cool to include a paper pattern—a sewing pattern—so readers could make the Lila dress with the jagged neckline, and that photograph, her *Portrait of a Lady Undone*, would make the best cover, and it's a good title, too.

I come up for air and Teresa finally speaks. "She sounds fascinating—great story. Really unique." I'm going to be a writer, a biographer. I will not smile in my author photograph. "Maybe *too* unique."

I fumble for my lighter and a cigarette. "What do you mean?"

"I don't know if it's *relatable* enough, I'm not sure if Lila's story is *universal* in the way publishers are looking for."

"But the *Ordinary Lives* series…"

"I don't think her life was ordinary enough—she had her issues, her struggles, but not the ones everyone can understand. Most readers are looking to connect with the subjects of these books and Lila's life was so different, her choices were unusual—I'm afraid she'd come off cold."

"She wasn't cold, she was lonely, and it doesn't get more universal than that." I'm defensive now. Teresa is not getting it.

"Lonely is fine, but she chose that life and I don't see readers relating to that. There has to be a connection or the desire for connection and she made a conscious decision to remain disconnected. Do you see where I'm coming from, Sara?"

"You mean she didn't have a family."

"It's not a personal judgment, it's simply that most people do and it's those kinds of connections and similarities that make a story like this work—or not."

"I could send you some copies of pages from her notebooks—they're remarkable. It might make it easier…." •

"Look, Sara. I'm going to be straight with you. The appeal

of the Lila book is too narrow. Now, if we were to talk about something more salable like maybe a collection of your DOs and DON'Ts photographs or maybe a street fashion guide or a dishy trend-spotting how-to, tricks of the trade, that sort of thing, I'd love to represent you. Ellen mentioned that you've left *Snap* so it wouldn't have to be a branded book *per se,* but we can still play on your position as cofounder. Think about it?"

"Yeah, sure," I lie.

"Just out of curiosity—how'd she die?"

"What?"

"Lila. How did she die?"

I don't know. I never asked. Esther didn't say. I didn't care. Didn't I care? I am humbled and ashamed and I lie again.

"Heart attack," I say.

I have reached a new level of asshole. I am a dirtbag bigger than every dirtbag guy I ever dated in my twenties and there were plenty of them. I don't know how Lila died. I know nothing—nothing really—about Esther. She was a librarian at the Westmount library, she never married, she didn't have children, she's seventy-five and is kind and has liver spots. She likes me but she shouldn't. I'm an asshole, I'm a nightmare. I take another Polaroid. Tears blink from my eyes. A portrait of the author after realizing she's not an author at all but an asshole who doesn't know anything.

I don't want to wake Esther so I pick her spare set of keys out of the bowl by the doorway and quietly let myself out. I push and twist the childproof cap on the blue plastic vial as I walk. I swallow two Ativan. I have to pick up my dry cleaning.

One

The tranquilizers numb me enough to be able to sip a coffee and scan the shelves at Connections bookstore-café without crying before I walk up the block to the dry cleaner. I'm looking for a book about why I'm such an asshole and how to fix it and another one that will tell me what I'm supposed to do now. I collect books about depression, narcissistic personality disorder, borderline personality disorder and think I might have all three and be a sociopath. The books advertise help and comfort—I can start living a balanced life today!—but the words strike me as hollow. Even a healing stone seems more promising. That I count seven other people perusing the same section this early on a Tuesday morning makes me depressed— if I wasn't before—and I dump the pile of books on a display table and the counter girl I've seen before shoots me the dirtiest look. My cell phone rings and the counter girl points to a sign: a circle with a picture of a cell phone with a red slash through it. I swear the man in the green sweater thumbing through a book on bipolar disorder actually growls at me. I can't find my fucking phone, there's so much shit in my purse, so I take my coffee and flee to the safety of the sidewalk.

It's Susan the lawyer and she says she has good news. She's talked to Ted's lawyer and the *Snap* lawyer and nobody is acting like a prick—she doesn't use the word *prick,* but I like to think she wants to. The deal is in motion, Ted will buy me out, there will be papers to sign and would I prefer a bank transfer or a cashier's check. Susan recommends the bank transfer. "That's a lot of money to be walking around with on a piece of paper," she warns.

It is a lot of money, more money than I'd thought, not that this is money I'd often think about since I figured Ted and I would keep going and going, making fun of outfits and leading Trend Mecca Bootcamp weekends. Nothing would change, we'd never get old or have babies or move to the suburbs. Gen wouldn't have huge fake breasts and stop talking to me because of Ted wetting his mushroom dick inside that cunt Eva. It wasn't supposed to be like this. And I was never supposed to get bored with that life and be standing outside some self-help bookstore wondering where I'm supposed to be.

I don't want to go home or go back to Esther's. I can't sit at Connections with the counter girl glaring at me and the green-sweater guy growling. It's too early for a drink, not that I want one—my blackout night with Ellen was enough, at least for this week, though a glass of wine with dinner or a pint of beer at happy hour doesn't really count.

"Excuse me." A short, round woman with red cheeks tries to edge past me. She looks grumpy. I realize I'm blocking the entrance to Connections and step aside.

I walk to the corner and cross the street. The dry cleaner is another block up but if I pick up my cleaning I'll just have to lug it back to Esther's or to my apartment and I don't want to do either and I wish I had thought of this earlier so I could have made alternate plans. I could have gone to the art museum or had a pedicure. I still could, I suppose, do those things or something else entirely. I slump up against the *Satin Rules* building and watch the people at the intersection. Everyone has somewhere to go, a place to be. I have nowhere to go, no place to be. I have a pending bank transfer and dry cleaning to pick up. I need somewhere to go, I need a place.

"Waiting for someone?" It's George Jr.

"Huh? Hey. No."

"So you just like hanging out in front of empty buildings?"

"Something like that. I like the graffiti."

"Ah, yes. *Satin Rules.*"

"It truly does." I have no idea what I'm saying. Am I flirting? Am I retarded?

"I would have thought satin might go against all your rules," George says. I think he's flirting with me. Maybe he's retarded.

"I have no more rules." Who is writing what's coming out of my mouth? I'm not drunk; I blame it on the Ativan.

"What about your DOs and DON'Ts?"

I shake my head. "Done."

"Really?" He looks genuinely surprised.

"I am officially retired. Well, officially as soon as I sign the papers and sell my half of the company to my partner—ex-partner?—Ted."

"Business partner or partner-partner?"

It takes a second for me to get what George is saying. "Oh, God, no! Business partner, definitely. *Artner.*" I laugh as I say this.

"Artner?"

"Never mind. It's a joke."

"I like jokes."

"Maybe another time."

"Because you've got someplace you have to be, right?"

He's sarcastic and his words puncture my spirit. "Nope. No place to be."

"I'm just about to open up. I could make you a coffee?" His voice is warm, the sarcasm gone. He wounded me and I know he knows this and I hate that so I say no thanks and he tells me he'll see me around.

I watch George make his way across the street and past Connections to the bar. I sit on the pavement and root through my purse, not looking for anything in particular, but wanting it to look like I'm doing *something*. I check my home messages from my cell and wish I hadn't—there's only one call and it's from Eva, wondering if she can use me as a reference. "I *was* a good assistant, Sara," she says and it's true, she was, except for the part where she screwed my married partner in my home and fucked up my relationship with my best friend. I don't want to think about this.

I sit on the pavement for I don't know how long, but for a couple of hours at least because the quiet streets abruptly fill with people and I know it must be noon. I stand and brush myself off. I'm stiff and the Ativan has worn off, I'm no longer numb to the traffic and chatter and sun. I lean beside the *Satin Rules* graffiti and light a cigarette but quickly stub it out. There are too many people on the street and there's nowhere safe to blow the smoke. The *Satin Rules* graffiti is sprayed on a plywood board that is nailed over a window. A corner of the board has been hacked away and I bend over and peek through. I can't see much, but the sun catches the building at just the right angle and I can make out a curved counter, a staircase and a second floor overlooking the first. I lean against the building again, covering part of the *Satin Rules* graffiti with my back. I look at the For Sale sign. I have nowhere to go and I don't want to move so I pick up my cell phone and dial.

"People do this every day, Sara." Esther lifts a pile of Lila's magazines and places them carefully in a box. "They buy things, they sell things."

"I know, I know. But I didn't think it would be so easy," I say, sealing a bankers box with packing tape and labeling it *Harper's Bazaar, 1955-1957*. "Are you sure you're okay with this?"

"Of course, my dear. I think it's wonderful. Lila would be so pleased. I know you'll take excellent care of her things."

Esther has given me everything—all the magazines, the notebooks, Lila's clothes, the patterns for the clothes, a dressmaker's dummy. She even dug out her box of Stephen's paperback porn for me. I turned down her offer of the furniture, though. There's only so many dead woman's things I can live with.

"So are you planning to get a new roommate?" I ask.

"Oh, heavens, no," Esther replies.

Every day I make a point of asking Esther at least three things about herself. I keep a tally in my notebook just to be sure. Yesterday I asked her only two questions for her but have forgiven myself since there was so much going on with Ted's bank transfer to me and my bank transfer to a man called Mervyn who owned the *Satin Rules* building. Now I own the *Satin Rules* building and I have somewhere to go.

The movers take Lila's things away and drive them the two blocks to their new home. The boxes from *Snap* were deliv-

ered to the office of Susan the lawyer this morning and according to Susan, *they've taken over her office.* I told her I'd
arrange to have them picked up and delivered to *Satin Rules*
this afternoon. My books, my cameras, my clothes, my
computer and my music are all I brought from my apartment.
I didn't go back there. I hired someone to clean up my mess
and pack my things and get rid of everything I didn't want,
which was practically everything. I gave my notice to my
landlord via voice mail. Still, I couldn't help but cringe when
I thought about the movers and the mess in the living room,
the bloody condoms in the trash and the red stains on the rug.
"No one will care, dear," Esther said. "They do this all the
time—it's their job—they're not going to see anything that
they haven't seen before." I told her I'd spilled wine on the rug
and that my place was a disaster. The truth about the paperboy
and bloody condoms is not something Esther needs to know.

"So what are your plans for your first night?" Esther asks
as we pull up in front of the building. There are workers
prying the boards off the windows and blasting the grime
from the exterior with pressure hoses. There is a cleaning crew
inside, as well. The phone and Internet guys are scheduled to
arrive at two. You can hire people to do anything and this dis-
covery tickles me with infinite satisfaction.

"I have that interview with Ellen at seven for her book, but
other than that, I don't know. Read magazines?"

Esther laughs. "You have plenty of those. I'm so happy that
we'll be neighbors, Sara. You'll have to come by for dinner
at least once a week."

"At least," I agree, getting out of the car. As I step onto
the sidewalk I see a burly man readying himself to rip off the
plywood with the *Satin Rules* graffiti. I run to him. "No!

Wait!" The man stops and looks at me quizzically. "Hi, there. I'm Sara—the new owner."

"I'm Jean-Pierre."

"Look, Jean-Pierre. This is going to sound really weird, I know, but I was wondering if you could be extra careful pulling that board off."

"I will not break the window," he says, his English heavily accented. I think I've insulted him.

"No, no. I know you won't. It's just— It's just that I'd like to keep that board. I want it all in one piece."

Jean-Pierre looks at it. "*Satin Rules,* eh? Okay. It's to you." He shakes his head and shrugs.

I sit on the floor in the corner of the second-story loft, smoking and talking to Ellen. I can see the *Satin Rules* board downstairs, by the door. I'm using a half-empty plastic water bottle as an ashtray. It's disgusting and it smells.

"Sorry things didn't work out with the Lila book," Ellen says. "I really thought Teresa would bite."

I don't want to talk about Teresa or the Lila book. "It's no big deal."

"Very exciting about the new building, though. I can't wait to see it. What do you think you're going to do with it?"

"I don't know. Read magazines?"

Ellen laughs and I decide that's what I'm going to tell people I do if they ask. People are insatiable in their need to know *what do you do? What do you do?* Like the answer holds the secret key to who you are.

"Okay, so I want you to take me back to the beginning, not just the beginning of *Snap,* but when you first developed an interest in trends and realized that you had a talent for knowing what the next big thing would be." Ellen is all business now.

I liked fashion, I liked music. I've read American *Vogue* since I was ten and kept every issue. I spent my allowance and whatever money I managed to earn babysitting, even though I didn't much like babies, on imported records, limited-edition twelve-inch singles. I made my own clothes and shopped at thrift stores, which perplexed and annoyed my mother, who thought I should dress like a lady. This was ironic because she was anything but—single mom, too many boyfriends including, when I was seventeen, one of mine.

"Oh my God, you're kidding!" Ellen says when I tell her this.

"I wish I was. Don't put that in, okay?"

"Don't worry about it. But—off the record—what did you do?"

"I moved out. She moved to Victoria with some old rich guy."

"Do you talk?"

"No. But I send her a birthday card every year to remind her that she's old. She hates getting old. I think it was easier for her when I left. I was a constant reminder that she was aging."

"What happened to the boyfriend?"

"We got back together. Not for long, just until he went off to university in the States."

"You didn't go to university, right?"

"Nope. Ted did."

I worked as a fashion stylist and photographer for crappy little magazines for six years, but on my own time I'd take pictures of people everywhere—on the street, in clubs. Then Ted started writing articles for crappy little magazines after he

graduated. And one night he came over and got drunk and
we thought it would be funny to divide my pictures into DOs
and DON'Ts like in *Glamour* magazine, but without the black
bars over the eyes of the DON'Ts. Then we made this little
'zine and left it in all the cafés and bars we went to and pretty
soon people were talking about it and wanting to be in it so
Ted asked his dad if he'd loan us some money, which he did
because I think he was embarrassed that Ted's degree was in
English literature and wanted to be able to say he was a *pub-
lisher* instead.

"You see, it was all a fluke," I say.

"More like you were in the right place at the right time
with the right idea—like all successful entrepreneurs. It must
have been very satisfying to watch the business grow and see
people respond to your ideas."

"It was—for a long time."

"And now?"

"Off the record?"

"Off the record."

"Now I don't care. I'm tired and I'm guilty."

"Never feel guilty for your success," Ellen says.

"But what if your success was based on judging and making
fun of people?"

Ellen doesn't have a snappy, *Infinite Woman*–power answer
for this and neither do I.

I have a place but I don't have anywhere to sleep and I take
this as proof of my long-suspected retardation. I left my furniture behind, refused Lila's and now it's eleven o'clock and
I have no bed. I have no cigarettes, either, having smoked an
entire pack during my conversation with Ellen. I need to get

on the patch or something—but tomorrow. Right now I
need cigarettes and a bed. I could stay in a hotel. I have plenty
of money. I could take a suite at the Ritz and order truffles
and call all my friends to tell them I've taken a suite at the
Ritz, but I don't have any friends except maybe Esther and
Ellen, but she doesn't count because she's in Toronto, so I'd
have to hang out at the Ritz bar and make new friends. I could
stay for days—a week—and shop for beds all day. The staff
won't know what to make of me. I'll buy a turtle and a puppy
and I won't comb my hair. I'll play Eloise and crash a wedding
in the ballroom.

But I forgo my imaginary suite at the Ritz and instead
trudge up the street to the *depanneur* to buy cigarettes and then
to George's to celebrate and make myself drunk enough to
sleep on the floor of my new home.

I don't see George Jr. when I come in and I'm relieved. He
puts me on edge; he's never impressed. There's a stack of *Snap*s
by the door and I pick one up, slip into a booth and wedge
my body into the corner for optimum privacy and darkness.
I order a double vodka soda. Ativan dissolves into my system
as I wait for my drink and open the magazine. I scan the
masthead and am surprised to find my name there, at the
bottom, under the title *cofounder*. That was nice of Ted. I
consider calling him to say thank you for the recognition, for
making the buyout deal happen so fast and so smooth, but
then I remember what a shit he is and change my mind. I wish
I could talk to Gen.

I flip to page six, where my DOs and DON'Ts once were,
and there they are. I read the fine print. The shots have been
sent in by readers; there's an editor's note announcing the new
system and soliciting pictures.

See something on the street you have to share? Send your DOs and DON'Ts attention Eva B. at *Snap*.

Eva B.? As in Eva B., the home-wrecking cunt? I turn the page and there it is: *Eva B.'s Life of Style.* I flip back to the masthead. *Eva B., associate editor.* This is bullshit. This is wrong. And didn't she just leave me a message wanting a referral? What is wrong with Ted? How can he do this to Gen? I close the magazine and turn it over. On the outside back page is an ad: *Coming soon: Snap TV. Watch for it.* There's a list of credits on the bottom of the page, like on a movie poster. Produced by Ted, produced by Jack. *Inaugural online broadcast hosted by Eva B.* This is bullshit. This is wrong. This is going to make me crazy so I go outside to smoke.

A million scenarios race through my head but none make sense. Maybe Eva's blackmailing Ted. That can't be right. Gen already knows about the affair. Maybe Gen has finally come to her senses and left Ted and he's clinging to Eva and promoting her is his way of making sure she won't leave but she is because she wants me to give her a reference. I stamp out my cigarette and head back to my booth. I catch a glimpse of George Jr. behind the bar but scurry by unnoticed.

I finish my drink and order another. I take my cell phone out of my purse and punch in Eva's number. It's close to midnight but who the fuck cares. She's probably fucking some married guy; she deserves to be interrupted.

"Hello?"

"Eva. It's Sara." I know she knows it's me; she has call display.

"Sara, hiiii. Thanks for getting back to me. I wasn't sure if you would."

"So what can I do for you?" Saying this makes me nauseous but I want to—I need to—know what's going on.

"I know this is a delicate situation but I was hoping I could use you as a reference."

"Yeah, I got that from your message. Didn't you just get a promotion or something?" She doesn't know what I know or how I know it. Ted could have told me. She doesn't know I have to pick up the magazine to know anything about the company I started.

"That. Yes. And it's great and amazing to be working with Ted and Jack, but I have another offer."

The mention of Jack's name stings. "Another offer?"

"From Apples Are Tasty. They want me to be their new style editor."

"Apples Are Tasty?"

"They're expanding and it's a great opportunity for me to really get my name out there and put my stamp on something. And after everything that's happened at *Snap*…"

"Yeah, everything."

"I couldn't believe it when Ted wanted to keep me on after, well, you know, and I totally admire his commitment to the brand and not wanting to let personal issues interfere with that, and you were amazing to hire me in the first place, and I've just loved working with Jack this week, but I have to do what's right for me."

I hate her. I want to hang up. "Does Ted know? About Apples Are Tasty?"

Eva laughs. "No way! You know how he is about them. That's why I can't ask him for a reference—I need you."

She's talking to me now like we're old friends, war buddies, colleagues, equals. I hate her more. I want to hang up. "I'll have to think about it."

"Could you let me know by Monday? I'd really appreciate it. And, Sara?"

"Eva?"

"I'd really appreciate your discretion. I know you don't talk to Ted or Jack and that you and Gen aren't friends anymore, but if you could keep this under your hat that would be great. And hey, what are you doing for work now? I was talking to Ben and he said he ran in to you. He got the impression that you were taking some time off?"

I hate her. I hang up and throw the phone down on the table.

"Stood up?" George Jr. is smiling down at me holding my double vodka soda in one hand, a full bottle of beer in the other.

"No. Just work."

"I thought you didn't do that anymore."

"I don't. It's complicated."

"Of course." He says this like it's a given—that everything with me is complicated and weird and fucked up.

"Can I have my drink?"

"Only if you'll let me join you for a moment. It's been a long night. The ice machine went on the fritz and I had to run out to the gas station and buy bags of it."

"Did you just say *fritz?*"

"I think I did. Not cool? Sorry."

"No. It's fine. Sit down. I have no idea what's cool."

The Ativan combined with the vodka makes me slippery and I stop after one more double, before things get too *Valley of the Dolls.* I start drinking coffee and George is still sitting across from me as I explain the complexity of my situation minus the part about Rockabilly Ben the paperboy or the parts where I'm a total asshole.

"It sounds like you're ready to move on from all of that."

"All of what?" My eyes narrow and I slide my elbows forward. I cannot have enough analysis. George could not possibly talk to me enough about myself.

"The magazine and the people and the drama—it's too much. It would be too much for anyone. Let people sort out their own problems. Move on."

On to what? "But it seems so unfinished. There's no *closure.*"

"Did you just say *closure?*"

"Shut up."

"Sorry. But seriously, Sara, I think you're just making excuses and that's holding you back."

From what? "From what?"

"From doing the things you really want to do."

"All I want to do is read magazines."

"Then read magazines."

"And find a bed."

"I may be able to help you with that."

I think that George wants to fuck me and I'm flattered and he's cute and I like the banter thing we have going but I seriously need a bed. Maybe he means that we should go back to his place. Or maybe he means he has a beat-up futon couch in the back office that folds down into a bed that he's going to let me borrow until I find something more suitable. This, unfortunately, is exactly what he means. There's no innuendo, no hidden meanings, there's no flirting when you're carrying a futon down the street at 3:00 a.m. on a Friday night. At least the booze and tranquilizers are wearing off and I can speak without slurring, but the gallons of coffee are kicking in and

I'm jittery. This must be what people mean when they say *you just can't win*.

We drop the futon behind the counter on the main floor. "You don't want freaks staring in here at you—or maybe you do."

I have no window coverings. I put that on my mental to-buy list, along with a bed and plates and a sofa and everything else. I feel a pang in my stomach. I'm going to miss my peacock-feather-print wing chair.

I have nothing to offer George because I don't have a kitchen or a fridge, which I quickly add to the list in my head.

"So this is where you're going to read your magazines?"

"Yup."

"It's a great space. I have a guy if you need one."

"A guy?" George is gay? He has a guy? He wants to share or lend him out? The guy must be bi. George must think I'm desperate. None of this is good.

"A *designer.* He did my place and we're talking about giving the bar a makeover."

"You have a designer?"

"Don't sound so surprised. I also have magazines."

"What kind of magazines?"

"Magazines I think you'll want to read."

"Really."

"Uh-huh."

"And what do I have to do to take a look at these so-called magazines?"

"Kiss me good-night."

He's serious and I do and it's nice, soft—no tongue. He says he'll be by tomorrow with the mysterious magazines and as I lock the door behind him I question my liflong aversion to cheesy repartee.

I am awakened by pounding on the front door. It's light but I have no idea what time it is. I scramble to the front window and peer out. It's George. "Sorry. I didn't have your number." I let him in and walk immediately to the counter, pull a Sharpie out of my purse and write my cell number on his hand. I say nothing. I am not a morning person.

"What time is it?"

"Ten." He hands me a coffee and a bagel and a small square napkin from Connections. Good thing the Connections people didn't know George was buying the coffee for me or one of them—that counter girl, probably—would have surely spit in it.

"I can't believe you kept that." George points to the *Satin Rules* board.

"What? It's brilliant."

"If you say so." He sets his coffee down on the counter and heads for the door.

"I'm sorry," I call after him, although I'm unsure for once about what I'm apologizing for. Maybe I smell. I haven't had a shower even though that is one of the few things the space does have: a fully functional bathroom. "I'm not a morning person."

George props the door open with a box. "That's not a shocker." He disappears for a moment then walks back through the door carrying two boxes. He goes outside and collects two more, and two more after that. Finally, he picks up the box that he'd used to prop the door open and it swings shut. "As promised."

"The magazines?" I rush over and tear the top off the first box. "Holy shit!" I tear the top off another. "Oh my God!"

"You really love your magazines, don't you?"

"Do you have any idea what you have here?"

"Yeah, I grew up with them. My Dad was quite the connoisseur—all those long nights at the bar, I guess." There are hundreds of them. I'm overwhelmed. There are copies of *Nifties, Spree, Sir, Carnival, Knight, Dude*—I love *Dude* the most. Men's nudie pin-up magazines from the fifties and sixties fill the boxes. "There's some classier stuff in there somewhere, too, like *Esquire.* And a few copies of *GQ* from the eighties—I think those were mine."

I want to hug him, kiss him, I'll drop to my knees and give him a blow job if that's what he wants as a thank-you. "George, this is incredible. Thank you. I'll go through them and get them back to you as soon as possible."

"Forget it. They're yours. Keep 'em."

"Seriously?"

"Seriously. They've been sitting in boxes taking up space in the bar for years. Consider it a housewarming gift."

"You're sure you don't need them."

George laughs. "No, I don't *need* them. The Internet serves my needs just fine."

"Ooh, porn talk. And so early in the morning."

"I always say, it's never too early for porn talk."

I want to kiss him but I want to brush my teeth first. He steps closer. There will be no minty freshness. He kisses me. "Thank you," I say. We pull apart and I realize that he probably thinks I just thanked him for kissing me, which would be pathetic and make me seem sadder than I already am. "No, not for that." I correct myself. "I mean thank you for giving me your dad's spank mag collection." I clasp my hand over my mouth. I'm an idiot, an asshole, a retard. I'm not cut out for romance and cheesy repartee. But George just laughs and peels my hand from my mouth so he can kiss me again.

Open

George's guy is Australian and calls himself Timotei. I assume it's a nickname and that he wasn't named after shampoo but I don't ask because I know that anything is entirely possible. "You can call me Tim," he says and I am relieved.

Tim takes me shopping and brings me photos. He finds a guy—no, *the* guy, according to Tim—to build custom shelves for my growing vintage magazine collection.

George comes by in the mornings on his way to work and brings me a coffee and a bagel from Connections. I stop by the bar around seven and we eat together. Some nights I have a nap on my new, very proper bed so I'm rested if George comes by after the bar closes for a drink and a kiss. I haven't fucked him and he always goes home after a quick visit. But it's nice and I think it's normal and I have no other friends except Esther and Ellen so I'll take what I can get.

The new, custom-built shelves are spectacular. I run my hand along the grain of the dark stained wood and sigh. It's almost erotic, which would make me a freak, and I make a mental note to look that up online. There's a name for every fetish.

Esther comes by to help me unpack the magazines and put them on the shelves. Watching her bend and lift the heavy stacks makes me nervous, but she wants to help and I don't see how I can't let her. Tim shrieks when he sees what I'm holding.

"What?"

"My lord, Sara. Is that an original copy of *Flair* magazine in your hands?"

"Uh-huh."

Tim scampers over and takes it gingerly from me. "Do you know how many people would die—absolutely *die*—to put their hands on this?"

"Uh-huh."

"My friend Martin—he would *kill*."

"Bring him by. He can take a look if he wants."

"Oh, he'll want."

"That Tim's a funny little guy," Esther says after he's gone and I'm cooking my first meal in my new kitchen.

"That he is. Can you pass me the Velveeta?" I'm making Lila's casserole.

"He was awfully excited about those magazines."

"There are lots of us out there." I want to tell her about George but stop myself out of respect for superstition, or because she was friends with his dad, or maybe because I like him. I don't know.

"You know, I could ask around. I have a feeling there are boxes of these things collecting dust in my friends' closets and basements. They'd probably be glad to be rid of them."

"You think so?"

"Sure. People keep the strangest things for the longest time. I'll ask around."

"And books—ask about books, too, like those trashy paper-backs Stephen wrote."

★ ★ ★

I'm too wired to nap. I made Esther and I espressos with my new ridiculously expensive machine after dinner and made the mistake of having two. Now I'm shaky and tempted to pop an Ativan but opt for a beer. Since Esther was coming for dinner I haven't seen George since this morning and he was in a hurry. I could go down to the bar, keep him company, but that might make me look needy and like a loser with no life, which I sometimes think I am, but I prefer to keep that information to myself.

My cell phone rings and I jump. My intuition says it's George. It's not. It's Eva, wanting who knows what. I let it go to voice mail. I didn't get back to her about being a reference and her name is still on the masthead at *Snap* and nowhere to be found on the Apples Are Tasty site, so I guess she didn't get the job. Not that it matters, not that I should be reading *Snap* or logging on to Apples Are Tasty. But I can't help it and I know it's wrong and I always hide the evidence, burying *Snap* at the bottom of my recycling pile, clearing my Internet history after my daily visit to Apples Are Tasty, irrationally hoping that if no one knows, it didn't happen.

I listen to Eva's message. Her voice is chirpy, which means she must want something. And she does. She's heard from her friend Martin that I have this library of vintage magazines at my new place and she's working on this project and it would really, really help if she could come by and take a peek. I delete the message. *Come by? Take a peek?* Oh, fuck off, Eva. I pick up the phone again and enter my password. My service has a message retrieval system so you can undelete deleted messages within twenty-four hours of deleting them. It's a feature custom-made for people like me. I undelete Eva's message and listen to it again. *What fucking project?*

I distract myself with beer and unpacking. My magazines, Lila's magazines, George's dad's magazines and the books—they're all organized and shelved. All that's left are the *Snap* boxes.

Some of the boxes are numbered, some say *Personal* or *Misc.;* they each have *Sara* scrawled across the lid and the sides. I open box number one and find the earliest issues of *Snap,* even the old photocopied 'zines we made before we had a name or any money. Box two holds issues from nineteen ninety-five, our first year on newsprint and as a weekly, box three is ninety-six. There are fourteen numbered boxes, every issue we ever made, all in order, a perfect archive. I choose a random box and pull an issue off the top. January 4th, 2000, the *We're Not Dead Yet* issue. I flip to the DOs and DON'Ts page. I remember the DON'Ts—the guy in the tight silver jumpsuit at a New Year's party, the girl who tried too hard to be Bettie Page—but the DOs are a jumble in my head. Everyone always remembers the DON'Ts. People, when they meet me at parties, tell me about this DON'T or that DON'T and how they laughed so, so hard.

I get another beer from the fridge and go through every issue in the box, looking at the DON'Ts. I make myself look at their unsuspecting eyes and remember that the second after the picture was taken and the release was signed they'd bound off to tell their friends how they'd been shot for *Snap,* thinking they were going to be a DO. There were never any promises, but no one assumes they're a DON'T.

By the time I'm through the third box I'm drunk and my

hands are black with newsprint. I glance at the clock because I have one now and it's after two. I haven't heard from George and he should have closed up by now; it's a Wednesday. I'm nervous calling the bar—I haven't before—but it rings and rings and rings, no answer, no machine. He has call display on the phone in his office and the possibility that he's screening sinks in. I will march down there and demand to know why he wouldn't take my call. The reality is more of a weave than a march but I make it to the bar. It's dark and closed and I return home to more beer and my archives.

I sift through the DON'Ts of box eleven and there he is, in his dark suit and white socks. The socks make me wince, I can't help it, but it's George and the white socks shouldn't matter. It was years ago. He said he never did it again. We don't talk about the DON'T. He's made a joke of it once or twice and I didn't respond or laugh and he stopped. I'm dating a DON'T. But I don't care about DOs and DON'Ts anymore, I shouldn't, I can't.

I put the George issue aside and continue looking through fifteen years of DON'Ts. I do the math longhand in my notebook: 3,560 DON'Ts. I am personally responsible for making 3,560 people feel like shit. Most of the girls probably cried. Then there's the shunning and the therapy bills and the creeping thoughts that everybody knows, everybody at work, on the street, everybody in the universe knows. Three-thousand, five-hundred and sixty people hate me, they must. And George. It's a joke, it's a game, it's his revenge to date me—are we even dating?—and dump me. Giving me his dad's old magazines is part of the ploy to sucker me in, make me like him so he can hurt me, abandon me, mock me. He's the hero of the DON'Ts. They'll lift him up on their shoulders and carry him through the square. They'll burn an effigy of me using matches from his bar. I understand now why he didn't come by.

I pack a single suitcase and call a taxi at 8:00 a.m. I ask the driver to take me to the Queen Elizabeth Hotel, to the single room I've reserved. Taking a suite at the Ritz was too grand and I'm too small. I ask the driver to drive faster and take shortcuts—karma is right on my tail.

I take a shower and climb naked into the hotel bed because I can and call Ted on his direct line. I'm still drunk. He picks up on the second ring. "Let me guess—you want your job back?" I can tell he's joking, but he's not funny.

"You're funny. Look, I was wondering if I could get copies of all of the releases signed by the DON'Ts."

"From the last issue?"

"No. All of them."

Ted whistles. "That's a whole lot of paper, Sara."

"Can you do it?"

"I don't know. Everything's in chaos right now with you leaving and the Apples Are Tasty deal...."

"You hate Apples Are Tasty."

"I *bought* Apples Are Tasty."

"Wow."

"Yeah."

"So can you do it? Get me the releases? I'm staying at the Queen E. Just courier the originals if you don't want to copy them. I'll have them back to you by the end of the week."

"Tomorrow is the end of the week."

"Right. Well, Monday, then."

"What do you need them for?"

"I just need them, okay?"

Ted sighs. "Okay. But I need something from you. I need you to let Eva take a look at those magazines we've heard about, and Brian, too."

"Art director Brian?"

"Yes, art director Brian."

"Why?"

"They just need to."

"I can't believe you didn't fire Eva."

"Don't go there, Sara. It was a strictly business decision."

"And Gen's all right with that?"

"I can't talk to you about Genevieve." Ted only uses her full name when he's very serious.

"Fine. Just send me the releases."

"And I'll tell Eva and Brian you'll be expecting them when?"

"Monday. We'll do it Monday. In the afternoon."

Next I call Tim. He doesn't ask me why I want a three-fold card designed with the third fold being detachable by perforation with a blank outline of a body—not too sexy, more like my body, a regular body—with my face resting atop it. I shouldn't be smiling. I tell him I'll take a Polaroid and have it sent over to him. I dictate the text of the card. The front should be simple, no script lettering, but no Helvetica, either—something classic, a meaningful font. It should say: *DO accept my apology*… And on the inside: *You were never a DON'T.* "At the very bottom of the page it should say, *Now it's your turn to make me over*—that should be in parentheses. Then have my address printed on the back of the paper doll thing so people can mail it in. And I'll need envelopes and postage for all of them—two stamps for each, one to mail it out and one to go on the back of the paper doll thing so they can mail that back. Got it? And find a printer who can do it today."

"This really isn't part of my job," Tim says hesitantly. I tell him I'll pay him a thousand dollars and now it is his job.

I go into the bathroom and take three Polaroids of my face. I pick the ugliest one, fasten myself into a bra, slide one of Lila's rayon dresses over my head and take the photo to the concierge. I have no envelopes, no courier slips. I hand him a fifty and a crumpled Post-it with Tim's address and he says he'll take care of it. Then I take the elevator back to my room, turn my phone off and sleep until the boxes of releases arrive.

The cards aren't perfect, the font doesn't say *meaningful* to me, but there are 3,600 of them and they're paid for and obviously nonrefundable. The makeover paper doll is good. My body is a bit blobby, but my body *is* a bit blobby and my face looks tired, my makeup is smudged.

Tim personally delivers the boxes of cards. His friend Martin, the one who came to look at the magazines, has tagged along. I take the first release form off the top of the first of three piles I've made on the desk by the window. *Alain Gagne.* I open a card and write *Dear Alain* and sign my name at the bottom. I grab an envelope and copy out Alain's address. One down. Three-thousand, five-hundred and fifty-nine to go. I can do this. I have to do this.

Tim and Martin stare at me in disbelief. "You're kidding, right?" Tim asks.

"I have to do this."

"You're gonna need some help," says Martin. "If you're hiring, I'm very good at addressing envelopes."

"I need to do this on my own." I am a selfless martyr. I must fight sleep and hand cramps and all other distractions to be granted absolution. It is my responsibility. My mind flashes to the aisles of self-help books at Connections. Maybe this is my *journey*.

This is insane. My hand is shaking, my head pounds and no matter how many times I stretch my palm out it springs back into a gnarled fist. And then I get to Gen's card. I want to fill all the white space, write a thousand apologies, but I don't, and sign hers just as I have the boxes of others.

My eyes hurt and I can barely hold the pen, but there are so many more to do. Reluctantly, I ring the front desk and request a wake-up call in two hours—at 3:00 a.m.—and climb into bed. I sleep with my sore hand flattened under my pillow and dream of George.

I wake up sweaty and start again. My hand is stiff but I soon get a rhythm going. I try to block the pain with happy thoughts: images of rainbows and unicorns, magical fairies and butterflies. But all I can think of is George and Jack and Ben the Rockabilly Paperboy and Ted's mushroom-head dick and all the years I spent finding possibilities in impossible men who wanted me because I was bitchy and got to go everywhere for free. I'd boss them around and they'd do what I wanted, then they'd talk baby talk and whine that I didn't pay them enough attention so I'd tie them to my bed and fuck them until they shut up. It was always then that they'd tell me they loved me.

The concierge says he'll take care of the boxes—the ones of cards all stamped and ready to be mailed, and the ones of release forms to go back to *Snap*. I give him two more fifties for his trouble. I like this part—paying people to do things and the no-questions-asked.

* * *

George hates me. He hates me. He hates me. I've kept his card. It's addressed and stamped but I've kept it. Maybe I'll leave it at the bar, slip it under the door when I know he's not there. Maybe he'll have a change of heart; perhaps I should send a fruit basket. I know he likes tangerines.

There's a note taped to my door. I recognize George's handwriting. The fuck-off letter. I take a deep breath and unfold it.

Where are you? Call me. Come see me. I'm worried. G.

He's worried and he wants me to call. He wants to see me. It could be a trick, he could be stringing me along a little longer as per the instructions of the DON'T cabal. The effigy, the celebration in the square—it's not impossible.

I let myself in and gasp at what I see. There are black handprints on the walls, the counter, the fridge, the floor, the stairs. The boxes of *Snap*s are still out and empty beer bottles are scattered everywhere, some tipped over, others half-full. I clear them up and shove the *Snap*s back in their boxes and lug them one by one to the storage closet in the back near the bathroom. But the handprints—I need spray cleaner and a rag. I look under the sink because that's where people keep cleaning things and am for a moment surprised to find an array of chemical potions, sponges, towels and rags. Tim is nothing if not thorough. I snap on a pair of yellow rubber gloves just as I hear a knock on the door. George?

"New look?" It's Eva. And Brian. It's Monday afternoon and I'd completely forgotten they were coming to look at the magazines for their mysterious project. "It's cute. Very domestic."

I force a smile and invite them in. I point them in the direction of the magazines. "Please put them back exactly the way you found them," I say.

"Of course." Eva grins and bats her eyelashes. Brian says nothing. He doesn't look at me.

I strip off the yellow rubber gloves. I'm not going to clean while those two are here. I'm dying to ask what they're looking for, accidentally drop something near the long reading table Tim found for me at an estate sale in the Townships and catch a glimpse of their notes, pick up a snippet of conversation. But I don't. I make a vow of eternal dignity and plant myself at my computer, listen to my messages and check e-mail.

There are two messages from Eva, left before I talked to Ted, so sweetly asking me to call her back, saying that she'd really, really appreciate it if I'd let her look at the magazines. I delete and delete. I think I scowl and that isn't a very dignified look so I go instead for disaffected or stoic, but it's a challenge since she's sitting across the room humming and flipping through my magazines with her precious gloved hands. There are six calls from George and three from Esther. Ellen called, too, to say she was coming to Montreal again on business in a few weeks. Esther is excited—she's found *just a ton* of old magazines and books for me. This gets me excited, too, but I have to listen to George's six messages repeatedly before I call her back.

I'm not calling anyone until Eva and Brian are out of here. I don't need that little cunt eavesdropping, knowing anything about me, anything about my life. My e-mail is mostly spam and messages from local gossipmongers and *Snap* clients wanting to know *what happened? Call me! What are you doing now?* I'm reading fucking magazines. I shake the profanity out of my head and wonder if there's a patron saint of dignity.

"Hello? Sara?"

I look up from my computer. "George!" *Don't sound so eager.* "Hey."

"The door was ajar."

"Did you just say *ajar?*"

"I did. Where the hell have you been?"

"Away."

"I gathered that."

I lower my voice and nod my head in the direction of Eva and Brian. "We can talk about it later."

"Gotcha."

Eva's eyes are glued to us as we walk past the reading table and through to the kitchen. "I like the handprints," George says. "Did you do it yourself or did you pay someone to do it?" George likes to tease me about my newfound hobby of paying people to do things.

"It's strictly D.I.Y."

"I like it. Really. It's kinda cool-looking."

He's right. It kinda is. I'm not so horrified anymore—not by myself, not by Eva, not by the black handprints on the walls. The others, though, the handprints on the floor and the counter and the stairs, those will have to go.

Eva and Brian take what seems like forever to finish whatever it is they're doing and I'm impatient for them to leave. George couldn't stay long and is back at the bar. When he kissed me goodbye I felt all swoony and practically floated past the reading table where Brian had his head buried in an issue of *Vogue* and Eva sat ramrod straight, staring at me, watching me walk to the stairs and promptly trip up the first few steps, nearly falling on my ass.

I hunch in the corner of my loft bedroom and call Esther.

"Why are you whispering? Is everything all right with you, my dear? I've been concerned," says Esther.

"I'm fine. There's just some, uh, people here."

"You can tell me all about it when I swing by with June and Nick. You'll be home for a while?"

"June and Nick?"

"My niece and her husband from Winnipeg. They came in last night. They offered to help bring the boxes of books and magazines over to you."

"That would be great. But you know, I can send someone to pick them up." If tripping up the stairs wasn't enough to jolt me out of my kissy-floaty state, news of June and Nick certainly is. Esther has a married niece who lives in Winnipeg. I should know this. I should send Esther a card apologizing for being such a self-centered shit. I make a silent promise to get back to my three-questions-a-day, learning-about-Esther schedule.

"Don't be silly. We'll be there in an hour."

I yawn loudly and stretch my arms out and pace the length of the reading table, back and forth, back and forth. Every once in a while my hand cramps and I shake it and make controlled claw movements like I'm a one-pawed tiger in a community theater play or auditioning for *Cats*. If Eva gets the message that I want her to leave she doesn't show it. Rather, she yawns when I yawn and seems to move slower. Brian is shifty in his seat. He flips through his notes, checks his watch, rolls his eyes to the ceiling. But Eva holds out, not moving from her seat until Esther shows up.

"Oh, my, let me help you with those! Brian!" Eva's playing helpful and pert; she commands Brian to help Esther's niece and her husband carry in boxes from Esther's car.

I slide a box out from the backseat of Esther's old Mercedes but my right hand is lame and I drop it onto the sidewalk. I think I hear Eva, who is efficiently carrying two boxes, *tsk* me. A handful of vintage paperbacks spill out of the poorly sealed box. *The Single Girl* catches my eye. I crouch down and scan the back cover:

Who is the single girl? How does she live? How did she get that way? Here is a book which examines her problems—lesbianism, bisexualism, alcoholism, frigidity, nymphomania, narcissism, sadomasochism, or asexualism—and seeks to gain some measure of understanding of the various types of girls who get trapped by so-called single blessedness.

I stop reading. The book was published in 1961. Its cover is pink, the woman pictured looks forlorn. Not much has changed.

"You could at least get a lawn chair." George is looking down at me. He's grinning and I'm on my knees on the hot concrete with a book called *The Single Girl* in my good hand.

I shove the book back into the box, along with the others that are scattered around me. "I dropped the box. It's my hand, it won't—" George's grin fades. He takes my hands and examines them. "This one." I poke at him with my right hand.

"What's wrong with it?"

"It's fucked up."

"From now? From the box?"

"No, from before. On the weekend. It's cramped. I wrote too much. Come here." I lead George into the building.

Esther is unpacking boxes, piling books and old magazines on the reading table and chairs. "They wouldn't let me carry boxes, so this is the least I can do," she says apologetically as I stand there, hands free, pointing George in the direction of the kitchen counter to lay down the box of paperbacks. "George! How wonderful to see you! Sara didn't mention you'd be stopping by."

"Sara didn't know I'd be stopping by. Bar's slow, so I thought I'd pop in."

"I'm so pleased that the two of you have become friends," Esther says.

"We're definitely friends," George says.

Esther's eyes dart to me. "I *see*."

"I should help those guys bring in the rest of those boxes," George says. He lifts my right hand gently and kisses it. My face is so hot I'm surprised it doesn't start to bubble and peel away from my skull.

Esther stops unpacking and walks over to the counter. Eva, Brian, June, Nick and George rotate in with the last of the boxes. She wags a finger at me. "You've been keeping secrets from me, Sara," she says quietly so the others can't hear.

"I know. I wanted to tell you, but I wasn't sure what there was to tell. I'm still not sure. I mean, I like him and I see him every day—well, except that one night last week when he didn't stop by after closing the bar—but I'm not sure, I don't know—"

Esther pats my shoulder. "Relax, my dear, or you're going to have another one of those anxiety attacks of yours."

This reminds me that I have to go back and see that doctor to get a refill for my Ativan since my problems are, without a doubt, *persisting*. He'll probably want me to see that therapist he recommended. I guess I can always make an appointment for sometime after I see the doctor and get the refill and just cancel on the therapist if I decide I don't want to go. I know I should go, but it's hard for me sometimes to do everything that I should.

Right now, however, I should stop Eva from rifling through the boxes, pulling out issues of *Look* and *Glamour,* oohing over trashy paperbacks with titles like *Temple of Lust* and *Strange Nurse.* "We really need to sort those," I say.

"I can't believe what you have here—it's like a *library. Where* did you get all this stuff?" She tugs open another box and I pull it away from her with my left hand. She sticks out her bottom lip in an exaggerated pout. "Come on, Sara. I'll help you unpack."

"Sorry."

"I'll *pay.*"

"For what? To help me unpack?"

"To go through all this. Maybe borrow a thing or two?"

Eva wants to pay me to look at my old magazines and books. Eva's a pest and a manipulator. "How much?"

"I don't know. Fifty bucks?"

I snort like this is a grand insult and a little bit of snot sprays out of my nose. I absentmindedly use my cramped hand to wipe it. "Ow! Shit!" George picks my hand up and examines it again. There are no clues or any indication of my pain except that my fingers curl in as if I'm limply holding an invisible handbag.

"Okay—a hundred," Eva says.

What we're bargaining for I'm not sure, but it's sort of fun. Esther and June, Brian, Nick, George—they all watch and listen. "This is worth way more than one hundred." *What is?* I almost laugh at the absurdity of the situation.

"One-fifty. Come on, Sara. For a year."

Brian speaks up. "I'd pay two-hundred if, you know, I could just drop by when I needed to." Eva purses her lips in displeasure.

"How about this—two-fifty a year. You can come by Tuesday through Friday afternoons, from one until…" I look up at the clock in the kitchen; it's just after five. "Five. And if you want to borrow anything it's extra and you'll have to put down a deposit in case you wreck something or skip town."

"I'm not going to wreck anything," Eva says, scowling.

"Take it or leave it."

Eva sighs. "Fine. Will you take a check?"

I shake my head. "Cash only."

"Where's the nearest ATM?"

"There's one at my bar in the next block," George pipes up. "I'll walk with you. I should check on things."

"Fine," Eva says.

Eva and Brian trudge off to the bar with George and I don't like this but I know I shouldn't care. It's not like Eva is going to seduce George in a half block and fuck him on the futon in his office. I feel ill. It's hard for me sometimes not to care about everything that I shouldn't.

"That was quite the negotiation," Esther says, chuckling.

"I'm not sure what that was," I say.

"I think you agreed to let them join your library," says Esther's niece, June.

"I think you're right."

Eva and Brian return with their cash but George isn't with them. "He stopped at that *self-help* bookstore." Eva says this in an exaggeratedly sad voice, like George needs *help* and pity. "Here." She hands me the cash. Brian does the same. "Shouldn't we get a receipt or something?"

"I'm having cards made up. I have to take your picture. For your library ID. Just a sec." I find my camera bag in the kitchen but my hand is too sore to handle the weight of the camera body. I grab my purse off the counter and take out the Polaroid. I ask Eva to stand against the wall. She drops her chin and turns her head slightly, looking straight at the camera from beneath her eyelashes—she knows how to make her face most attractive in a picture. Then I do Brian, who blinks, but doesn't seem to care. "You can pick up your cards next Tuesday."

"You won't be open before then?" Eva whines.

"No. We have to get things organized," I say.

"Everything must be cataloged," Esther says.

"Fine, then. We'll be by on Tuesday. Will there be a party?"

Why would there be a party? "Of course there will be a party," I say. "And your cards will be *laminated*."

Eva and Brian finally leave and I flop onto the couch in the main room across from Esther, June and Nick. "What am I going to do?"

"You're going to open a vintage reading library and throw a fantastic party," Esther says.

"It does sound really cool," says Nick, who up until now has said nothing.

"What's it going to be called?" June asks.

I groan. I just want to read magazines and trashy old paperbacks, not think of names and throw parties. The board with the *Satin Rules* graffiti is propped up against the wall beside the couch. Tim and I keep arguing about what to do with it—I want to hang it, he wants it gone. "The Satin Rules Library and Reading Room." It's good. I like it. My years of trend analysis and general bullshit are put to good use. I can see the logo. We'll do a newsletter for members, but more like a 'zine, like the way *Snap* was about a million years ago. There will be no DOs and DON'Ts. It'll be about reading old magazines and books and other things I like. Strangely energized, I spring up off the couch and grab my Polaroid. I push my feet back against the wall until my heels touch and hold the camera out in front of me. I smile and the flash goes off.

"This looks fun," George says. He's back from the bookstore and sees Esther, June and Nick gathered around the reading table waiting for the pictures to develop. I've taken one of each of them and have made them lifetime members of the newly anointed Satin Rules Library and Reading Room. I have to get one of those machines that makes the ID cards with the hard lamination.

I ask George to stand in front of the wall while I take his picture, too. "What's with all the pictures? You're not back to your old ways are you?"

"No way. No DOs. No DON'Ts."

"Good."

"Stay there." I stand next to him and tilt my head toward his. I hold the camera with my good hand and push the shutter button. George looks confused. "This one's for my notebook. I'm trying to make one like Lila's." George looks more confused. "I'll explain later."

"We should be going, dear," Esther calls out. "I'd like to change before dinner."

"You're going out?'

"I'm taking June and Nick to that new tapas bar that was on the *Snap* MUST DO list last week."

"Oh." My mood deflates. I know nothing of that new tapas bar that was on the *Snap* MUST DO list last week.

"I'm sorry, dear. I shouldn't have mentioned—"

I cut her off. "It's fine, really, Esther. Call me tomorrow and let me know how it was. And you two…" I say this to June and Nick. "I'll get your address from Esther and send you your cards."

There are thank-yous and handshakes and awkward hugs all around and then George and I are alone and I notice that he's holding a rock in his hand. "What is that?"

"It's for you. Here."

"No. Wait. I have something for you." I pick a white envelope with his name on it up off the counter and hand it over.

I take the rock from him—it's black and smooth. "What is it?"

"It's a healing stone. For your hand."

"You bought me a healing stone?"

"I did." George laughs, then he reads the card aloud. *"You were never a DON'T. Now it's time to make me over. Do your best DON'T."* He holds up the paper doll. "Oh, I'm going to have fun with this."

"Go to town. That's what it's there for. I'm thinking I'll cover that wall over there with them—if anyone actually returns them. It could look cool."

"You sent these out?"

"To every DON'T I ever put in the magazine. That's how I fucked up my hand—writing them out."

"They have things called computers and printers now, you know."

"I wanted to do them by hand. I had to."

"I know," he says and pulls me into a big hug.

Satin Rules

George says I need a business license and I know he's right but I'll deal with it later because right now I need Timotei and his friend Martin—or at least one of them—to get up on that fucking ladder and put the *Satin Rules* sign above the door.

"You should have it coated," Tim says in his Australian accent, which is getting on my nerves so much today I don't think I could ever have sex with an Aussie. Not that I really would have before, I don't think—too blond and tanned and *g'day-mate* pep for me. "It's a piece of *plywood*. It's going to look like shit."

"That's the point," I say.

"I'll do it." Martin takes the drill from Tim's hands and climbs up the ladder. Martin has agreed to be my occasional slave in return for a free membership to Satin Rules. He wrote *cash only* on every invitation since I didn't think of doing that before the invites were printed and I don't have a credit card machine or account or whatever it is you need to take Visa. People will complain. I'll tell them it's part of the D.I.Y. throwback aesthetic of Satin Rules. This makes no sense, but people will nod and someone will inevitably use the term *old-*

school and I'll smile and grind my teeth because they might pay me two hundred and fifty dollars a year to sit at my reading table and flip through books and magazines. Martin the occasional slave will also be making the laminated membership cards at the party. I've made it clear: no more freebies; everybody has to pay. I need to make money because *I am a successful female entrepreneur embarking on a new and challenging venture.* And it's the only job that will allow me to read old magazines all day. Shit. I'll have to give Ellen a comp membership, too. She's coming in tomorrow for the opening party.

The party, the party, the party, it's all about the party. Esther volunteered to catalog all the books, all the magazines, code them and make old-fashioned sign-out cards for them. What's not so old-fashioned is the deposit charge that's neatly printed in the upper-right-hand corner of each card. I have to get this credit card business straightened out. George said he'd help.

I look around the space. I'll block off the stairs to my bedroom loft with something. I make a note to ask Tim or Martin to find that something. I don't want random people wandering into my bedroom, looking at my stuff, taking things, smelling my panties. People do this, I know—I had a boyfriend once who did.

Jack is coming, so is Ted and, of course, Eva. I sent everyone at *Snap* invitations and have an ad in tomorrow's issue. I'm going to be a bigger person, I'm *growing,* I have a *healing stone,* which as far as I can tell is a cheap polished rock rebranded and sold for twenty bucks. I was feeling big and all about *growth* last week after a day of rushing around the city with Martin and Tim, buying this, getting that, checking things off lists. I was feeling big and so absolutely inflated with personal growth I could burst after postering the neighborhoods with photocopied announcements of the Satin Rules opening and leaving stacks of handbills in cafés. It was exciting and reminded me of the early days of *Snap* when I'd walk through the city, distributing copies of the magazine myself, taking pictures, talking to people, stopping for drinks. It was the same, sort of, but with assistants and I didn't bring my camera and I'd duck behind Tim or Martin before I had to talk to anyone because I don't like people very much. But I was polite to one particularly annoying Bjork wannabe with bad breath and this, above all else, was tangible evidence that I was indeed *growing*. So maybe it wasn't so much like the early *Snap* days, but we did stop for drinks and after too many in the sun I ordered Martin to send invitations to the opening to every employee at the magazine.

Ted called the next day to congratulate me and said he'd be there. Jack e-mailed. Eva left an obnoxious voice mail asking if there was anything she could do to help. *Yeah, build a fucking time machine so we can go back to the day before you fucked Ted or, better yet, the day before I met you, and I could have my best friend back and everything would be fine, not the big clusterfuck that it is.*

But I don't think I want to go back. I want to read old magazines and kiss George. I want to shush people when they make too much noise in my library. But I do miss Gen, especially when I have to walk by the bus-stop posters advertising her upcoming album and reality TV show and her huge fake breasts. *This fall…fall in love all over again. J'taime Gen-Gen.* Gen has a reality TV show and a new album. She has a kid and huge fake breasts. She lives in the suburbs and wears high heels with three-hundred-dollar jeans. *That's* a clusterfuck. I want to plaster myself behind the fresh drywall that's gone up on one side of Satin Rules' main floor. I could live there with the rodents who will probably move in soon and I could think about what a hypercritical shit I am. So what? So Gen has a reality TV show and huge fake breasts and everything else, she was still my best friend. So she stayed with Ted after he fucked Eva's cunt with his mushroom-head dick. So maybe that is a total clusterfuck and I'm a judgmental bitch who maybe isn't *growing* much but for God's sake what was she thinking?

I don't know because she doesn't come to the party and I don't ask Ted about her. I just have a drink and wait for the Ativan I took five minutes ago to kick in. It's my last one. I'm seeing that doctor again on Thursday and I made an appointment with the therapist for Monday when Satin Rules is closed so if I want to go I can but if I don't I can finally go pick up my dry cleaning and spend the rest of the day reading old magazines in silence, alone. But that is six days away and now there are people everywhere, all over my place, laughing, drinking, touching things. I think some are buying memberships. They're all talking at once.

They're talking about the half-filled wall of DON'T paper dolls I've received in the mail. Some are meticulously colored with pencil crayons, some have haphazardly drawn boobs and pubic hair and nothing else. One card simply has *Bitch* written across it. Gen hasn't sent hers in.

They're talking about me and Ted and me and Jack and me and Eva and what happened—they all pretend they know what happened but they don't. No one asks and some people point and whisper when they see me talking to Ted and Jack and not having a terrible time. Jack is running *Snap TV* and is moving to Montreal. He says he'll give me a call when he moves; he has a couple boxes of stuff I left at his place. He doesn't seem mad and I don't hate him.

They're talking about my turn as a judge on *Stylemaker*. The episode aired on the weekend but I completely forgot about it. Diane's at the party. She says she'll send me a tape. She says I was a big hit and that she'd like to talk to me about the possibility of being a permanent judge for next season. I won't do it, but I don't say no.

They're talking about Eva and the rumors that she'll be running the Apples Are Tasty site since Ted bought it and giving it something I hear someone call a *retro look and sensibility.* "And she's the face of *Snap TV,*" whoever is talking to the *retro look and sensibility* guy says.

Killing yourself at your own party is generally considered a bad idea, I'm sure Lila would agree. I walk heel-toe, heel-toe in her highest black patent d'Orsay pumps and smartest black pencil-skirt suit that I hope makes me look like a sexy librarian but more likely makes my ass look bigger and rounder, but I remind myself that was very much the style in Lila's day and people seem to like the look of those days or they wouldn't be here. As I wind my way through the room eavesdropping, saying hellos, looking like I'm on a meet-and-greet mission but really looking for George. I'm feeling very Lila. I had a duplicate made, well, Martin had a duplicate made, of that picture of her—the *Portrait of a Lady Undone*—and it hangs in the library. I'm going to write an explanation, a dedication to accompany it. I am, but not tonight.

Across the room I see Eva with her Montreal red hair the same shade as Esther's. She's with Rockabilly Ben of the perfect cock and the paper route. *What is he doing here?* They're talking to Parrot Girl, who I can't believe I let in and who's carrying a camera and has that fucking parrot on her shoulder.

I consider calling the animal control people or the humane society or whoever is in charge of keeping pets out of parties. But then, if I did that then the in-charge people might notice that there are too many people here and that there are drinks and lots of food and I think I might need a license for that and I have I license for nothing. I hunch down and slip behind the crowd, still watching Parrot Girl. She's smiling and laughing and asking people to pose for pictures. She's pretty— and touchy, she touches everyone she talks to on their shoulder, their arm, their back. Eva says something to her and Parrot Girl grins, but as Eva turns from her I'm sure I see Parrot Girl's eyes narrow and her grin briefly disappear. I convince myself that Parrot Girl dislikes Eva, *hates* her. For this alone I should give her a comp membership instead of calling the in-charge animal people, but then that fucking parrot squawks and starts talking, saying, "Party, party, party," in its awful parroty voice and people are laughing and pointing and saying things like, *how cute.* I don't need animal control or Parrot Girl thinking she's extra fucking special because she got a free library card. No, I need another drink. And Parrot Girl can get in line and pay for her membership just like everyone else.

I find George in the kitchen talking to Ellen. George pulls me to him and kisses me on the neck but I wriggle away. I find the bottle of pink champagne I had stashed, pop the cork and pour a glass. "Are you okay?" George asks.

"I'm fine, I'm fine, I'm fucking fine. I'll be fine when this is all over and it's quiet again." I pour another glass after I knock back the first.

"It'll be over soon enough," says Ellen. "Maybe you should save the champagne for later—after everyone leaves."

George nods. "And we could share it when you can finally relax."

"I am fucking relaxed." There is a woman wearing a *baseball cap* walking through the front door. I know this is an open opening, but *come on*. I want her gone. "Where's Martin?"

"He went to get more film," George says, his voice even and slow.

"We bought a ton."

"It's gone," George says. "The memberships are a hit."

"Great," I say unenthusiastically.

"What is going on with you?"

"Nothing is going on with me." I reach for the champagne bottle but George picks it up and puts it on top of the fridge.

"Do you want to go for a walk? Get some fresh air?" Ellen asks.

"Hey, Sara." Fuck. It's Rockabilly Ben.

"Uh, hi, Ben. Ben, this is George and Ellen."

"Nice to meet you, *Ben,*" Ellen says. I want to kill her. I told her about Ben—all the hideous details—late one night when I was tipsy and waiting for George and was much too close to the phone.

"Great party," Ben says.

"Thanks," I say.

"Well, I think I'm gonna split—have to get up early."

"Of course," I say. "Thanks for coming."

As soon as Ben is out of sight and out of earshot Ellen lets go a whoop of hysterical laughter. "I'm sorry, I'm sorry," she says as she doubles over.

"Who is that guy?" George asks.

"Nobody."

"He's a *paperboy*," Ellen says. I will kill her. I will open a drawer and take out a knife and slit her throat.

"I don't get it," says George.

"It doesn't matter," I say.

"Oh, come on, Sara—you can tell him."

"Did you fuck that guy?"

I don't want to lie to him. I don't look up at his face. "It was a bad night."

"You fucked a *paperboy*."

"He's an *independent adult carrier contractor* according to his card."

"Paperboys have cards now?"

"Yup."

"How was it?"

"Did you just ask me *how it was?*"

"Sure did. So?"

"Uh, I'm going to go talk to Esther," Ellen says as she hurries out of the kitchen and away from the conversation. George is laughing now, but I'm still going to kill Ellen.

"You didn't answer my question," George says.

"I'm not going to answer your question."

"That good, huh?"

"I didn't say that."

"Didn't have to. If a guy is bad in bed a woman will tell you right away. If he's good, she won't say anything."

"Oh, you're so fucking smart."

"What'd he do that you liked so much?"

"George, I can't talk about this here."

"Yes, you can. What was it? Did he hold your hands behind your back and fuck you really hard?"

"George!" I growl at him.

"He did, didn't he?"

Did I tell him about Ben? I couldn't have. Did I? I set down my champagne glass. It's empty, but it's a gesture. If I told George about Ben I will never drink again. "I am not having this conversation with you here."

"Then how about over here?" George grabs my arm and drags me through the crowd and past the barricade blocking the stairs. He pulls me up behind him, up and up, past my bed and into the tiny bathroom Tim had installed. "So Ben held your hands behind your back and fucked you really hard, huh?"

"I never told you about Ben." *Oh, God, I hope I never told him about Ben.*

"You told me what you like and got me all hard, but you were so drunk it wouldn't have been any fun." I have no idea what night this was. There were several to choose from. *He doesn't know about Ben, not everything.* "But you're not too drunk now."

George turns me away from him and I'm facing the corner. He hikes my skirt up over my ass and reaches his hand around and between my legs. I'm wet and he fucks me hard with his fingers. Over the din from the party below I hear Martin's voice calling my name. George and I stop and I pull my skirt down and step toward the door. Martin stops calling.

"Get back in your corner," George says. It takes me a moment to realize he isn't joking. He's serious, there's no sign of playfulness in his expression. I face the corner again and he places one hand against each wall. He's careful with my right one—he knows it's still sore. He pulls my skirt up again and my panties down. He pulls my hips toward him and I arch my back. I think he's going to spank me, but I'm not sure if he will or when or how hard and this makes me wetter.

He waits, not touching me, just looking at me, exposed and wanting. I want him to spank me and fuck me. His hand slaps my ass and instinctively my back arches higher and I push back against the wall, the pain in my right hand the last thing on my mind. He spanks me again—harder.

I can feel George move in closer. His cock brushes my ass and I want him inside me and push myself against him. Very deliberately, he spreads my legs and pulls me back to him. I push my ass up so I can take him. I keep pushing myself back into him in hopes that he'll slide his cock into me, but he slaps my body back into the position he wants. I'm dripping and swollen and my thighs are sticky. Finally, he rubs the tip of his cock between my legs, on and over my clit and I think I'm going to come right then, but he pulls it away.

"Fuck me, George. Please."

He says nothing and is perfectly still. I can feel his eyes on me, watching my body shift and relax just slightly. And then he guides his cock inside me with one hard push just as he spanks my ass with his free hand. Once. Twice. So many times. My body jerks and twists. I try to dig my nails into the walls. For a moment, I want to get away, push him off me; it's almost too much—the fucking, the spanking, his cock and his hand. I push my whole weight against him as I come. George pulls out and comes on my ass. He straightens up. "We should get back downstairs," he says, zipping up his pants.

"I guess we should." I am dazed. My body burns and my head is fuzzy. But I am completely relaxed and George is the most delightful surprise.

Ted is lurking at the bottom of the stairs, talking to Esther and shifting his weight from one foot to the other like he always does when he's impatient or has somewhere to be. "Hey, Sara, I gotta run. I said I'd be home by midnight."

"Ah, curfew," I say. "Well, drop by sometime."

"Yeah, let's keep in touch."

What kind of a fucked-up conversation is this? "I hope everything goes well with all the new stuff."

"Thanks. And I know this is going to be great for you, Sara. You've always had that sixth sense—you always know what people want at the right time. You're lucky."

I watch him leave to see if Eva follows but she doesn't.

Ted's right. I am lucky. I'm luckier than everyone here. No matter how much I fuck up I'm the luckiest. The glow of sex with George fades. I'm lucky to have him—it's all about luck, right place, right time, but to think that everything, all of it, has all been purely about luck, is depressing. I'm the rich lawyer who wins the lottery twice, the fifty-year-old woman who wants a baby and gets pregnant just like that, I'm the girl who flukes through her life and gets to read old magazines for a living. And I'm the girl who needs a drink. And since it turns out that I didn't tell George about Ben I permit myself to have one, as my personal promise never to drink again would have only applied if I had. I go to grab the bottle of pink champagne from the top of the fridge, but George already has. He hands me a glass. I think about him fucking me in the bathroom. I love it. I think I love him, but I can't because it's too soon and I'm tired and fucked up and my nerves are rising and I wish I had more Ativan.

George puts his arm around my waist. "You should be enjoying this," he says quietly into my ear.

The party is clearing out as people move on to another or go home to bed. It *is* a Tuesday night, after all. Ellen and

Esther are the next to leave. Ellen is swaying like a metronome but never too far to the left or the right to actually fall. I've reconsidered killing her, but she'll definitely be paying for dinner when we go out next time she's in town.

"Looks like it's going to be a big success," Ellen says.

"Yeah, I'm lucky, I know."

"It's not luck, Sara. It's good business sense. You're a born entrepreneur." Listening to Ellen drunkenly navigate her way through the word *entrepreneur* is both painful and amusing.

"I am a successful woman entrepreneur," I say teasingly, my mood lifting.

"You are an *Infinite Woman!*" she shouts.

"Shh," I say. People are looking. I see Eva roll her eyes as she shrugs on her vintage fifties jacket. *Oh, fuck you, Eva.*

"I think I'll drive this one to her hotel," Esther says in reference to Ellen. "But don't you forget it's casserole night tomorrow. I'll expect you at six. You, too, George."

"We'll be there," I say. I look at Esther's face, the thin wrinkled skin that sags, the age spots makeup can't hide. It would be okay, I think, to be old and like Esther. I smile and bring her into a close hug. "Thank you for everything." I try not to cry.

"Oh, Sara dear, this is all your doing and I'm so proud. And I'll be in on Thursday to help you with the catalog system." Esther is teaching me how to run Satin Rules like a proper library.

The last partygoers finish their drinks and leave in packs. I wave goodbye to Martin and Tim and to Diane, who is leaving with Jack. I don't want to think about that. But maybe they could be artners. Maybe she likes cuddling and girl-bossy sex.

I wave to Eva in hopes that she'll leave and I won't have to talk to her, but she walks her old-lady orthopedic shoes over to where George and I are standing. Parrot Girl is a pace behind.

"This has been a super night, Sara," says Eva. "And you know I'm going to be your very best customer." *Oh, goody.*

"Excuse me." Parrot Girl speaks up. "I'm Camille. I'm a photographer for *Snap* and Apples Are Tasty. I'd love to get a picture of you two." She's grinning and readying the settings on her camera.

George moves so his body is angled half-behind me, ready to pose. I elbow him gently in the stomach. "Sorry, not tonight," I say.

"Okay, whatever. Sorry to bother you," she says. The parrot squawks and says, "Party, party party," for the trillionth time tonight and no one is laughing and thinking it's cute anymore.

"Jesus, Camille —can't you control that thing?" Eva chastises her. Parrot Girl's face burns red.

"I'm sorry, I just—I couldn't find anyone to look after him tonight, I didn't want to bring him." Parrot Girl looks at my face but not in my eyes. "He's my mom's—or he was. She died and he freaks out if he's left alone and then my landlord gets pissed and threatens to evict me, so I can't just leave him there and most of my friends don't want to look after a *bird,* you know. So I'm sorry I had to bring him."

"It's okay," I say softly and touch her arm. The parrot swoops his head down and raps his beak on my hand. I jump back, sure he's going to bite me.

"He doesn't bite. He likes you," says Parrot Girl. This is new. Animals never like me, but I still don't trust the squawky thing and keep my distance.

"Can we go now?" Eva's voice is demanding and shrill; the goodness-golly-gee Eva has fully transformed.

"Just a sec," Parrot Girl says, unzipping a pocket on the front of her bag. The parrot squawks again. "I meant to give this to you."

It's the DON'T paper doll of me on which she's scratched out the word DON'T and replaced it with DO. She's drawn blue short-shorts with white piping, soccer socks with stripey tops and cowboy boots. With a metallic gold marker she's drawn a shiny jacket.

"Thank you, Camille," I say and take the card from her. Then I head to the kitchen to get a roll of tape so I can paste the card up on the wall with the others.

★ ★ ★ ★ ★

Look for Pamela Klaffke's next book in stores
January 2011.